Travelling Light

J. L. Morin

New York
Harvard Square Editions (HSE), Ltd.
www.HarvardSquareEditions.org
2011

Published in the United States by
Harvard Square Editions (HSE), Ltd.

ISBN: 978-0-9833216-2-0

Harvard Square Editions web address:
www.harvardsquareeditions.org

Printed in the United States of America

For My Mother

"Morin's Mackenzie is a vivid and vivacious protagonist, judiciously aware of the power of her sexuality and fully in charge of it. The voice sparkles."

— DON TINGLE
Author, *Imperishable Bliss*

"The author admirably dramatizes this, using an intelligent everywoman, who sees the origins in the jealous and depersonalization of her own marriage."

— Not Another Book Review

"It's a bit of humor, chick lit, history, creative nonfiction and detective story rolled into one."

— JUDITH SMITH
Arizona State University Media Relations

Fact

Slavery has endured into modern times. There are now at least twice as many real slaves on earth as there were at the height of the trans-Atlantic slave in the late 1700's. The UN has set up the Voluntary Trust Fund for Victims of Trafficking in Persons to combat this hell on earth. Professor Kevin Bales of Free the Slaves estimates that there are 27 million slaves worldwide in the year 2010 — men, women and children captured and violently forced into unpaid labour who cannot walk away.

"The collective impression of such future Europeans will probably be that of numerous, talkative, weak-willed, and very handy workmen who REQUIRE a master, a commander, as they require their daily bread; while, therefore, the democratising of Europe will tend to the production of a type prepared for SLAVERY in the most subtle sense of the term."

— Friedrich Nietzsche, *Beyond Good and Evil*

"I prefer to call it what it is which is modern slavery. And with 27 million slaves worldwide, I would say that we have an epidemic."

— Demi Moore, Actress

Chapter 1

Styxos

It is a universal truth that friendship between man and woman escaping the bonds of flesh can free an entire circle of friends. I had an inkling of this the summer of the dig: a silver glint that disappeared beneath the waves.

A whiff of this fish kept me awake at night breathing negative ions and brine. We sailed away from Alexandria's obelisks and secrets and headed northwest toward Styxos. I expected nothing more from the island than the usual anthropological stockpile, but couldn't fall asleep. My body refused to succumb to the boat's gentle rocking. I stared at the moon, seagulls crying, *Vain! Vain!*

What was this feeling in my stomach? There was no one to have this ache about. Had I fallen in love with the sea? I sailed through the hours in that platonic state.

I remember how the moonlight sliced into the cabin as I stumbled out onto the deck and closed the door behind me quietly so as not to wake up the babies.

The change in my husband's personality had become more pronounced since we set sail for his homeland.

Bonds of flesh grown fragile, he avoided eye contact. How could I break the spell and turn Charon back into the man I had married? His shape was camouflaged by the night, but I could see his fierce eyebrow connected in the middle above his nose as he carried his great hammer around the deck. Charon had been up most of the night fixing the boat. He turned his back, still not speaking to me, and ferried us back in time toward the blind underworld.

My eyes explored the abyss of black water in that enchanted hemisphere. The sea rose, *voluminous,* and sprayed my boatman's shaggy cheeks. I thought how handsome he looked, probably the same mechanism that had me remembering only the good times. The waves heaved in the darkness. We sailed through this sad region forever.

A hint of dawn lit the backs of the gulls flying above the boat. Land. Gradations of blue and grey mountains receded into a cloud of dust, a storm in the Sahara. The crack of dawn turned the island shadow into yellow rock. Digging in Styxos would present its own challenges. The island had grown out of active volcanoes in the Mediterranean Sea distributed along an arc structure above earthquakes with focal depths greater than 100 km. Its foundation is high in K_2O versus SiO_2 which increases with the depth of the underlying magma. This explains the high level of potash in the earth.

The waves lapped at the sides of the boat. I scanned the sparkling horizon for my husband's mother's house, which I would discover was nowhere near the shore, and savoured what was to be the last cool breeze for an eternity. "It's beautiful, isn't it?" I asked.

It wasn't meant to be a rhetorical question, but Charon's only response was a grunt. Styxos might turn out to be the kind of place where the most aggressive got the biggest cave. I let him get off the boat first and gave him some space. I was afraid to admit that Charon was one of those Styxan men who aged badly. By his forty-sixth birthday, he had become insecure. Being close to me was a threat to his identity.

There was a market set up in the port, and Charon hurried ahead to talk to the people behind the stalls. I set foot on the island and looked around for clues as to its personality. The kids ran in circles after the seagulls. The dark Styxan men were curious about my blond hair. Seeing me walking alone, they began to follow me. Charon turned down an aisle that led toward jagged cliffs hidden in dark shadow. I looked over my shoulder. Sure enough, three men with furry eyebrows turned left after me. Charon was quite far ahead by now. A man with a crew cut and a tattoo on his neck stepped in front of me and blocked my way. The three men behind me closed in. The vein on his neck bulged under the tongue of the serpent tattoo and sent a shiver down my spine. I called our son, "Justin!" Charon looked up and yelled at Justin to stop chasing the sea gulls. The men looked at each other. The soldier-type surprised me by growling in English. "They're yelling at the same kids." The three men disbanded.

The children came and hugged me. "It's big," Justin said, looking around. "Styxos island?"

"Yes," I said, trying to calm my voice, "a special one. Every island has its own character. One might be known for mythological battles, another for her gay nightlife, another for cave dwellings . . ."

They say that somewhere on Styxos lies the entrance to Hades. The locals discount the myth, though, since it's bad for tourism. But they admit that there are ghosts on Styxos. That energy has consciousness on Styxos.

Timeless bawd with her creased shores.

I was startled to hear this spoken with the authority of a chorus.

And lapsed allegiances.

I looked around expecting to see a group of old women in togas. But there was no one. The blank cliffs stood behind me. Indeed, the very rocks seemed to have an opinion.

Watching merchants load up a camel train from the hold of a ship, I felt a wave of panic and knew I'd stepped into the past, or several simultaneous pasts. Could it be that time really did work in loops here? A motorcycle scooted through the dusty port. Peasants in sneakers haggled with relics from the days of Poseidon in the open market where a man in rags was selling all manner of junk, the helm station from a shipwreck, a clepsydra. *For when the clocks stop.* In the split second as he handled a piece of junk, something caught my eye. I turned and saw that his hands were translucent! This discovery sent a bolt through my bones. I gathered the children around my knees and limped away.

The fragrance of eucalyptus grew stronger as we drove into the noonday sun along the seaside and past a fenced-off ghost town that had been occupied by troops since the invasion. Tumbleweeds gathered in the streets. The silhouette of war-torn hotels was an eyesore. "Why would Muslims take over a whole city and never use it?"

"For the same reasons they have built a wall to divide our country, Mackenzie" Charon said. "This city was a jewel. Capturing it and leaving it here to rot, was the ultimate act of jealousy." Wires dangled in front of the graffiti.

A crime that continues to be committed.

A veiled woman floated on a kickboard like a clownfish in the water.

People swam in front of the ghost town as if at any tourist beach in acceptance of the war that had passed there. And why shouldn't they? It was the land that was occupied, not the water. In fact, after a half century of abandonment, the water looked extremely clean. "A Florida real estate tycoon bought up those hotels." My husband pointed to some crumbling sky rises. "They're next to the site for a new train station." Renovations had started on the edge of the ghost town where a few fish *tavernas* had opened up. The speculation had begun.

We arrived at the house, a white, boxy affair set among a smattering of the same. My mother-in-law came out of the downstairs apartment to unlock the wrought iron gates. The keys clinked against the metal, a lever was released. Several in-laws filed down from the upstairs apartment. They didn't appear to have changed, not that you ever really got to know your in-laws, or whether you should hide displays of affection in front of them. The gates screeched as they ran along the ground.

It began the second day on the terrace overlooking the garden: a very loud monologue from the neighbouring house invaded our peace. At first, I ignored the voice.

Surely whatever the woman was complaining about would be resolved, and since we only had one neighbour in close proximity, we could get on with our quiet. But there was no answer, so she kept asking. Why was she so loud? Her voice was a stain that wouldn't come out. Was she deaf?

It hadn't rained in the springtime. Bees were buzzing around the watering can and crawling inside for a drink before the last drops evaporated. Blended with the drone of the bees were sobs coming from the other side of the garden wall, and I realized the voice was talking to someone on their terrace. My husband's mother went on stringing green beans. She was my only company most days while my husband went on his tiresome visits, apart from my fellow anthropologists on the early morning digs near the old amphitheatre. We were looking for the fabled mouth of hell.

"Bees," my husband's mother said, as the loud woman continued her monologue next door. My husband's mother caught a glimpse of a man in uniform coming down the street, and stopped stringing. The mailman passed our gate and went up to the next-door neighbour's and called up to the terrace, "Are you alright?"

"Fine," the neighbour wailed from her terrace. Over the wall, I discerned her large body clumped on a small wooden chair. She resumed her sobbing.

"No, she's not fine." My husband's mother stuffed the beans into the seat next to her, hopped to her feet and shouted over the wall in Styxan, "How can you be alright when you insist on that racket? You're making yourself sick. How many years has it been since your husband left you? *My* husband is *dead*, and *you're* crying." She tugged her black mourning dress down over her frame, her eyebrows ruffled like feathers and fixed on her neighbour like a hawk on its prey.

Her eyes gleamed in tacit understanding at our house: *What's left in life if you can't make fun of your neighbours?* Our neighbour's house was to become a reliable source of diversion.

The elderly neighbour, self-conscious in her flowered dress, sobbed, "Never mind." The loud neighbour called to the old lady from inside the house. The elderly neighbour didn't answer. That's when *she* appeared on the terrace. The younger woman was showing off her thin waist and wide hips in a tight summer dress. Parts of her mane of black hair had been straightened with an iron. I glanced across the fence again. She must have been about my age, but had undergone a completely different process of enculturation. The woman stunned me with her stare across the fence. Then she quickly ushered her mother inside of their house.

My husband's mother went up to the wall after them. "For God's sake, he was only your husband! You're not even *related* to him. Let his mother cry over him. Fancy crying over someone else's son!"

The mailman closed the mailbox and went away. I watched him stop at the next house where there was another family sitting on the terrace. They erupted with laughter.

All that digging for hell at dawn with a pickaxe, and here it was blowing around the neighbourhood like so much summer dust.

Fancy crying over someone else's son!

Chapter 2

Collectivists

I'm not sure how my life changed its course to make me care about this place. One minute I was up on the hundred and seventh floor looking out at Manhattan, and there was that ad saying 'Private Island for Sale' in my inbox. The turquoise sea on my screen looked inviting. Not that I had the *time* to go there. The price tag was two million dollars. I felt like I had been wasting my years in New York. I should be sun bathing everyday. There weren't any buildings or people in the picture. The absolute solitude seemed a little extreme. I would adjust my fantasy to a more moderate destination. I began researching populated Mediterranean islands.

Who would have guessed that crashing that Styxan VIP party at that hotel was a decisive move? I followed a group of merry-makers into the glass elevator and ascended the missile-silo atrium. When we got to room 7892, my eyes adjusted to the darkness, and I realised that everyone was wearing black: I was the only woman in the room. And I was wearing a red dress. Immediately Charon's dark eyes were on me. "What are *you* doing here?" he asked, as if he had been waiting for me all his life. The connection was strong in that sea of pheromones. Being with him felt so right. I could tell by the way he glanced back at me that he felt it, too. We talked about our dreams for the future, and he said "It would be nice," at the same time as me. He could read my mind! How much did he already know about me?

After going through a shelf full of modern anthropological studies, I now know that this was just Pseudo-Simultaneous Awareness Disorder, which is due to abnormal awareness oscillation creating the illusion of simultaneous awareness. Abnormal awareness oscillation is rapid switching between two modes of conscious awareness — your own sensory awareness, and social awareness of others. Awareness oscillation becomes abnormal at the point when the rate of oscillation is so rapid that an illusion of simultaneous awareness is created, often resulting in marriage.

On the way home, I ran through the memories of him and wondered what he meant to me. He was a diplomat with a Ph.D from a collectivist civilisation, and his group over individual orientation had to be approached with a measure of cultural relativism. He fascinated me. Still, I had the wherewithal to let him chase me until he hunted me down. He came to my apartment with a bottle of Styxan wine and his picture in a frame, and he never left. After two days, I went to the gym and the grocery store. When I came back, he was furious. I was shocked when he yelled, "Where were you?"

"I told you where I was: at the gym and the grocery store. Don't you believe me?"

"I was jealous." He hugged me.

"It's OK. Don't get angry." I hugged him back.

"I'm learning," he said.

Individualist and collectivist societies both have their downfalls. We are susceptible to loneliness, and they suffer from fear of rejection, almost the same thing. Charon was a challenge. A throwback from another era, but intact with a warmth that was extinct in New York, land of fear of intimacy, impotence, the exploited and abused. There was a dearth of real men. He was the answer to everything that was wrong with America. Coddled people, weak with antibiotics, isolated, unable to socialise without drugs. Charon's group consciousness was the answer to social ill. "I don't like being alone," I told my stepmother on the phone.

"You'd better not marry him, then," she said.

The second time his temper flared up, Charon said, "I'll fix it." He was a friendly man, passionate about me, jealous of my friends, deliciously demanding in bed. So what that he had no sense of humour. A sense of humour only protected you from a million little aggravations everyday. He couldn't laugh at himself and tended to think that everyone else was laughing at him. Maybe that was it. He didn't get it, and in the end, he cracked. I didn't pay much attention to that aspect at the time, though. He had enchanted me with his conversation. He would watch the people in the room, and I would watch him.

The wedding was on Santorini with its cliffs falling into the sea. Violins led the parade of guests riding on donkeys through the town at dusk.

At first, I was impressed with Styxos because the divorce rate was only 10%. I thought a Styxan man would value family above all else. Now I realize it's just because the women put up with everything. They should keep their men in line! You think you can go around the world taking the best from every culture, but some people take the worst: French fries from Belgium, copies from China, infidelity *à la française*. Many compromises later, I was married with two children on the terrace at our house in Israel. At first he was so gentle with the children. He would sit down on the floor and let them climb all over him. He tirelessly trotted them on his back around the house.

What happened to our connection? Now it was blocked, pheromones dried up. His father had died, and Charon had receded into his cave. They say that it only takes one person to save a relationship if they really want to. I was determined to find my husband again. Maybe he was getting sick. "Did you take your cod liver oil today?" I could tell by his seriousness that he was about to tell a lie.

"Yes."

A letter had arrived. My husband sat down across from me with the torn envelope, his smile froze on his face as he handed me the letter. It was in Styxan, but I recognized two words: 'posting' and 'headquarters'. I handed it back to him without saying anything.

He looked angrily at me and translated the letter. Our diplomatic posting to Israel was over. Our application for an extension for another year in Israel had been refused. My husband was being called back to the Ministry of Foreign Affairs on Styxos. I got my wish. We were going to live on a Mediterranean island.

In Israel, we'd lived in a secured compound on the beach with a mango tree growing in the garden. My cosy life consisted of walking the children to preschool and tooling around the neighbourhood with a double stroller. Now, my main concern was the high ratio of the trace element rubidium to silica in the soil suggesting the profound depth of the volcanic activity under Styxos, which originated in dehydration of oceanic crust under the sea due to the counter clockwise rotation of Africa relative to Eurasia. The geologists on our team had found the spot where the water released had worked its way to the surface in a hydrous melt scattering potash and other alkali on the way, and thought they could deduce from whence it came. I wasn't so sure. What interested me about Styxos was the depth of its origins. Tectonic shifts subject rocks to higher temperatures as they become buried deeper in the earth until they become wet molten rock. The metamorphism of its underlying rock occurred at temperatures higher than 200 degrees Centigrade. There is nothing extraordinary in the theory that hell is close by. Turn up your body heat two degrees and a slight fever turns reality into a persecutor. The world becomes a threatening place.

On Styxos, it was eight degrees hotter than Israel, and there were no swimming pools. The northern population had converted religions several times. The last invasion — an echo of past tragedies — exacted no blood. In the North, they were calling themselves the 'Jarmuth', a disputed Biblical name not recognized by the outside world, but they were allegedly Muslim. Although occupied by eastern mainlanders, they passed as star-bellied democrats.

The complicated political environment on Styxos is outside of my scope. Moreover, I soon realised that my theories about the island had been whitewashed by history books printed in America. I regretted not properly learning the language, a mixture of Maltese, Arabic, Greek and Hebrew. My ignorance on this score no doubt contributed to my feeling of safety, as long as I could ignore the troops in long-sleeves patrolling the old city with IMI Galil assault rifles. We stayed put and prayed that they would open the road to the beach. A shadow rippled across the garden path as a blackbird skimmed overhead.

I remember how Charon's volatile temper had improved at the thought of going back home. In a wave of wellbeing, I had agreed to the children learning his culture and language. "You can lead the work on the dig at the old amphitheatre. It's a small country." That was a voluntary job.

Here was his plan: while we were waiting for our furniture to arrive from Israel, we would stay at his mother's house. "It will only be for a few weeks." This must have been when I lowered my expectations.

He began to slip into delusion. Now here I was between my false husband in a fantasy world and our loud neighbour, who did not appear to have any man or children and could afford to negotiate every decision. I ignored the old place with her crumbling walls and bees buzzing around the watering can. The neighbours watched us from their terrace, no doubt in amusement at my predicament.

A New York day passes like a month at these temperatures, where unbolting the shutters is like opening an oven. The heat melted not only electrical appliances, but also barriers between the years.

Styxos fickle liar: one minute cool night, and the next, the scorching hot fires of Hades. No respect for time, shameless bawd, passing late and comprehensively, looping into the past.

The present was a mirage on the horizon.

I was surprised at how much of my husband's collectivist personality resided outside of himself, in the architecture, his friends, his title, his possessions. Our family resources leaked from his pockets, and I wondered when his network would start to give something back. If only I could establish myself on Styxos, I wouldn't have to depend on Charon so much. Maybe improving my own social life would restore some balance to our relationship. I watched the house next door for any sign of friendliness, but the neighbourly relations I'd inherited seemed to be a truce at best.

We shopped around for an apartment, but nothing suited my husband. I looked at his rugged profile, black brows of Charon searching the horizon from the roof terrace of a three-bedroom. A white moth fluttered around the terrace's cover of pink and orange bougainvilleas as bright as summer lipstick, but all he saw was a labyrinth of indecision, sprawling apartments obstructing the view of the Styxos mountain range. Styxos would never give away her charms without a sacrifice. My husband scowled, looking through the clotheslines for her fickle mountains. A lizard scurried down the wall of the building and froze in the shadow of the bougainvillea. "A lizard! A lizard!" Justin cried.

All of the apartments we looked at were in much better condition than Charon's mother's house. Would my husband find fault with them all? To my horror, when our furniture arrived, he said, "With all the modernization going on, it would be a good idea to update this old place." He paced back and forth within the peeling walls stopping to meditate on the trinkets blanketing the surfaces. "In this house I never know where to start."

The curtains on the house next door parted. The loud woman was peeping at us. I stared back at her, but she held her post. I went to the window and drew the shades. The nerve of that woman!

I was determined not to panic in front of the neighbours, and tried to see the bright side. Why should I impose my view of the situation, since it wasn't my island to begin with? Too often foreigners come to such places and see things in terms of their own cultures. Charon broke the news to me that his salary was a quarter of what he had earned in Israel, ending the revelation with, ". . . as you well know."

This was news to me. What was he trying to pull? "But everything's twice as expensive here!"

"It's an island. Everything has to be shipped in."

"A quarter!" I swallowed, sure that I wouldn't have forgotten such a shocking piece of information. The extended family chimed in. They had missed Charon all these years. And it would be good for his mother. "My husband is dead," his mother pleaded. "I don't have a husband!"

Our furniture went into storage.

"We have to paint the house," I said.

He seemed happy for the first time in a while. "Do you know how to paint houses?" We bought some white paint and started to move all the old furniture into the centre of the room. The sweat poured from my body. Soon there was a mountain of old trinkets in the living room: a stuffed bull with one horn left, imitation Chinese vases, miniature plates with the names of Greek islands painted on them, chipped glasses and broken clocks, brown curtains and dismal framed prints each with a soul of its own. His mother picked up one of the sleeping souls and grumbled, "This bull was expensive." I threw a tarp over the whole pile.

I was standing in my undergarments with a dripping paint roller in my hands when she brought in an over-sized red envelope. "Don't touch the doorway!" I said. Her eyes smiled at me, before she disappeared back into her territory, the kitchen. I glanced at the envelope and continued painting. There might be some opportunity somewhere. I might get to know my in-laws' favourite TV shows, or the songs their children knew on the piano.

"It's starting to look like a new house," Charon said.

"We have an appointment to look at an apartment this afternoon."

Charon's face turned red. He started to curse in Styxan and then began ranting like an animal. "Oh, whore!" — the catch-all expression they used when organization fell apart, things started to not work, boundaries melted. The children ran out of the house. His mother ran out. God fled. Charon had argued himself back into the womb. He didn't want to be understood, and went on in Styxan. If I showed any understanding, he tore me to pieces. I was only real to him in so far as I refused to understand him. He treated me as if I didn't have feelings. Indeed, I couldn't feel anything with him. The veins on his neck pulsed with purple blood and the animal sounds started. He burst into English. "You don't understand anything about Styxos! *You* move out!" He went on ranting in Styxan. There was nowhere to go. His horrible sounds invoked all manner of evil spirit. He went on with a long tirade, shackled me into my degraded status in his tribe. How to break free?

He yelled and threw a fit. I knew that this hysterical persona of his was a false self. In fact, hysterics pretend that they are not experiencing any gratification, that their lives are meaningless, and that they are just going through the motions because they are being forced to, while secretly, the very activities they complain about are fulfilling their desires.

"That energy could have been used to fix the house," I countered. But he was arguing specifically to burn up energy and avoid such a leap into the fearful unknown. Fighting was his retreat into a zone of familiarity. He preferred to rant. He was terrified of making any kind of change. The more he tried to preserve his identity by denying my humanity, the greater a threat he felt me to be. He desperately negated my being, yet failed to exist alone. I knew he went around visiting because without other people, he couldn't maintain his sense of self. "I'm trapped in the circle I've entered!" he had said after visiting with friends.

"If you were secure, you wouldn't worry about whether people treated you like a person or thing," I'd said.

Or, "A crust of lava is forming around my feet!" Everyone was a Medusa ready to turn him into stone. He had to strike first and dehumanise the others so he could safely relate to them: dehumanised people and phantoms. He was not autonomous, and felt neither separateness nor relatedness to me, just familiarity. He oscillated between the extremes of merging identities and complete isolation. How had I become such a threat to the survival of his self? Was I ready for his regression? Where had we left the path for these gloomy woods? I was proud that I didn't cry. Instead, I stumbled into the bathroom, nauseous.

After washing up, I felt like a human being again. I came back into the living room. Charon was gone. The house was silent. I was in a lamentable situation, but wondered if my life was worse than Charon's. The way I saw it, the biggest risk in marriage was being stuck with someone I didn't love. Someone who became weaker with each rejection. Avoiding a pathetic creature every day who I couldn't love would be worse than getting yelled at once in a while. Were there only these two extremes? Had I chosen my trap? Charon's venom enhanced his beauty.

There was the red envelope, sitting on the shelf. Somewhere in the back of my head, I dreaded the moment when the shock would wear off. I opened the invitation. *Millennium Investor's Gala.* What had had happened to my green evening gown from before we were married? I turned the card over. At least the dress code didn't say *burqas.*

Chapter 3

The Internationalists

The gala was billed as the most fabulous event in the history of the island: a dinner organized with the motive of attracting business investment, everything from offshore oil to trains.

Big deal. I put the invitation down and started painting the second wall of the living room, miles away from Charon in the kitchen with his mother.

What I wouldn't give to reclaim those days when we first fell in love. Or to just have an open conversation again. When did the change come? It had snuck up on me. It was only a slight difference in his personality at first. The stress of his father's death. I thought he would get over it, but it was taking so long. Some days he would be the calm affectionate man I had known for years, and other days, he was a different person, a stranger. His temper flared up so violently, and I knew he was thinking he'd like to kill me. For the first time, I was afraid of him.

I turned the invitation over and re-read it. The gala was to be hosted by both the Christian and Muslim communities. The Styxos government was spending enormous sums on infrastructure to float the new island-state. The end of economic division between the Christian south and the Jarmuth north was in sight. At least the invitation looked legitimate. There was a parking pass and a map. I put it back into the red envelope.

Offshore oil? The island certainly had olive oil. If I was going to win Charon back, first I would have to find the right dress. Years ago, I gave up on packing for every eventuality. Travelling around to archaeological sites on a boat, you spend most of your time in a bathing suit. You can't foresee galas; no point in suitcases full of unworn clothes. And still no dress.

The gala's immediate financial beneficiary was the new Taylord's department store on the main street flanked by all the big American retailers. It had just opened up across the street from Martin Keel's. Taylord's fashion director, hired away from Saks in America, was holding a private 'showing' for gala invitees. Taylord's was filled with the magical perfume of new clothes mixed with warm muffins. They had turned up the air-conditioning and installed coffee carts in the aisles of the elegant new store to stem the rush of Saturday morning shoppers. Invitees enjoyed free coffee and muffins as they mingled with other tastemakers in advance of the gala. It was rumoured that an *haute couture* fashion show would precede an audience parade down the catwalk.

A German woman was holding up a gold *lamé* pant suit. "Feel how supple it is!" her Arab friend commented. The cash registers rang. A saleswoman wrapped a coral chiffon gown, and ran a platinum card through the machine. At Taylord's everyone had dressed for the day. For many, this was the real event.

Shoppers strolled through the large atrium on the first floor. Eyes met amid the smell of newly minted couture imported from Paris and Milan. A dozen women from Iran, Dubai and Saudi Arabia had unveiled and purchased staggering evening gowns for six, eight, and nine thousand Styxan shekels. The event pumped up retail sales for the island-state. The papers said the Styxos Taylord's was on the map as a store that could introduce a number of big couture lines to the tremendous new market on the high-styling threshold of the Middle East. With all that investment, there must be a dress here that could help me manage Charon's anger. Warm colours were out. I found one with green pearls that would do nicely.

In those days, I kissed him when he came to pick me up, and enjoyed feeling in his possession. In the car with the air-conditioning on, I wished I'd worn more than this green wisp of silk. My cheeks were flushed red. How ironic to look nice when I felt lousy. If I could have been healthy every time I had to go to a cocktail party, my life would have been more enjoyable.

Charon pulled into a side street and parked the car. At first I was relieved to be outside in the heat. Charon passed me on the pavement. "How much was that dress?" Another rhetorical question. He walked several paces ahead of me. The humid city waited for us with construction sites. I was determined not to rush, as Charon turned down a depressed alleyway. Strolling to the gala, I felt a pang in my chest as a young couple stepped into the alley ahead of Charon. When was the last time Charon had reached for my hand like that? I knew I was feeling jealous in the car when my husband started complaining that everything that was wrong with his life was my fault, but was I getting so old that it made me sad to see a happy couple? I couldn't help saying, "That dress is too low-cut in back."

Then I saw that the man had a crew cut and tattoos on his neck. He started pushing the blonde down the sidewalk in front of us. She pleaded with him and sounded like she was talking backward. A Russian? The way she looked in her silver gown, she couldn't have been more than eighteen.

"Fashion's not the only business the gala is attracting," I said to my husband.

"She shouldn't have married him."

"I don't think they're married, cupcake." I had seen the papers. There was a large population of 'sex tourists' in Styxos, and after being repeatedly colonized, Styxans had one-upped the new species of foreigner by prostituting the new tourist class, mostly Russians. She looked back at me. A look of recognition and implored me for help. I averted my eyes, and felt immediately guilty.

"The Big Boss is watching us, Snake!" the blond warned. "He will not be happy if you damage goods."

The skinhead let out a murderous growl. "Big Boss will get his goods one way or another. He doesn't care if it's you or someone else." He pushed her again, and she fell down.

Snake saw us. His eyes locked with Charon's. Charon averted his gaze into the distance. Snake reached down and helped the girl to her feet.

I instinctively stopped. "What did she mean by 'he's watching us!' Who?" Another rhetorical question. Charon just stared at the road ahead. "Isn't that the soldier we saw at the port?" The couple moved ahead, distancing themselves from us.

"You're imagining things."

"No, really. Don't you remember?"

"I don't know. They all look the same to me."

Snake shoved her again. Poor exhausted creature. That's when I noticed the bruises on her neck.

"Snake!" the girl pleaded with him.

"Come on, let's move!" Charon took my arm. We reached her cheap perfume. *Firebird.*

Charon was pretending not to hear me, so I had to hold up the conversation myself: "We should call the police."

"The what?" Charon sneered.

"They don't pursue this kind of case, do they?"

"Mackenzie, who do you think controls the cabarets? Police, judges, military officers, and they enforce their interests with death threats."

"Didn't Styxos agree to some international laws when it became an EU candidate?" I asked.

"Agreeing is one thing. Sex is another . . . law." I tried to get him to elaborate, but he just knit his brow. He'd blocked further communication. What was this statue? I had to free him. I had seen his beauty. He could be that person again, if I could just handle him the right way.

The couple had reached the avenue ahead of us. A group of Styxans surrounded us. I hugged my shawl around my bare shoulders, suddenly realizing that everyone was staring at me, the blonde trophy at Charon's side. Did my fair complexion mark me as another woman for sale?

The estimates by the time of the gala were forty thousand sex workers trafficked to Styxos to handle the increased demand. This hidden form of prostitution was notoriously hard to measure. They said forty thousand workers meant over two hundred thousand people falling prey. That seemed like a low-ball estimate to me. Frontline sex workers were managed by money launderers and arms traffickers. The big jump in force, fraud and coercion of cross-border trafficking didn't result in increased arrests.

Dark locals in jeans and hoodies gave way to guests in evening attire at the entrance to Hotel Ben Gurion. My husband showed our invitation, and we walked through a corridor of hedges to the swimming pool. We had arrived.

Everyone who was anyone was there: Israeli investors, ambassadors, CEOs and Ph.D.s; all the good island families, from the local philanthropists to the founders of AnimalSafety4Styxos; a thousand heavily-perfumed women, some with aquiline noses and glitter spread across bare shoulders. The ex-Soviet money launderers behind the real estate bubble were showing off their latest shopping spree. The investment banks were there with offshore meta-risk managers balancing portfolios on flexible vehicles. The UN presence was discreet. European Union diplomats worked the cocktail party to schmooze heavy hitters into drilling for oil, lining the roads with bicycle paths, or installing Styxos' first train.

The sun and the wind had been ignored and raised a dust storm in the Sahara that filled the sky over Styxos with a red pallor. A 112-degree heat wave had the *maître d'* moving the party inside to the vaulted ceilings of the air-conditioned lobby. He was persuading the guests that they would be more comfortable inside the hotel where they wouldn't have to stare at the swimming pool in their coattails. The crowd started to filter out of the courtyard along with the last plate of tuna kebabs. Strands of French escaped the rumble of Styxan. A group of francophones was clustered under a eucalyptus, oblivious to the hostesses motioning guests inside. As I wiped the fish juice from my lips, my elbow bumped a woman. *"Pardon,"* I said.

"Et bien, vous parlez français?"

"Mais oui! J'ai habité à Paris," I said.

The wide-eyed black woman smiled and took my hand with an open spirit that couldn't have survived a season in Paris. She wore a long wrap-around skirt with a tribal pattern, a scarf for a belt, and, of all colours, a pink blouse. "I'm Vanessa."

"Excuse my French, Vanessa. I'm going to study."

"That's, *'Je vais étudier.'"*

"Je vais étudier."

"See, it's not hard. Just say, *'Je vais* this and *je vais* that. As long as you're *je vai-ing* you're probably alright."

"Sorry I'm such a disgrace . . . no makeup on." It was so hot.

"You look natural." She was a Frenchwoman from Martinique, and had come with her two children to find a house to rent before her husband joined her 'definitively' on the island.

The French families seemed to do that. The men would usher their wives and children out to wherever and stay behind living in empty houses to finish up with a knife and a plate and nobody to watch them.

As if they could escape the chorus.

To me, willingly bringing on such solitude was unfathomable, and I couldn't imagine a Frenchman burying his sex drive under diapers, meetings and reports. Unless he wasn't really alone. Did they find other lovers?

Of course not.

Funny how woman ignores what she doesn't want to see. My mother had told me if a man travels, you can be sure he is unfaithful.

One of the French diplomats was offering Vanessa his *canapé.* "Your husband sent you ahead *alone?* He's not worried someone will steal you?" I ignored their crude worldliness and concentrated on the sound of their language. Not that French is *better* when you can't understand it. It's just that the romantic sound floated up to the tree tops where blackbirds flitted from branch to branch.

How committed was Vanessa to her marriage? Incurable styxophile, I had only spent a week away from my husband since our wedding, and it was a long week. During that week, time rolled out like an expanse of sea with nothing on the horizon, inviting several ghosts from the past. On the second day into the week, a hole seemed to open up in my stomach, a sensation I hadn't felt in years, and I tried to remember whom it was about. There was a startling awareness of the men around me. They seemed to propose themselves as options with the insistence of Penelope's suitors and made me feel as if I owed them something. In debt and hungry. The gray line that divided the sea and the sky disappeared, and ghosts were trying to get into my boat. Finally, my husband returned and drove them away. I paced around the living room as he assembled his briefcase. I'd wanted to mention the ghosts, but he was late for work.

"It must be hard to leave your husband and move to your next posting alone. When my husband went away for just a week, I called him every night to make sure he was in his hotel room."

Vanessa laughed a deep laugh from the pit of her stomach. Her dark skin shone in the twilight. "I'm convinced there are some things in life one cannot experience as a couple." I was struck by her self-confidence and didn't ask for an example. It sounded like an adventure. Here was someone comfortable with life on the borders of two cultures.

Chapter 4

The Arab

There was a drumbeat. I looked around the cocktail party with its chatter. They had set up tall tables outside with white table cloths for the *hors-d'œuvres*. Waiters passed in ritual with trays of skewered meat. The summer twilight set the mountains ablaze behind the white cityscape. Pale reflections shimmered on the surface of the swimming pool. The conversation among the stragglers in the garden was light.

Observing this ritual under the spell of Vanessa's musk, I smiled as she presented her colleagues, the staff of the French Embassy, each more charming than the last. The careful selection of the French diplomats cannot be exaggerated. After finishing the appropriate schools and passing the necessary exams, further subjective criteria are applied. As a result, they are all handsome — every last one of them, men and women — not of any particular brand, but in their own surprising and unique ways. Their charm is full of a natural curiosity that comes across with more force since they have had to make the effort of living in foreign countries. My husband's dark eyebrows were unfurled. His whole physique was engaged in conversation with a Frenchman whose hair was the colour of sand. It had been a long time since Charon had met such a distinguished gentleman, so self-deprecating and discreetly dressed. My husband smiled, *content among peers.*

It was wonderful to hear Charon talk. When he was in public he could really turn on the charm. I was proud of my husband's accomplishments and had often thought of him as a rare specimen, in the beginning. He was smart, handsome, and hard working. It had taken me a long time to find this fluke in the Styxos machinery, where hiring is done on the basis of who your father is. Now that we were in Styxos, his healthy mind in a healthy body seemed like an oasis in a nepotistic breeding ground for mediocrity. Returning to Styxos hadn't been easy for him. I knew he felt like a foreigner in his own country, so he must have been relieved to be a part of this international milieu.

The cicadas had awoken, their rhythm accentuating the comfort of the shade. Vanessa whispered from the umbra. "Your husband's new friend is the *directeur général* of the number one French transportation concern." The Frenchman turned to look at me. His dignified air took my breath away. The thoughtful lines carved on his brow fit the position, but it was surprising to meet a *directeur général* with so little gray hair. He couldn't have been much older than we were. I caught myself staring at his handsome face when his eyes flashed with annoyance. He afforded me a dismissive nod, "*Bonjour,*" and dissolved back into conversation with my husband.

I stared in shock as a woman in red butted into their conversation. My neighbour's daughter! Before I knew it, Niovi was demanding of me, "How do you do?" Her urbane non-question caught me off guard. I don't remember answering at all. There was nothing ordinary about her. Her satin gown hugged her curves. She was conspicuous. She commanded the group with an easy voice. She shined. I struggled to reconcile her attire with the discovery that she'd gone to high school with my husband.

I like to think of myself as athletic, whereas this Niovi was feminine in every sense of the word. She knew how to put herself together. Here was a woman who had dispensed with everything masculine, who probably never appeared in public without her makeup on. Her mane of long dark hair descended past her slim waist to her high and exceptionally wide hips. With those obscene hips, the red satin was very brave. Her femininity masked the strength of her voice. "Niovi is a singer," my husband explained. I had never met anyone like her. I realized from the whispers around us that many of Niovi's fans had come tonight . They were as eager to get a glimpse of her as to meet each other so they could talk about their idol.

Niovi made a big fuss over my husband, who was revelling in her attentions. The circle closed around them and I stumbled backward. I tried to console myself with the knowledge that the lives of stars are usually unenviable. The guests watched Niovi enchant my husband. "It's been too long! I'll send you an invitation to my garden party." She would be throwing the bash at the house of the *directeur général*. They were engaged!

"Garden party!" I heard Niovi's fans whisper. The star's shining personality warmed the circle of Styxan fans like the sun ripening apples. It seemed like Styxans loved nothing more than to talk about Niovi. Would she find her soul mate? Or was this foreign businessman just a pastime? How far would they be able to get with each other? Could he bring her back down to earth? Could she make him want a baby? And then there was the question of marriage.

She'll never marry.

What motivated this class of people to lead their lives in the public eye?

I overheard that Niovi was thirty-six years old and just as frivolous as ever, as if time for a family could be delegated along with other minutiae. There she was, reaching for the next apple with immortal vigour. The locals pedalled their criticism of the Frenchman. He was too removed from tradition on the subject of marriage. It had been in the tabloids. The couple was planning a family, but without any mention of even a small, sacrificial wedding.

What could be the rationale behind such an arrangement? "It's French," one young Styxan said. Royals had sired thousands of illegitimates over the last millennium, including the heads of many modern dukedoms. Here was more proof that aristocracy bloomed even stronger after a revolution.

"It's not only French. It's American, too. Forty percent of American children are born out of wedlock," I offered.

A young Styxan scowled. "Children born out of wedlock might be good for seed sowers, but there are no advantages for the woman."

Or the children.

There was a wave of general agreement. The chorus had spoken. Niovi might be able to make him father a child, but husband a wife? If time weren't ticking away, this difference of opinion would have seen her moving on. Instead, she had listened to the Frenchman and let him impress her with his slick city ways. She had agreed to set the wedding date later on.

My husband handed the *directeur général* a cream-colored business card. I looked down at Niovi's feet and the straps of her black stilettos that wound around her calves all the way up the slit in her dress to her knees, a misanthrope's dream. My husband bulldozed a pleasantry I was trying to formulate and told Niovi about his recent promotion at the foreign office. He expounded on the higher aspirations of the spirit, and then betrayed himself with a sidelong glance at her cleavage. The muscles on his face tightened.

Not that I was worried. Wasn't he a faithful husband and kind parent who had never demanded *too* much from me or the children? I found myself standing between him and Niovi, who suddenly reached for my hand. "Nice to have met you, Mackenzie." The island *fiancée* flashed a Cheshire cat smile. How she charmed everyone. "Come, Farouk. It's hot out here," and she plucked her fiancé away.

Farouk! His name spoke of sand. A *directeur général* from the desert. I tried to hide my surprise as I searched his face for a sign of Arab roots. There was no trace. But then 'roots' were pluralistic, by nature denoting a variety of sources. Farouk looked back at me with furious blue eyes and a visage as *rive gauche* as de Gaulle's. Was he afraid I would mess up his game? He turned his striking profile. The pit in my stomach opened up. I watched his back as they walked away. Niovi's servitors followed her wide derrière.

He should be with you.

I looked around to see who had spoken. No one was there. Farouk's and Niovi's souls seemed to linger where they'd stood a moment ago, laughing and talking in a cloud of smoke with the waiter dancing around them. Soon there was just the view of the pool and a shaker of salt on the table. The *apéritif* was over; the guests had all gone inside. "We're the last to leave," I said.

"As usual," my husband agreed. Arm in arm, we left the courtyard.

"Farouk is a fine man," my husband said.

"He seems to think so."

Police cars flashed in the street below. Eight cars escorted the President of Styxos into the parking lot.

Chapter 5

Foul Play

Our way was suddenly blocked by a small crowd flowing out of the hotel to watch the president get out of his black Mercedes. The president was forty-seven years old and good-looking. We followed his escort into the air-conditioning under a regiment of chandeliers. A waiter offered us each a glass of champagne. We stood in the centre of the red carpet watching the president shake hands with dignitaries and pose for the press. They had him in front of a metallic screen and white lights. There were three TV cameras.

"They say he led a sheltered life, apart from four years spent at university in London." Vanessa was at my side. Then the cameras turned on the crowd. We tried to pose for the press, but they wanted Farouk. The white lights ignited Farouk's eyes as they fell on mine.

"He's staring at you," Vanessa said.

"No he's not," I whispered.

Vanessa was laughing at me.

"OK, where is he from?"

"Paris. Can't you tell? *Vive la différence.* Farouk inherited his mother's 7th arrondissement complexion."

The president didn't stay long. Enclosed by his bodyguards, he edged to the back of the room. A man in a uniform opened the glass door. The president slid through the door, and stepped into the evening heat. He meant to leave by the pool gate.

Night had fallen. The men's shoes echoed on the tiles. The pool lights illuminated turquoise water. The bodyguards padded obediently behind the president outside the picture window. The president had started to loosen his tie when his body went rigid. What happened? Had someone shot him? I didn't hear anything.

But the president did not fall. He stood there, frozen, looking down, as if struck by some hideous scene at his feet. His hands blocked out the sight, and then he looked again in disbelief. The bodyguards surrounded him. Our alarm increased, watching him aghast at the sight.

Footsteps sounded on the pavement. The president's men dispersed around the swimming pool and took control, yelling orders. A siren wailed.

Who would do such a thing?

There was a strange electricity in the air. The guests hurrying to the picture window blocked our view. The first row of guests recoiled as if in outrage as the next wave cascaded against the window. The crowd was impenetrable. An unholy field of energy seemed to be coming in through the window, telling without words that reality had shifted, that I must be ready.

We will see you through.

How did energy know to turn into matter? I knew I was being touched by a spirit.

Death is separation from herself and communion with us.

Now the president was pacing up and down in front of us on the red carpet and talking on the phone. "This is bad press!" And right at the pinnacle of our bid to accede to the European Union. "The ten o'clock news *better* mitigate the embarrassment. Yes, say that! 'The police report indicated no evidence of foul play.' " The president left half his escort at the pool and sped away in his black Mercedes.

In his capacity as *directeur général*, Farouk managed a pained smile for *la presse française*, to the chagrin of Niovi, whose Mediterranean temper was beginning to cast a long shadow. Farouk's eyes flashed to mine, and I had to look away again.

"He has to be correct in all his relations to compensate for his darker roots . . ." Vanessa was saying, "Underneath his mother's Parisian snobbery is the emotional reservoir of his father's Egypt. Look at him. You see his masochistic endurance? His unwillingness to react?" I watched him, standing there perpetuating an illusion that everything was under control.

Niovi descended on one of the journalists. "That's the Middle East bureau chief of the International Press Agency," Vanessa said. Niovi begged to differ on the story and antagonized the bureau chief into getting on the phone with their Paris office.

"What's going on?" I asked.

"There's something in the pool, but I can't see what," Vanessa said. "People are getting trampled at the window."

Charon remained planted firmly on the red carpet. "And if they all go to hell, is it OK if we don't?"

Questions flew from all corners. Bodies pressed to the window and shrank back. On this first night of the ensuing battle of the sexes, the carpet of the hotel lobby danced with male and female shadows. Farouk pressed his forehead to the glass. He didn't show any sign of recognizing the bureau chief's wife kneeling by the poolside with her pocket camera. She was a journalist who had survived a cult of sexy mergers: made to work for the new chief, she got her revenge by marrying him. Through someone's legs, I could see her hold her camera just above the water to take a close-up shot.

Vanessa followed my eyes. "Farouk does not like swimming," she said. "He says he prefers to escape from the heat with a cold shower."

"Really?" Charon and I said in unison.

"Maybe it's part of his culture from generations of desert dwellers. He'd rather retreat with a good book to his air conditioning than put on his swimsuit and get to the neighbourhood pool. He says he refuses to *stew* in the Mediterranean. He finds excuses, like needing to finish a report so he doesn't have to join his colleagues at the seaside."

Looking back, I'm convinced that Farouk's separation from the horror that night was an expression of this layer of his personality. I can see him shored up in his study in search of clues to his deepest feeling, taking down a leather-bound companion from the shelf and contemplating the celestial mathematics of interrelationships.

Beyond his tall figure, a form floated in the water, tail disappearing in the depths of the pool.

Chapter 6

Monstrosity

I was seized with fear watching the monster undulate facedown. A long piece of seaweed twisted in the mild current. I let out a whimper, unable to control my panic, but there was no need to feel ashamed. Farouk was no longer aware of me. He seemed absorbed in his own reflection in the window. How could anyone be so egocentric? Was he noticing his hair greying around the temples? Not that I don't find a touch of gray attractive in a man. An air of responsibility would come in handy in the ensuing battle. I could picture his family *château*, a bulwark of strategic importance against the kingdom of Spain, the natural strength of its position being reinforced by fortress after fortress, and how good the wine must be in that region, once it had been decanted.

A dark liquid curled in the water. But Farouk didn't seem to see the form floating beneath the surface, tail disappearing in the depths of the pool. The conversation bubbled around him at the window as the ambulance arrived. What was wrong with Farouk? He did not seem to hear the other guests around him surmising about the blonde waif's nationality, *Russian? Moldavian?* Her arms spread out to the sides to embrace her wedding with eternity. Her scarf twisted in the water like a piece of seaweed. The long, silver train of her dress undulated like a fish tail.

That silver dress. As they lured the body over to the side of the pool, I saw! It was the blond girl from the street! Her square jaw was clenched shut. Her blue eyes were frozen in a look of terror. My first taste of death. I would have envied her fate if I had suspected the evil that was to come. I pushed my way over to the window next to Farouk and pressed my face to the glass. He shook from his reverie as soon as he saw me, turned on his heel and walked away.

I was shocked. How could he hate me so much? He hardly knew me. Languages rang in my ears. No one admitted to knowing the waif, but they bubbled her name, Grushenka, age, nineteen. I listened to the gossip around me for a clue as to the girl's identity.

"Of course the circumstances are suspicious," Niovi echoed.

"What do you think?" a reporter asked.

Niovi's voice raised an octave. "She was fully clothed. Obviously she was not going for a swim! This was a premeditated crime. But watch how the tribunal will handle it. The criminals!"

A reporter scribbled greedily on his pad.

Someone should have shut Niovi up for her own sake. Why wasn't Farouk at her side? Farouk was waiting helplessly. I wanted to straighten him out, but I knew it would only set Niovi off again, so I waited for my chance.

Farouk stood in the back of the lobby as they dragged the woman from the pool. The silver gown clung to her hips. The train fanned out from her ankles like a mermaid's tail. Niovi's voice rose above the din. The woman's blue torso was lifted out of the water. They pulled a thin arm to turn her over. "Look at those!" The mermaid's dress clung to her bosom, a sublime final act.

"Those aren't real!" Niovi squealed.

I stifled a nervous laugh. That would be in tomorrow's paper. More reporters crowded around Niovi. She composed a headline, *Call Girl Hits High Society*. She stalked the press, convincing them to jump to the wildest conclusions. The battle seemed to take on a personal significance for her. Could Niovi have known the dead girl? I watched her as she went from reporter to reporter. Why did she badger the media? Did she know more than she was letting on? Her outrage peaked just as the head of the International Press Agency got a hold of her. "Travelling light!" Niovi cried. It was all over. "Without Your Body!" The reporters soaked it up. The next day the story would appear in all the mainland papers. *Bottoms up on Styxos!*

A pained smile was frozen on Farouk's face. He was powerless to rein in Niovi. Her black hair seemed to stand on end. Zeal flared in her deep brown eyes, matriarchal eyes burning for justice. Flanked in an hysteria of window-shoppers, Niovi seemed capable of organizing a suffragette contagion. When she stalked off to talk to the police, Farouk's face turned ash.

The *maître d'* hurried about the scene of the crime trying to calm the guests. He whistled to the wait staff. That the death of a call girl might slow the wheels of business investment on gala night was beside the point. There were guests to feed! The waiters moved the lobster gazpacho. Dinner was served. Hungry and unsure of what was expected of them, the guests shuffled on to the next attraction. I stifled *my* indignation.

The great room was set up with orange tablecloths and silver candelabras fit for a séance. The tables were laden with crystal goblets for red and white wine, and still larger ones for water. I was relieved to find place cards on the tables — left to their own devices, the Styxan men would have congregated on one side of the room and left the women on the other. Tonight there would be no need to scramble for a seat on the border of two very boring conversations. A waiter skirted off leaving a course of stuffed grape leaves and pheasants oozing fig sauce. My nose started to itch as it always does when encountering delicacies of this calibre.

A widescreen video flashed a picture of languid, bombed-out hotels waiting timelessly for the obelisk of capitalism to open them again. Plans were revealed for a rail line linking the airport to the ghost town. To christen the renovation of the abandoned city, Shakespeare's Othello would play in the streets where investors could relive the dark wanderings of the jealous Moor.

Businessmen on Styxos were talking about dredging the water around her ancient quays for container handling. One of Farouk's competitors pointed to a pie chart showing that one high-speed train was projected to increase tourism by 20% in the first year. My husband whispered, "Farouk says Styxos isn't long enough to run train *à grande vitesse*." But Farouk was not available for comment.

The guests watched the red and white wine being poured. There was a rustle of starched shirts trying to drown out the keynote speaker's litany of foreign invasions. The French diplomats perked up during the French invasion, and without toasting, discreetly drank the wine flown in from Bordeaux earlier that day.

The Italian diplomats bowed politely to the French ". . . with Styxos finally surrendering to the legacy of Italy." During their rule, they had made plans to turn the town into a little Venice, but instead the Ottomans had demolished the palaces and mansions. Here the Muslim islanders feigned indifference. Video clips of modern technological symbols flashed across the screen, ending with the clean, high-speed train itself.

The next speaker was supposed to be Farouk. One of his colleagues stepped up to the podium and made excuses in a thick French accent before introducing the proposed clean machine, faster than any other train in the world. The maximum gradient was to be 3.5%, quite steep for a railway. This meant there was little need for tunnelling in the heat. The islanders perked up at the news that the line would pay for itself in less than ten years. They felt the tugging need for a railway to connect them with their long-lost real estate.

The Muslims grumbled. Civilization would exacerbate their problems again, leaving everyone with new expectations. Look how modern medicine had abolished the need to have more children, imposing new requirements on their sex drives, upsetting natural selection. The Christians rolled their eyes. They had been missing a train for so long that it seemed ignorant to argue the point. When the subject of a railway was broached, they exchanged knowing glances, and changed the subject to pâté versus caviar and Grushenka, who, someone

42

guessed, had been involved with the mafia. An Ex-Soviet diplomat was saying, "Now look what they've done," to the tabletop.

"At least you have something to drink about," his wife consoled him in earnest. As the Russian couple set to work on another round of vodkas, I studied my husband's expression. Just when his avoidance of the subject had restored my sense of security, Niovi swept past our table.

Her gaze swiftly caressed my husband and locked onto mine. A chill ran down my spine, as if she had projected a passive envy from her eyes. I was paralyzed — my eyes still connected with hers — and I felt my energy being drained away as if I were a shrinking star collapsing inward. I had seen the opposite of the look of love. It wasn't hate. It was envy, in her eye, as if despite all her talent and good looks, she couldn't rise above her meanness, as if she had nothing of her own to feed on except her envy of . . . the life in me.

Chapter 7

Theory of Lite

I felt devoured. What if the eye, the organism that senses light, also transmitted a light — or darkness — of its own? The hypnotic stalking of a lion is known to bewilder antelopes and other quadrupeds. Its stare renders them incapable of moving as they are seized and eaten.

Surely that eye, the seed of a dark star, projected as much as it saw, half-closed behind the veil of envy, radiating from a woman who could reflect harm simply by looking at me with hunger. I tried to keep a sense of proportion, and rationalized that she probably wasn't aware of the spell she cast. It was hard enough to find women who could be role models. After all, she was one of the most talented women, one of the few professional women around. But the power she possessed! To imagine her eye looking into the passage of Farouk's soul, unconsciously dealing its curse through the forces of nature, so much greater now that the victim was her loved one. There was no denying that eye.

That night I started to develop my own theory of light. I began to understand why Charon had become so evasive once we moved to Styxos: just as Medusa had frozen heroes with her stare, being the object of another's awareness was a great risk among Styxans. I would learn to stay out of the black sun of their scrutiny. The Old Testament mentions the belief in a force projected by the eye. In a flash, I understood what modern culture had almost repressed. This is why people on Styxos believed in the ancient Sumerian superstition of the evil eye. The word 'evil' seemed unfortunate because I was sure that as a bearer, Niovi did not mean to curse me in particular. But, as the British say, I had been 'overlooked', touched by a gaze that remained too long.

The press stood ready at the back of the room. I watched Niovi march up the steps to the stage, and braced myself for another embarrassing scene. I guess every town has a fanatic, and if it doesn't have one, it fabricates one. There was a hush in the audience. Her conceit fed by the exercise of unquestioned authority, Farouk's fiancée unhooked the microphone to start her next tirade.

But instead of ranting, she sang a very high note. The piano tinkled like crystal, shattering as her voice broke through. The rebellious beginning took the audience by surprise. By the second bar we were in her hands. She stalked lazily downstage on the downbeat, now in touch with a deeper part of herself, the guitar and snare drum playing softly to the hypnotic rhythm. They said it was a new song, and some of the notes evaded her voice. She was not always master of the gifts she possessed, but when she got it all together and kneaded out the chorus, you could tell she had grown up with music. She slipped effortlessly out of her atonal rendition — *Without you, my dreams will take wing.* The Asia Minor melody slid down her torso and piled onto the floor

A green spotlight quenched her red dress and camouflaged her limbs in praying mantis hues. It was impossible to maintain a casual interest. Even if I couldn't dispel my fear of her inner state, I was fascinated with Niovi. I struggled to avoid her gaze, to not fall under her power. I reminded myself that 'fascinate' and 'bewitch' were confined to malevolence in earlier times. She was not necessarily an evil person *per se,* but I felt her dark influence lurking, ready to invade those she beheld.

Outside, the moon lay on its back in the sky, the old moon shining in the arms of the new. A dark disc circumscribed within the yellow crescent. It was precisely this phase of the eastern moon that the witch had adopted for her headdress. She had painted her large eyes like those of the Egyptian goddess Isis, whose symbol was the crescent and disc. But the horns of Niovi's crescent were prolonged, like the horns of a cow. The ox-eyed woman was beautiful in this half-bovine state. The symbolic horns of the crescent moon, upon which the ancients relied for protection against malevolence, caught the stage lights. Her song mounted in a plea to free her occupied city.

Guests whispered. Representatives from a mainland recording studio were in the audience. Would she get a recording contract on the continent?

I remembered that charms against the evil eye were called *corno,* 'horn'. As a piece of archaeological fieldwork, her costume with the disc of the sun resting in the crescent of the moon seemed appropriate, but the real genius was in the universal theme, "a woman's envy of her captor," according to my husband. Niovi didn't need to *assume* the role. She made full use of her power over us.

Steeped in Virgil, Niovi recast ancient Isis as Ceres, and Osiris as Bacchus adorned with the telltale horns. The anthropologist in me was hooked. I couldn't take my eyes off this goddess of real estate wearing horned crescents in her hair. Hera and her line had lost their identities as monotheism gained sway. These divinities had all been rolled into one: she was Diana. How modern it must have seemed at the time, recasting all those deities as mere attributes of the one!

And we were there.

Now that we were back on track after the death of the call girl, I looked down at the programme. Its Styxan hieroglyphics were ensconced in photos of terra cotta figures meandering around the entryway to Hades, reputed to be hidden somewhere on Styxos. This gave me plenty to dig about. If we didn't unearth enough pots, I prayed that we would stumble upon the mouth of hell.

There was a stunned moment before the applause erupted. A strobe played on Niovi as she threw her arms back and walked to the edge of the stage. In the strobe, you could see the line of goddesses in her wake. She started to sing again, immediately silencing our hands with frightening beauty. The locals knew the poet's new single by heart and sang along. The eerie eastern melody had struck a chord among the young women of the day. "This is a departure from her usual repertoire," a fan commented. I noticed for the first time that many of the women in the audience were wearing evil eye charms. There it was again. Envy was widely believed to be a poison that kills. An official chuckled, and was rebuffed by a fan who said that it was an observable fact, "Jealousy kills."

After much prompting, my husband translated a bit of the programme for me. "It's about an evil spirit who possesses Zeus' lover. A vestal virgin plays her magical lute, and the enchanting sound draws the spirit out of the vestal virgin. After many complaints, the spectre finally announces that she is none other than Zeus' wife, Hera, who possessed Zeus' lover out of jealousy." The public eye watched the horns of jealousy shine on Niovi's head, turning Farouk's happy and cheerful mate into the angry Hera. The music subsided, and Niovi was herself again, a petite woman with a mane of curls and wide hips. The applause was genuine. The part of her soul that thrived on recognition —Niovi's *thymos* — revelled in the applause, thirst momentarily quenched. We rose from our seats. She disappeared behind the curtain and then came out again, her gown a vermillion flame. Then the flame went out!

Chapter 8

A Reasonable Vice

The moment Niovi disappeared behind the curtain, the guests started talking about Grushenka again. How had she stolen so swiftly into the spotlight? Was her ghost simply handy? Were people using Grushenka as a tool to ignore the business deals underfoot? As the evening wore on, the 'truth' started to come out. An Italian business-man in his late forties had spent a night with Grushenka at a seaside resort. She was expensive. She was *bella!* He confirmed rumours that she kept men going from club to club under the strain of seeking pleasure until morning, and hardly went to bed.

"I met her, too," the busboy said.

"You did?" I said. "Well what was she doing here?"

She was trying to get in without an invitation. "She said she was here with one of the guests. She was a talker. She told me that a guest — I won't mention any names — this guest had proposed to her. I thought it was a lie, but she was wearing such an expensive dress. She wanted us to let her in as his accompaniment — without him."

"Which guest?"

The busboy pursed his lips and glanced across the room at Farouk.

"That's impossible," my husband said.

"He's taken!" I said.

"I know," the busboy said, "and we didn't believe her, but she hitched a ride on the arm of the ambassador of Turkmenistan, so we had to let her in."

"Everyone likes Farouk," my husband insisted. "He's a fine man. If he did anything questionable, I'm sure he had his reasons for it."

But what about Farouk's withdrawal after the girl's death? It fit.

"I don't mean to implicate anyone," said the busboy, "but I don't think that she was the type of girl who would take his reasons into account."

"Maybe you should talk to the police."

"Oh *putain*! Oh whore!" The busboy's breath smelled of alcohol. "They don't want to know. They have their own story for cases like this. What do they care who invited her to the gala? He didn't kill her. He was with us the whole time. It was probably a mafia job, maybe a suicide. She probably got punished for trying to run away. No one cares if Mr. Farouk proposed to her, or if it was a game. So what if he was seen with her in a cab or wanted to make everything legitimate? For the police, she didn't exist in the first place. The fact that she's dead simplifies things."

"Exactly," my husband said. "One way or another, she stopped playing the game and got punished. Whether they killed her, or somebody drove her to kill herself is a matter of semantics, isn't it?"

I glared at Charon.

"I mean, for the police."

It appeared that the murder of Grushenka was the perfect crime. It was executed with premeditation and a long-established alibi. She never existed in the first place. The institutions erected to uphold the law for selected Styxans had rationalized her away.

The chief of police had been passing from table to table, questioning the guests. The busboy ran off just as the chief alighted at our table. He planted a chair in between us and straddled it. The police chief had eaten so much he was short of breath. "Just a few brief questions," he said. "Nothing serious, my friend. The police force pretends to pay us, and we pretend to investigate murders. Are you a friend of Farouk's?"

"I just met him tonight," my husband said. "He struck me as an upstanding citizen. I can usually tell right away."

"What about the girl? Ever seen her?"

My husband shook his head. I looked away.

The police chief scribbled on his notepad. "Collecting information is a delicate art. I prefer to do it myself when possible. Thank you for your input. It has been illuminating."

"Really?" My husband's eyes sparkled with pride.

"Well, I'm afraid that we already know who did it." Without disclosing what evidence had cemented the fate of the unlucky suspect, the police chief glanced across the room at Farouk, folded his notepad and restored it to his inside pocket. My husband and I looked at each other.

As soon as the inspector was gone, my husband headed toward Farouk, who was smoking in the corner of the room. He was leaning against the wall, looking more like a victim than a criminal. I shuffled through the dinner party after my husband, who was quickly saying hello here and there on his way over, but was apprehended by an old friend. I lingered on the fringe of the lengthy boast my husband had launched into about his tax-free car. I could feel Farouk's eyes on me, and broke free and headed toward him. I needed to see him under pressure. I looked forward to seeing confirmation of my theories about Farouk. As I approached, he remembered his manners, pushed his body off of the wall, and stood at attention.

He looked away quickly and then straight at me while I was admiring his nose. His eyes swept over my bare shoulders as if to say, *Wasn't that the point?* I felt naked. Ambivalence gripped us both. It was tangible, and had to be coming from him since it smelled male. I tried not to feel this cowardice, and found something to say. "So you're a smoker. I was a smoker for seventeen years."

"Seven or seventeen?" he asked, searching my face for a sign of my age.

"You know just what to say."

He looked trapped in his coattails.

I immediately regretted imposing this formula on him.

He was forced at last to exhale a curl of smoke. "You think what I say is worn out? Why not? I suppose it is. Did you know, even when you read the gospels, there are 180 similarities between the Egyptian god Horus and Jesus? Every miracle, every teaching was present in the Egyptian writings thousands of years before, with pictures of the shepherds visiting the infant Horus, even pictures of the visit of the Magi. No *matteur* how much we try to possess them, good stories have a life of their own."

I watched the smoke curl out of his mouth and encircle his argument that Jesus was a bastard. He was tempting fate. I couldn't find my voice but wasn't going to get sucked into his game. At last I managed to say, "If you quit before forty, you have almost the same chance of escaping cancer as someone who never smoked."

He drew the smoke back in with a snort. "How did you quit?"

"When you have a baby, you have to quit," I said, at the risk of sounding American.

"But not if you're a man."

"These days it's almost the same thing."

"Hmm. It's too late for me, but I only smoke after meals, and I smoke these cigarillos." He contemplated the brown stick in his hand. "The smoke never gets to my lungs."

"You could take a vitamin supplement."

"People don't usually die of cancer of the mouth, so it is, you see, a vice *raisonnable*."

"I'm sure you are always reasonable."

"Quite." Up until now he had readily pointed out his own weaknesses, so I wasn't expecting an arch reply. Vanessa had hinted that Farouk's mother had been disinherited for marrying an Egyptian. Surely he was not about to succumb to public scandal on the verge of making his infrastructure bid. The show must go on. I looked into his draconic mouth, full of the pleasure of a reasonable vice. "And is there such a thing as a reasonable crime?"

He was taken aback. "Ah, Mackenzie. That would be a lack of *caractère*. It takes a weak personality to make a crime reasonable, to justify it, and then institutionalize it. Yes, there is plenty of that, starting with philosophers and politicians who turn crime into constitution. And then there's the church. No one can be expected to be good all the time. You see, even to be friends is dangerous." His eyes had wandered throughout this speech, adding to his aristocratic lack of conviction, but whatever was phony about him suddenly evaporated when he looked into my eyes and said the word 'dangerous'.

I fought back a wave of fear. "If you don't believe in anything, why bother whether a vice is reasonable or not? As long as there are no values, everything goes, for you."

"*Moi?* I never met her."

The busboy had said Farouk knew the girl.

"You've got the wrong man." The smoke curled out of his mouth. "I didn't kill her."

"Who?"

He glared.

"But you condone it."

Farouk's spine arched again as he watched something over my shoulder. I turned to see a police officer approaching. He asked Farouk with alarming familiarity if they could talk in the lobby. "Alone."

I was stunned by his karmic precipitation. Did Farouk have a police record?

"Excuse me, Madame," Farouk said. He crushed out his cigarillo and hurried after the officer.

So. He had a reason to be afraid.

Chapter 9

Catwalk

I managed to throw back my shoulders and forge my way to our table. The smell of charred meat filled the room. Waiters were carrying plates of grilled lamb dripping with juices and tomatoes stuffed with wild rice. The manager of Taylord's led the way through the tables, saying, "People always find an excuse to spend money," and revelling in the prospect of making more sales in the coming days. I found our place cards. My husband was already seated. He poured me another glass of red wine.

Thoughts of Farouk and the waif overtook the beginning of the *hors de prix* fashion show. I felt a wave of nausea when the audience *oohed* at a catlike model marching down the runway. There was that emptiness tugging at my stomach, even though I'd made up my mind to despise Farouk, who was in the lobby.

The next model's hair and physique resembled Grushenka's. She wore an Elizabethan theme gown with a push-up bodice and a skirt that fanned out into a chessboard pattern. Black and white diamonds painted onto the silk in perspective sprang from the horizon of her waistband, with a large pawn and king sewn into the foreground above the hem. The blonde model wore a garland on her haughty head, green eyes glaring out at us in search of her end game. When her turn was over, she marched to the corner of the stage and stood motionless. Her hoop skirt swayed on the gigantic video screen.

The women in the room looked as uncomfortable as I was, all trapped behind bishops and knights, dreading our turns. The next piece came out, a short black leather mini dress laced up the back like a shoe. The model strode out onto the catwalk, all legs and straps, her face hidden behind a fan.

A string of frilly evening gowns floated by. An Italian model flounced the see-through fabric 'for the woman who couldn't do without luxury.' Her gait sent the ruffles floating. The frills that had covered her breasts ascended in the ventilation. Her eyes swept the crowd with bold indifference. The audience watched spellbound as long scarves flapped in the wind machine. We gasped when the ruffles on the hem of a coral job got caught on a poor model's heel. She flushed to match her red eye shadow. Three women in headscarves at the next table chuckled. The model regained her balance, hiked the dress all the way up around her waist freeing a pair of concave, runway thighs, and thrust her nose into the air. The applause was loud. The designer peered from his facelift with pride.

But the height of the show was a perky brunette in a cocktail suit, who strode out onto the catwalk to a modern version of *Summertime*. She had appeared on the scene holding a tiny blue purse to match her powder blue miniskirt. A trumpet whined, *Aw your daddy's rich.* Walking away, she executed a half turn as if looking for someone she knew. She pretended to snub him. Then, she unbuttoned her cocktail jacket and let it slide down to handcuff her arms in back, tiny purse dangling behind like a padlock, breasts pointing up from an excuse of a silk camisole. "Look at the cameraman!" my husband said. "He's going to drop the camera."

I'll never forget that night. Catching the tide of the fanfare, Miss Styxos appeared on stage wearing her banner, and announced that it was the audience's turn to walk down the catwalk. Her voluptuous body moved through the chairs. She invited several women in scarves and dresses with swooping necklines, albeit opaque, up onto the runway. She grabbed my arm, but I tugged it back. My husband held onto my other hand, and all of my misgivings about him melted away. Two women from our table got up to join the final parade.

Of course once our own women were up on stage, it was obvious that the models had been far too thin. But most people had to agree that the models' chiselled bodies showed the clothes to their best advantage. The guests still at their tables felt suddenly self-conscious. The lights sharpened our imperfections. "Should I put my jacket on, or keep it off?" my husband whispered.

"You're fine either way. You look very dignified in your blue ascot." Women noted what their competitors were wearing. With the middle-aged contingent onstage, our remaining tablemates sank into debate. It seemed that everyone had known Grushenka better than the others. Rumour spread around the room. She was that meek girl in the back, the one who'd given good massages until she disappeared one day. "Nonsense!" the woman next to me practically yelled across the table. "She was a parasite who thrived on disintegrating marriages." An elderly couple supported this argument, saying she answered the impossible exigencies of religion: there was too much love with no object. "Lucky her, to be freed from such strange games."

The stories multiplied. "Her lover had confessed to the police."

"No, to a clergyman."

"I heard it was a classic mafia cover-up. She was one of those women terrorists posing as somebody's wife."

"She was just upset that she wasn't invited.'"

"We saw Grushenka in a Gucci bathing suit with an ambassador at the hotel swimming pool, but then her 'colleagues' came walking along the poolside in G-strings with a lack of modesty that betrayed them all."

"Could she swim?"

"That's nothing." She was a former president's mistress. *A lesbian. A witch.*

I listened to the chorus elaborate how she had been brought to Styxos when she was sixteen, supposedly to work as a tailor's assistant: she was confident in her sewing and eager to be in a position to send checks home to her mother and blind sister. She was an uncommonly beautiful girl with classic Russian features, golden blonde hair, and long legs. Maybe she would find a husband on Styxos, her mother had told her. When she arrived at the island establishment, she was shown to a bedroom above a cabaret. The room smelled like a candle that had just been put out. Her naked roommates stared at her with accepting dispassion, and it was then that Grushenka understood her situation. She gasped, seeing that one of the girls was handcuffed to a bedpost.

The other women left 'for work'. Grushenka sat on her bed staring out the window. A man with snake tattoos on his arms burst into the room. He liked pain, and felt the surge of endorphins about to enjoy hers. "Why you sad at me?" he accused. "I am your master. You've never had a master before. You have a lot to learn." She shrank against the headboard, a translucent shape, travelling light above the candles.

And then I saw her! The white ghost of Grushenka flushed from head to foot. *Afraid.* Her form was vivid behind the candelabra. Her eyes wide, understanding his pleasure. She watched him unbutton his pants, ready to carry off his blood-dripping, virgin prey.

Chapter 10

Travelling Lite

Early next morning, my husband got a call from the wire service. Half of the English desk didn't make it in the morning after the gala. They needed back up.

"I'm an anthropologist, not a journalist."

"What's the difference?"

My mother would have divorced him then and there, but my mother had died a long time ago, alone. I was determined not to make the same mistakes. Getting a divorce on Styxos would mean giving up the children. The courts always ruled in favour of the Styxan parent, and the Styxan grandparents ended up taking care of the children while the foreign mother sank into poverty and struggled to visit.

"Today's news is tomorrow's relic." My husband found me some work clothes.

I refused to take this seriously. To argue would be to admit that I had become a part of Styxos, whereas *I* would be leaving one day, with my kids. He dropped me off at the wire service. I stood in the doorway of the newsroom. A short, balding man in a wrinkled shirt sat me down at a computer. Three executives padded by my desk. I murmured, "Good morning," which all three eagerly snubbed. They filed into the adjacent glass office for a meeting.

As soon as they were engaged in animated exchange, the Arab desk lit up. A cloud of cigarette smoke rose to the ceiling. A bearded man in a gray sweater and black jeans slid his Coke can into the middle as an ashtray. The other desks typed away at their stories and watched the glass office out of the corners of their eyes.

Everyone sucked up to these three kings so they could offer up their nuggets to the speakerphone. The French regional director and his chief editors from the US and UK spat into the speakerphone in the centre of the robust Holstein's desk. Holstein rested his belly on the veneer and cocked his beefy head toward the speaker phone. That crackling voice seemed to be all that was left of the antichrist who had lived and breathed newspapers longer than anyone could remember. It barked in Journalese, "Parker, my concern has been piqued by this watershed of crucial arms smuggling pieces coming out of the Middle East!"

Parker evoked his best Journalese. "I didn't mean to lambaste you, but we are slated to sound like an obituary. I was merely noting that the arms contraband angle was overblown, adding that this focus could have the undesirable effect of sparking undue negative sentiment."

The French Regional Director concurred in his heavy accent. "*Weaders* are weary of this watershed of death tolls, especially in light of embattled US troops which have moved for closure in the aftermath of the contraband *cwackdown*. In a nutshell, our arms-related copy has *wratcheted* up too far in a bid to slate American success stories for the Christmas season."

"Exactly," Holstein's lips pronounced. "We need to shatter the stillness with something softer." The three recurrent magi stood up and looked at each other meaningfully.

Moments later the outcome travelled around the newsroom. Enough of violence spawning suicide bombings! They were missing the real story. What was the real story?

"If it bleeds, it leads," someone called. The fat Holstein padded over to my supervisor and mumbled something. As soon as Holstein was out of sight, my supervisor walked past his reporters. They all avoided eye contact. My supervisor, a short man with a shiny head who smelled like tobacco, came to me and began to explain the situation.

It was then that I got a chance to write my first Grushenka story. I tried to follow his instructions about writing the lead: "It has to hook the readers from the start and get them to proceed on to the second sentence, or the article will be dead." I thought it would be a struggle to describe the battle of the sexes I'd witnessed between Niovi and Farouk in the hotel lobby and the discovery of the dead girl, but it came by itself, not from me. I was only typing out an incantation, and it was coming from somewhere else. I squeezed my eyes shut and a teardrop fell on the keyboard. When the first paragraph was done, I went back and obsessed over breathing some life into the second sentence as a springboard to the third. Soon, the story was growing out of the prototype, my lead. Grushenka had made her debut.

The next day, there was that strange electricity again as she went from headline to dust bin and got picked up all over the Middle East. Wire stories have a life of their own as journalists from all over add pieces to them for as long as an item is newsworthy. Background was added from other stories including one about the skinhead Snake who had been picked up for questioning the night of the gala. He claimed to have come to Styxos "to get back to the ancient ways." He liked the warmth of the people. They made him feel more comfortable than before he lost his eye. Yes! He only had one good eye. The other one was glass.

Grushenka got pasted into newspapers and TV broadcasts everywhere, offering some relief from the residual smuggler stories that ran that day. Grushenka was travelling light over the IPA wire.

I shivered when I realized it was Holstein himself who was leaning over my shoulder asking for more. "Make it your business," he hissed. "Find out where she worked."

My colleagues sneered at me.

My bald supervisor came around again, and whispered, "That's how you know you wrote a good article: you get a kick in the butt."

Chapter 11

Serial Monogamists

The paper lay on the breakfast table. *Ex-Soviet Call Girl Dead after Botched Escape.* My husband's mother was talking about her to Niovi's mother over the wall. From what I could make out, Niovi's mother hadn't liked Farouk from the beginning. He was rude. She could see through his haughty foreign airs and disregard for Styxan customs to his true character. He had been heard saying he'd rather die than stay in Styxos. "That foreigner doesn't know how to live!"

Charon's mood was better that day. He seemed happy to be going out with me, even if it was only to the embassy. Maybe things would be alright after all. Before we got married, he had promised to do something about his temper. "I'm learning," he would say, a loveable throwback. "I'll stop yelling by the time we have kids," he'd said. Maybe he was just a little bit late.

We'd taken the front-page Grushenka story with us, and I read it out loud in the car: they'd found an expired plane ticket to the mainland in her name. The national interest in the high-speed train had kept Farouk out of the paper, but I knew the scandal was not going to evaporate. It seemed Farouk's fiancée had rightly blown the whistle before the lovers could elope, but too late to save the call girl. "So that's why Niovi was fuming at the gala!"

The police said they only wanted to determine the full extent of Niovi's involvement. Niovi, usually comfortable in the spotlight, was allegedly shocked at being detained for further questioning. There was a quote smearing Farouk, "His French spirit is corrupted through loveless lust, his sense of meaning rusted through distaste for work. He's not exactly a man of steel."

"Talking badly of one's family is like spitting into the wind," my husband said. "Not that Farouk is her family, but then, Frenchmen often don't marry their spouses."

"Niovi would never fall for that," I said. "Styxans have to be paid dowries to take responsibility for a family. She's not naïve. What Styxan would marry her after she'd been used by a Frenchman? Look here, Niovi says, 'When I became famous, I swiftly disentangled my real essence from my public personality. I'm making new friends now. All personal contracts are up for review.' "

I folded up the story. Vanessa's black arms waved us into our mid-morning appointment with M. Montaigne, a diplomat who had set out to perform reconstructive surgery on our past.

Two circles of sweat graced his armpits. He took off his glasses and put them back on again. "Two serial monogamists have found their match." We all laughed and relaxed into our chairs. "You have come to the embassy to apply for French nationality for your two children, a process you started when you lived in Israel."

"Yes." I thought of our adorable bunnies, a towheaded four-year-old boy and his two-year-old sister with a tummy like a ball, at home with *saba*. We wanted to move to France someday, and getting French nationality for the children was the first step. The paperwork was complicated by the fact that we had moved around so much, and had both been divorced and remarried. The French citizenship was coming from my first husband, a Frenchman. The paperwork had multiplied exponentially, and M. Montaigne had to go beyond the usual prescriptions to fully understand the intention of the law to figure out which family each document was supposed to come from.

Montaigne sifted through the mountain of paperwork. At length he closed the file and looked at each of us. He sighed, "Since there were no children from your previous marriages, no harm has been done. We will fix everything!" He deduced the missing paperwork needed to obtain French citizenship for our children. "What you need is a new *livret de famille* for you and your husband. We will apply for it now." Montaigne had just begun the scramble to obtain this new document, when he suddenly stopped. "You started this process four years ago!" Some of the supporting documents had expired. "*Aïe.* You should have registered at the consulate in Israel." With all the moving around, the file had never been completed, and now the babies were children, with no citizenship. "This is turning out to be an interesting job."

"On account of us?"

"Not only you. Also because of the arrest." He gave a telling look.

"You're joking. They didn't arrest Farouk!"

"They did. Don't repeat this, eh? It's an open secret that Farouk spent his first night in jail. They say he fainted."

"Oh, whore!" my husband murmured in French.

"He is one of those people who never learned how to steal. Not that it's a good thing to steal, but you have to know, in case you need to steal a loaf of bread to save your life. Everyone should know how to steal a loaf of bread. Don't you think so, Mackenzie?"

I nodded my head tasting the stale bread.

"With a little luck, it won't be in the papers. We are trying everything in our power to get him out on medical grounds. His girlfriend is trying to do him in. She's hysterical. This is as modern as Styxos is going to get. They're not even married yet, and she wants everything: his five-bedroom house, both cars, the bank accounts. She's becoming an opportunist. She is trying to steal what could have been hers. A real peasant. His lawyers have given up on trying to convince her that if she keeps him in jail, he will lose his job, and would never be able to pay for damages."

"Do you mean the wedding is off?" I asked.

"I do."

"This can't be going over well with the authorities. Everyone was hoping that Farouk's company would build a railway on Styxos."

"You have understood everything. The authorities have managed to keep his name out of it so far. But this is a devout society. The letter of the law is very strict about this kind of thing. She has gotten it into the international press, so the letter of the law might have to be applied. The point is her family is trying to keep him in jail with claims that Farouk is responsible for all the evil on Styxos: smuggling, sex slavery, the divorce rate, and all manner of criminal behaviour. Her family will dispute the procedure that was followed to register the case for trial, and they will have to start again. It could take months. Maybe longer. Now your own predicament seems easy, *n'est-ce pas?"*

"A piece of cake."

"Don't worry. Just follow the prescribed path: *la civilisation française.* We will help you through these levelling experiences and on to felicity."

"Felicity, marital happiness. There's a word that's practically dropped out of our language."

"Not ours!" He began to re-create me in the files of the French government, applying for my new birth certificate (on French soil!) and registering me at the consulate. While the first round of papers was being stamped, signed and sent, my husband skimmed his address book and made Farouk his business. Everyone wanted to talk about the public trauma. My husband repeated the nuances of the Grushenka scandal in a phone call to the Styxan Minister of Trade, and then in another one to the Archbishop. It would be something if he could get Farouk out.

Charon was pacing back and forth in front of the window. I wasn't sure of my Styxan, but I think I heard him say, "That should fix him."

Chapter 12

Male Conspiracy

I imagined Farouk in jail, the sun shining through the bars, a striped shadow on the floor. Why should I care so much? Maybe he deserved to be there. But they didn't have enough evidence to lock him up. The dead call girl nagged at me. How could I find out what really happened?

Charon actually closed his eyes when I walked into the bathroom while he was shaving. When did he stop looking at me? "Do you know of any cabarets?" I asked.

"What's that supposed to mean?" I prodded.

"There aren't any cabarets. Maybe there were a long time ago, but they shut them all down, at least in our neighbourhood."

I came at him from several angles, but couldn't get him to say anything more. He uttered some curse in Styxan.

I'd have to study harder if I wanted to figure out exactly how I was damned. Until then, I had to cope with his sullen nature. "The more you feed your fantasies, the weaker you become in reality," I said. "You go ahead and live your imaginary life. I'm living a real one."

Charon was in a foul mood for the rest of the day. *I'm learning,* hah! Not only had he stopped learning, he'd forgotten how to cook. "I'm going to take a walk," he muttered to his mother at nine p.m. I knew that at this time of night, this meant, "I'm going to get something to eat."

I'm not sure when it happened, but one autumn day I needed to know for myself. I think it was the dying leaves. Orange leaves burned on the trees, and the question burned in me. What was this male conspiracy? I had to know. The task had started out as a burden, but now life was less painful on a mission.

I found a grammar book in a dusty cabinet and started making vocabulary lists while the children napped. After a month of study, the results started to show, at least to me. I didn't mention my progress to anyone else. In fact, somewhere in the back of my mind, I'd decided not to let anyone know about learning Styxan.

If I was going to find out anything, it would have to be from beating the men at their own game. I'd have to ask other women. I was curious to hear more about the house next door and Niovi's involvement with Grushenka. I went to find my husband's mother covering the vegetable patch over with dead leaves and casually asked her about the neighbours.

"Oh bother," she said in Styxan, and then went on in very polite English, "That house? And the other and that — all my mother's," she said.

Apparently, the whole piece of land had once belonged to my husband's grandmother until she got to thinking one day: *They say time is money, but at the end of the day more money buys less and less time.* At the end of life, even nuisances show themselves for what they are. *Loans.* So his grandmother sold the land to Niovi's family. "Big mistake," Charon's mother said. She shook her head to the sobbing from the house next door. "They were friends of my family. Were." And now this racket from the house next door. "Always everybody watch that house, good or bad." She passed the time before lunch telling me about her former friend and how their two families grew side-by-side as the best of friends and enemies. When their family became the object of a debilitating divorce, they became just neighbours. Everyone talked about the ex-wife who got to keep the house, and the ex-husband who immediately remarried a blonde foreigner half his age. The old neighbour went on living in the house with her daughter, 'the girl who could sing'.

Each day began and ended with the sounds that arose from behind that wall. The only respite was Niovi's singing. They said she was as famous as you could be on Styxos. We pretended not to watch each other over the wall. I knew my fair complexion must seem exotic to her. To me, her world was as inaccessible as a scene painted on pottery.

We had a certain complicity. Her family had known my diplomat husband since his childhood. They said he aged overnight when he came for his father's funeral. Without his father, there was no more time for my husband to prove himself, and suddenly life had fallen short of his expectations.

My husband's father had had big expectations, and the singer next door was not considered a good enough match. So, the boy went abroad and came back with a blond styxophile, me. No one was good enough for their son, but it was too late. The match had already been made.

Loving a foreigner was ideal for me. We went beyond language. What filtered through to the international level was not only exotic, but of a higher order. For years. Until we came to Styxos. Here I am with a changed man. I still couldn't figure out why he was closing off the relationship he fought so hard to create. There had to be a way to heal and repair our marriage. Charon had become a temperamental and not-very-romantic lover. But everything has a flipside, and my husband's was that he was a *real* man. We'd played no games, promptly married and had two wonderful children. At least we had that.

"Not like old days, before the war," my husband's mother said. "When I was girl, we had sunshine and dust. Families had many children to finish with only two! No foreign women, no problems they bring."

I remember trying to ignore these styxocentric remarks. They were only natural.

"In the days, a boy had one toy." A hoop. He loved and took care of it, dreaming of becoming just a man. There were not ten thousand things to buy. You savoured time under a eucalyptus tree. Some people said that life was hard. "Compared to what?" my husband's mother said. "Our city was rich! Dirt roads, bicycles. What you want? We had more *time*." There was time to stop and visit, or to sit in the shade of a eucalyptus tree and talk without a cup of coffee, without a cigarette, *with someone*.

"When Niovi's mother was young girl, she very beautiful. Very. Now finished. Crying. Me not beautiful, now old, not crying!" They way I understood it, when Niovi's mother was a girl, she went to market every day with dust in her nostrils to buy fruit and vegetables. One day, a gust of wind raised her skirt revealing her sturdy village knees. That was the day the stranger came down off the mountains, wearing a well-pressed tweed suit and carrying a suitcase. The newcomer lay in wait like a magnet while the familiar men at the coffee shop watched her voluptuous figure going inevitably to market. An oversized cross swung at her throat, her whole body bent on the task. In a fluster, she quickly looked around to see if anyone was watching. She blushed at the stranger, and was surprised at her body crying out to her. What was this mystery?

The smell of sweat and eucalyptus pervaded the coffee shop. The men rustled at the sight of her skin as she twisted to yank the brown wool back down over her knees. The stranger crossed her path outside the market. They were looking over the white *calocassi* roots, a food that took on the flavour of any sauce. Fingers touched on the stalk, eyes locked. She looked at her feet and felt fire. There was no means of escape.

The stranger laughed.

She watched his fingers touch her chin. She smiled up into his brown eyes and smelled his arms pulling her into the future.

It was hot out. The men in the coffee shop didn't move as they ordered another round of island coffee, each with a glass of cold water, in the shade of the terrace, and swallowed their sighs. She walked faster than usual through the dust, past the coffee shop, contest over, secret door open.

The stranger proved uncommonly industrious, and soon became a police officer, bicycle and all. His parents had died when he was a boy, but he managed to learn a few things. He laboriously taught Niovi's mother to read, and she applied herself with determination to the task until she could write a grocery list and copy a telephone number. He asked her to marry him the day after she turned twenty.

"Nobody marries a Muslim," she told him.

"Nobody marries a Christian," he said. He had already converted from Judaism to avoid persecution, and now he would have to convert again. Change names, become someone else: nobody. It was the only way to be allowed to have a soft young thing. His imagination wandered where it liked, leaving his body burning on the threshold. There were only a few 'mixed' marriages on Styxos, where locals said, 'Who is your father?' instead of 'How do you do?' With nobody as her father, how would the daughter fend for herself in matters of career and marriage?

Their love was cast in optimism, but its glow faded with each year. They had known happiness in the heat and dust, with Niovi on the way. But after the *coup*, their little family recoiled on its own flesh, and the arguing never stopped. Husband and wife grew old early. They watched the children they adored divide cell by cell against themselves until the *non-Christian* part of the family, their father, disappeared. He had been seen with a new blonde woman, a foreigner. "Did she ever come to the house?"

"I see her in his car one day," my husband's mother said. From then on, Niovi's mother cried next door every day. Niovi had a lot to sing about. I listened for her voice in the racket next door, and wondered how to bring up the subject of Grushenka to her. "Were there any other foreigners at the house?"

"Not that house, but the other and the other. Many foreigner!" She waved her hands to indicate the epidemic of divorces since the fall of the Iron Curtain.

The mountains swam obliviously in the heat behind my husband's mother's house. I had no leads, and there was nowhere to go. It seemed like I would never see the sea in the occupied area on the other side of that purple range. I joined my husband's mother on the terrace. "Come, Mackenzie!" she said to me, scooping the beans from the chair next to her. A reply did occur to me as I looked at the chair, a short speech to the effect that one needed some exercise to keep fit, and what a fine day it was for a swim. That would have been simple before the invasion. But these words might seem cold, considering the wall separating the Christian south and the Muslim North that cut us off from the beach, occupied by the Muslim troops 'for security reasons'. I sat down.

That's when I heard Charon's voice in the driveway. He was talking on the phone. I'd given up on everything. I think I was even about to surprise him with a few sentences in Styxan, when I heard him say, "She's not worth her weight. Just kill her if she won't do it. Dump her body in the sea."

My feet stuck to the floor. I tried to catch a glimpse of his expression — well of course he was joking — but his back was turned to the window.

Chapter 13

A Real Santa

Still reeling from my eavesdropping episode of the previous day, I was growing more apprehensive by the day, but was still too much in shock to confront Charon. Just being around him was enough to make the hairs on the back of my neck stand on end. But until I had a plan, I knew instinctively that I had to try to live my life as if everything were normal.

All of this happened just as the holiday season stole upon us. I had been expecting relief from the Ladies' Consortium Christmas Party 'for the families' from the diplomatic community, but it was not to be had. My husband suggested that he would drop me and Alex and Justin off at the party.

I didn't want to confront him until I had more to nail him with, but I couldn't help saying, "Do you think I'm going if you aren't?" This provoked a Mediterranean tempest, and the children were soon copying their father while I tried to wrestle Justin into a tight T-shirt. My husband stopped yelling to ask whether any other men would be there. "I'm sure the *fathers* from the *civilised* countries will be there.

"And the 'men' from the third world countries will not? Is that what you're saying?"

We arrived at the hotel, where they had set up a jumping castle and face-painting booth. There were over 100 guests there, but there was only one man: my husband. "You can go to the gym," I told him. "I give up on the Ladies' Consortium. I don't see why I should go to their functions at all."

"It's O.K. I'm just adjusting." Our children were crying, and Charon looked uncomfortable, but he insisted on staying. "It's not the first time I'm the only man." Finally, Justin sat down in a circle with a bunch of children passing around a box with a present in it, and my husband and I had coffee standing up with Alex wrapped around our legs. One of the Ladies' Consortium organizers came over and started talking to my husband about 'Santa Claus'.

"Even Santa will be a woman!" I said, but my husband didn't laugh. That's when I realised she was asking Charon to be Santa.

I sat the kiddies down at a crowded white banquet table full of children and mommies. While the children were immersed in chips, Jell-O, chocolate cake and fruit tarts, my husband tipped out the door. "I feel sick in my tummy," Justin said.

"You do?" Alex was still eating and eating chocolate cake, pudding, tarts and Jell-O. She was too little to be left alone at the table, so I couldn't take Justin to the bathroom.

Suddenly, Santa appeared! He was nice, but not plump. A right merry old elf! And Justin laughed when he saw him, but Alex said, "I wanna my Papa," the chorus to a little rap song she'd made up waiting in the car while Charon bought an overpriced medicine cabinet. I told her Santa looked an awful lot like Papa. As angry as I was at him, I had to admit he was not bad in red with his dark eyebrows, despite the white beard. "I believe in him," I lied. But baby girl did not agree, and sulked, closing her big eyes slowly with an expression that said, *You are sooo wong, Mommy.* Santa made a big fuss over the children, I'll have to give him that, and he only knew our kids' names. "Who wants balloons?"

"*Ego!* I do!"

"Me!"

Man, woman and child struggled together over the spoils. Justin and Alex were impressed that he knew their names when he handed them their gifts. They got Indian play sets, which solved everything (except the choking hazard) with canoes and horses, and weapons! There was a lot of playing and a little less quarrelling when we got back to his mother's house.

Chapter 14

Roots

For all my skill at digging for pottery shards, I had a sinking feeling that I would fail the powers that be at the wire service with my ineptitude at investigating the Grushenka story. I had come to fear that I couldn't unearth anything of value if my life depended on it. It was hard to dig while suppressing the shock I'd felt after Charon's latest complaints, about the black marks from the exhaust of passing cars on his mother's house. I had to focus on my job.

The first time my boss called me into his office, I prayed that he wouldn't mention my probation period. "Have you found anything?" the editor-in-chief asked me.

It was spring already. "I'm working on it."

He twirled a pencil between his fingers and sprung some Journalese on me. "I see. Well, history has emerged! There are other crucial items to capture. The business investment the gala attracted cracked the fissures in the island's political deadlock. Occupation leaders announced that the wall separating the two communities will be torn down. Unfortunately, we have a lot of reporters competing to cover those items."

People more related than I was.

"Sorry, Mackenzie. There's no work for you here."

I had let everyone down. I cried on the couch at my husband's mother's house with the TV barking about the wall coming down. It was big news, and everyone wanted a piece of it. Foreign reporters appeared on the screen. The colours swam, but I could make out that economic reunification was the current fad among walled cities. Would the island also accede to the European Union like a long lost archaeological fragment? Styxans came out on their porches like beetles in a fire to talk about the possibility of accession. To me, it seemed more likely that Styxos would sink.

I was afraid to stay on Styxos, but I was imprisoned here. Charon would never let me leave with the kids. I caught sight of his briefcase on the chair across from me. With my heart in my mouth, I quietly slid the latch upward and opened it: papers, nothing extraordinary. I thought I heard a sound and was about to close it, but then I saw him outside the window talking to the neighbours. I went on unzipping the side pocket and reached inside. Napkins, business cards — a condom! I dropped it. Fury rose in my veins. There was no going back now. I took out all the papers and combed through them. What was this? A bank account in his name with 150,000 shekels in it. He had never said anything about that. We had spent my inheritance on groceries over the past five years. If we had that kind of money, there was no need to live at his mother's house!

By the time I heard Charon's footsteps in the hallway, his briefcase was back where it belonged. I swore to myself that I would not say anything. I would watch for more signs of infidelity without letting on that I knew. After all, what did I really know? It was an unused condom.

"Hello," he said.

"Hi." The sound dropped from my mouth.

"What's wrong?"

"*You're* asking *me?*" I couldn't help myself.

"What do you mean?"

The blood rushed to my face, and I burst into tears. My hands tore open his briefcase. "This! You're carrying condoms around in your briefcase?"

"It's not condoms. It's a condom," he stalled, thinking. "It was for you," he said at last.

"You lie!" My hands were beating his chest. "What about us? What about our children?" In one swift movement, he dragged me into the hallway away from the window where the neighbours might see me, his hand over my nose and mouth. I tore at his fingers. "I can't breathe!"

"Be quiet," he hissed. "Get a hold of yourself. Now that you're in Styxos, you find out what I really am, and you don't like it. You never liked me. You married the wrong man. You tell the whole truth while hiding the soul — even worse! What do you think you're doing going through my briefcase?"

"I'm your wife."

"Not if you act like that. DON'T TOUCH MY THINGS!" He slammed the door and was gone. I sat there for a long time with the TV going in the background wondering what to do.

My dilemma was swept away by the historic events of that day. An upheaval next door drowned out the noise from the TV. Our loud neighbours were arguing, and I could see Niovi's figure full of animal grace pacing up and down the garden wall. I put everything back in the briefcase and closed it. Niovi's mother had gotten a call from a cousin on the other side of the wall whom she'd never met. "We're here!" they yelled into the phone, in English! During the separation, each side had forgotten the other's language, and had to use English. Niovi had her phone on loudspeaker. "We came through on the old road where they broke the wall. But we cannot come to your house."

"Why not?" Niovi asked the cell phone, her dark mane touching her high hips.

"There are too many of us!"

I watched Niovi come out of the driveway with no makeup on and head for her car as if she had waited for this moment for decades. She threw her keys and her wallet on the seat and yelled to her mother that she was going to meet their Muslim relatives at the checkpoint.

"Wait! You have to bring them here," I heard her mother say in Styxan to Niovi's back, already disappearing down the driveway. "They said they have to get back to the North soon!" Niovi said. A stripe of sweat appeared on the back of her dress.

Her mother ran down the driveway after her and caught her arm. "They crossed over the wall for the first time in so many years and they have to get back?" The emotion played across their faces. "Without coming to our house? Tell them that your mother is offended!"

I heard more scurrying in the driveway next door. Niovi's mother was taking boxes out of the car so that they could fit more relatives. "You can get a taxi for the rest of them." Instead, Niovi ran across the field and got her cousin out of his big house. They drove off in two cars to pick up the long lost relatives.

Within an hour, fourteen Muslims from age five to sixty-five strode up the driveway next door. Fat ones, little ones, tall ones, ones with moustaches. They kissed and shook hands, trying to pronounce all the cousins', uncles', great-uncles', and nieces' names, mixed in a flurry of English. For once, I could understand what was going on over at Niovi's house. Thank God for the name 'Mehmet' — there were three of them — and also for the communication barrier between the young generation of Muslim and Orthodox Styxans, who had forgotten each others' languages in all these years of separation and could only talk to each other in English. But after listening for a while, I remembered that there was a beauty to not speaking the local language. Styxan was such a ritualistic form, so pleasant to hear in the background, and as long as you couldn't make out the content, you could still go on with your own thoughts while listening to it. If I had to go back to understanding what everyone around me was saying, I would have to go back to listening to a hundred nitwit thoughts a day. I would understand what Charon was saying when he cursed. Our marriage might not last. Wasn't it just after I'd learned French that my first marriage had fallen apart?

The whole obliterated family squeezed into all the chairs they had in the circle of shade on the terrace under their umbrella, with Niovi hovering over them. It was a hot summer Sunday, and the grocery stores were closed. One woman got squeezed out from under the umbrella. "Never mind," she said, and sat on her chair in the bushes. They had coffee and juice while Niovi's mother, who at no moment in her life had been seen eating, emptied the refrigerator and started cooking everything she had. At least she had meat in the freezer and plenty of potatoes and salad.

And then an amazing thing happened. There was the smell of cigar smoke, and Niovi's father appeared in the garden under the lemon tree, alone. Niovi stood up, and after an awkward moment said, "Papa?" The ex-Muslim tapped his cigar. Niovi's mother pretended he wasn't there. She looked down at her feet and just went on serving the drinks. One-by-one, his kin stood up. He dropped his cigar in the dust just as the relatives erupted around their blood. He threw himself into their arms. Words rolled off their tongues in their native languages. It was a good noise. Someone stopped in the street to look up the driveway. Everyone was crying, even me. One of the men took off his shirt and wiped his face.

It was a day full of bright sun and dark shadows. Charon was standing a few meters away from me watching the scene. I didn't talk to him, but we had struck a temporary truce. His silhouette blurred in the afternoon light. Looking at him out of the corner of my eye, I thought I saw his shadow was elongating. And then it was there! A ghost just like Charon's father moved forward and separated itself from Charon's body. A cold chill riveted through my spine. The feeling that gripped my stomach was sickening. The ghost drifted across the lawn. It went through the garden wall and attached itself to the others hugging Niovi's father.

I hurried over to Charon. He put his arm around me! I could feel him again. He let me hug him. I could feel that he was craving support and understanding. I had a fleeting thought that there wasn't very much of him left. Or that there wasn't very much time left. He started to tell me about playing with Niovi's long lost cousins just like the old days when he used to run to me with so many things to tell me. My husband was here! "I was so sad when my father died that I wanted to do everything he had ever told me to do," he was telling me. "I thought maybe that would bring him back." What a relief the end of Charon's silent treatment was. He had been buried under the ghost of his father. I believe it had encased his soul. It wouldn't let him out to see the light of day.

Lunch was ready. Niovi brought all the chairs through the house into the shade of the front porch, and everyone squeezed around the dining room table. They'd put a chequered tablecloth over a card table for the children. What a fine day. A day without luxury, in the accepted sense. They ate slowly, making sure there was just enough food for everybody. A big family of strangers, they listened to the children speaking their languages and ate an unimpressive lunch of meat and potatoes.

Time to come in from the fields.

Three of the Muslim uncles gave Niovi's mother their passport applications. They would be needing passports now that they could go through the Christian south to get into the European Union. Their tweed suits blended with the brown chairs on her terrace. The trip across the checkpoint had taken three hours because of the long lines of cars transporting thousands of islanders through the hole in the wall. I looked up from my book to see Niovi's mother handing them a bottle of water from the fresh spring of the men's native village up in the mountains, on our side of the wall. They took the bottle and burst into their own language. *Their own water was famous in the South!* They were happy to have a special bottle of our daily drinking water. I was wondering if they would drink it, when I felt the chill in my bones again.

There in front of us was the ghost of Charon's father wafting back across the lawn toward my husband! "No!" I screamed, but Charon let out a sigh of resignation. The ghost touched Charon' body, which stiffened. Charon breathed all of the air out of his lungs. Then, he inhaled the ghost in one whiff.

Chapter 15

Gains from Trade

I dreamed of Grushenka. She was journeying with us back to Israel. My husband, Grushenka and I were all glad to leave Styxos and vowed never to live there again. The children were excited to see the house again. They skiddled right into their baby pool, and my husband sat down next to them with a stack of books. I picked a mango and sliced it. "Do you want some mango?" My husband grunted, which I took as a 'no' and gave it to . . . Grushenka.

I awoke with the taste of mango in my mouth. The shock came rushing at me like a brick wall. My marriage was a lie. Rage filled my veins. I softened my voice. "Did you have any dreams?"

"No."

"How can you dream of nothing?"

"OK," he said. "If you must know, I dreamt that I was a snail stuck to your back." He pulled the blanket up over his head.

There was no way *not* to confront him with it. "What were you doing with a condom in your briefcase?"

"What?" He didn't roll over.

"You heard me," I said to his back.

"No I didn't. Say it again."

I grabbed his shoulder and turned him over. Then I pried open his eye and glared into it. "There was a condom in your briefcase."

"What were you doing going into my briefcase? Stay out of my personal things." It was not his voice.

"That doesn't explain the condom."

"There's nothing to explain. You're imagining things."

"You can't have a family if you are cheating."

"There is no family!" He roared, and threw off the blanket. "Don't bother me again!"

"Either you're faithful or I leave."

"Ha! Go ahead and leave!" He ran out of the bedroom and started yelling at the kids to get ready to go to the pool.

"Be a father!" I yelled back at him. "Get their things ready for them. Antisocial. I know why you want to go so early in the morning. Because you know we won't come with you so early in the morning, and you'll be able to make your phone calls. Make your damn phone calls later!"

Now that I knew what Charon was about, I was disgusted at the thought of sex with him. I had to give up on this imposter. If my husband was in there, I couldn't find him.

My new abstinence went smoother than expected, and I realised that I had been the only one initiating sex for quite a while anyway. Now that I thought about it, I'd spent the whole year negotiating him into bed. The last time before I found the condom, he'd said, "Like robots."

Ha! As if by dehumanising me, he defused any power I might have over him. He'd saved himself from being engulfed.

What a fool I was, saying, "Let's feel something."

He had a rash. He'd been telling me that it was psoriasis. He also had a new position he'd shown me in bed, and I'd thought he was clever for thinking of it himself!

I lay there for a long time trying to adjust to the new reality, wondering how or where I had missed it. Men must really think women are stupid. We believe in fairytales like love and marriage, that an animal on his way to war with the taste of blood in his mouth could be a prince. Were we all victims of their conspiracy? One of the necessary symptoms of Charon's personality being represented by a ghost was that he saw all of his actions and relationships as meaningless, since they were dissociated from his true self. He was safe from direct experiencing as he remote controlled his mask. His soul withered, excluded from participation in the world. Creative relationships were no longer possible. If I confronted him with it, he said, "You're engulfing my soul! I don't know who I am anymore." My biggest problem with this was that my children needed their father's true self. I had to find it.

The telephone rang. I picked it up and said 'Hello', but it was a miss-call. I realised I was listening to a conversation from the inside of somebody's pocket.

"Only fifty shekels?" A woman's voice. "I need to buy clothes for our daughter."

"Take it!" It sounded like Charon, but I couldn't be sure.

That afternoon, Charon returned home and started moving his things into his mother's bedroom. His mother obliged him and dragged her bed out onto the terrace.

Every morning I woke up to the shock of an empty bed. Out of the forgetfulness of sleep, memory would come rushing back, a brick wall. Smarting, I would be faced with the end of our family. I would spend the day churning out arguments that I couldn't use on Charon. No argument had worked on him before, and none would. I could not leave without the kids. I could not leave. The only way out was to not think about it. To think about other things. My mind played tricks on me, made me forgive him, rationalised that I had not *caught* him with another woman. I'd only found a condom. I could not leave my children. I would have to stay. I had to find a job. But there was no job market.

How to find meaningful work in an outpost? Efforts to make a country out of Styxos had failed. *Rapprochement* had been put to a vote, and hard reality caught up with the euphoria of the wall coming down: the southern Styxans voted no to union. Only her southern appendage could hope to begin accession talks to join the European Union. Northern Jarmuth occupation leaders got jealous watching southern diplomats move off of Styxos, onto the continent and into Brussels neighbourhoods. But despite their pangs of regret, it was too late to reverse the failed vote and reunite Styxos. The European Union had learned a lesson from the islanders; now the road to accession to the EU was guarded by a Sphinx, its lofty head mad with hunger, its languid eyes blinking. *Answer my questions, ply the law.* The doubtful monster held up a long list of Problems: the whole country was working part time, there had been so many religious conversions to evade taxes that the magnitude of Christian philandering rivalled the harems in the Muslim North.

There were too many benefiting from the *status quo*. Whether fighting over religion or real estate, people fell with stunning homogeny into a culture of Problems. On the enigmatic rock at the crossroads to the Middle East, the Problem was the solution. The EU caught on. The storms in the Sahara kicked particles of iron and topsoil, and now, when easterly trade winds carried these vast clouds of red dust laden with immigrants across the sea to the EU, there was a stubborn, red-tape sphinx in the doorway. Member states that didn't necessarily want to admit a Muslim country were able to hide behind this large, plastic sphinx.

I got a job interview at a community college for young women. The men had all gone to the mainland to study. The first round of interviews went well, but the last person vetoed hiring a foreigner. Now I realise that if my husband had come with me to the interview, they would have given me the job . . .

Time nibbled at the *status quo* and wore down economic barriers between our side of Styxos, her coastline indented with a multitude of steep and rocky coves, and the occupied side, with its long white beaches. Rays of business optimism shone through political deadlocks to these forgotten beaches, punctuated with abandoned hotels painted in warm terra cotta colours.

Two months had gone by when a wonderful thing happened. The aged occupation leader up and died. Sudden hope filled the air. Anyone could see that the island of Cerberus had the makings of a tourist trap. It was

Tuscany with endless beaches. The dry Styxan heat and Mediterranean culture made her the next choice spot for colonies of mainland retirees.

This is when Farouk's picture hit the papers. Farouk was like a sunspot. I shouldn't have looked at him with open eyes. Now he was everywhere. I looked away from his black and white picture all day. I had to save the paper, since there was an ad for a job at a new hotel on the back page. I walked through the dunes on the outskirts of town at dusk toward the hotel. Sand crunched underfoot. The expanse of sand rippled up to the twilight sky. The sand seemed to go on forever, and just beyond forever lay Farouk. I felt him close by in his parallel universe. I came out of the dunes and brushed myself off under a neon sign. When I opened the wooden door to the hotel, I immediately realised what kind of place it was.

"You the new girl?" The bartender said. There was a pole in the middle of the room.

"No!" I folded the ad into the newspaper. "I was just looking for the reception."

"It's closed."

"Is that why you're looking for a receptionist?"

"Old. We forgot to cancel ad."

"I came all this way! Next time put your phone number in your ad."

"A smart one. Maybe I like you. We don't get many clients here, few men from the construction company, some soldiers."

My eyes adjusted to the dim barroom.

"Glad they caught him?" The bartender indicated the newspaper I was holding with Farouk's picture on the front page.

I held it to my breast and felt less alone. "No," I said. I couldn't get Grushenka out of my mind and had an idea. "I mean, I don't know for sure that he's the one who did it. What do you think?" What was I saying? There was no proof that he hadn't done it.

"I don't think anything. I hear what the people say."

I leaned forward on the bar showing some cleavage and took out my wallet. "You think he did it?" I held out a twenty shekel bill.

His eyes narrowed as he reached for the bill. "Now I remember. Sure he did. I know him," the bartender said. "He's been here, looking for Russian girl."

"Really?" Ah, the scoundrel. How could I have entertained any feelings for him?

"Everybody like to talk about her and him these days. I tell you." He wiped the counter in front of me. "What would you like?" I looked around the barroom. There were no customers. My legs were shaking, so I settled onto a barstool and ordered a beer. He put the glass on the coaster. "She had an apartment in back. They locked her in during the day, but the key was in the lock outside the door. He visit her there. What you think? She was tied to the bed."

I choked on my beer. How could I have cared for such a low man? And I thought he felt it too! My imagination was cruel.

"Why you surprised? She was a nice girl. Nice body, blond hair. We let him talk to her in the café across the street."

"We?"

"The owner. Sit down! It's OK. He not here now. Not for another hour."

I was fishing in my pocket for more money to pay for the beer when he said, "It's not so bad. She was on the

93

'closed system'. She could go out of the room to the café for a few hours. It's worse in other countries!"

I slammed a five-shekel note on the counter and didn't wait for the change.

"He try to leave the island with her. This is what happen when you try to escape. The foreigner stopped coming. She dead, he in jail. It is not easy to leave Styxos!"

I took off my shoes and hurried back through the dunes. Thoughts of Farouk increased, even though I suspected his involvement more than ever in that heinous crime. I looked back at the hotel lights. The wind had erased my footprints in the sand.

The cheap Jarmuth labour force descended to build new roads, sidewalks and bicycle paths for wages I would never accept. The Styxan economy with the Protestant work ethic left over from the most recent colonists absorbed them. Israeli infrastructure spending spurred growth and kept the population heterogeneous. The economy chugged along despite the R.O.W. contagion of recessionary spirals. For me, other than volunteering at the dig, there was no job to go to, and everything was always closed. "It's a public holiday," my husband said.

"Not another holiday! What are we celebrating this time?"

"Forgiveness."

Random acts of kindness, from presidential pardons for convicts to cash for the handicapped unleashed every species of hypocrisy on this day, but I swallowed my indignation when I heard that they had pardoned Farouk. He was out of jail!

Chapter 16

Blinding Memory Schnapps

The heat abated and brought on a desert winter. With the drop in temperatures, the past decoupled from the present and let us be with the holiday season. Political animal that he was, Charon wanted to go *out*.

An advantage to living with my husband's mother was that she could baby-sit anytime. The children slept in the room with her, and we were able to go out in the evening. The only obstacle was getting there. Charon was a nervous driver. "Did you take your cod-liver oil?" I was managing Charon's mood with fish oil. I couldn't get him to take Omega-3, but cod-liver oil he trusted, since his mother had made him take it as a child.

"Yes."

"Good for you. Let's go."

In Styxos so many invitations flowed in that I often didn't know what the occasion was until we drove up in the car. We found ourselves at the Romanian military attaché's residence, a sprawling mansion with wings cropping out of ever bend. "Ah yes! That's right," my husband said.

There, in the middle of a group of colonels, lieutenants and generals was Farouk, a head above the rest of them, clad in a dark suit. I still had on my red hat, which he must have spotted instantly; the women were easily outnumbered. The uniforms came to life around the dining room table. An officer with a trim moustache was pouring a clear liquid along a line of tiny glasses. What landed on the table evaporated immediately.

The officer lovingly served up a glass. "Farouk! You must try my *Blinding Memory Schnapps*." The men laughed, downing their schnapps and slamming their gold-rimmed glasses down on the table. "It's homemade?" Farouk took his glass and downed it in one shot. The others with more fat on their bones started on their second round. I was just thinking how Farouk didn't scare me as I'd expected when he turned his profile in dark tweed and his black turtleneck. He looked at me for a split second, and I knew defences would be useless. It was suddenly hot in the room. I took off my gloves.

I caught his eye, but he looked quickly away, a piercing overreaction. What reason had I given him to be angry with me? He had turned the tables, as if *I* were the one at fault. His gaze darted around the group. He managed to strike up a conversation, which died right away when he checked whether I was still watching. Farouk turned away again, a stallion chafing at his bit. He broke free of the military group and was trying to leave before I could say hello. Trying to exit, he glared over my head as he pushed past me.

"Farouk!" I said.

He stopped in front of me, hands on his hips, listening to me in my hat, still not looking me in the eye. He was suffering, that much was clear.

"I'm *sorry* about what happened," I said to the open collar of his starched shirt. I gazed into one of his stubborn eyes, *fortress*. I laughed, and stood on my toes to kiss his cheeks. "Nice to see you again," I whispered into his ear. My cheek almost didn't touch his weathered face, but his soul welcomed mine in a wave, *together*. "We'll arrange a party," I said to his nose as I moved to kiss his other cheek, "With everyone." I watched his mouth as we separated.

"Soon," his lips said.

I could feel Farouk begin to relax with friends around. It was like standing next to a fire in the fireplace. Would his warmth be enough to chase away the chill of Grushenka? "Thank you, *mon ami*," he said, patting my husband on the back. Their colognes mixed with the smell of schnapps. Farouk's voice was hoarse. The shade of Grushenka travelling across the ceiling above him threw death's efficacy into question. I had already accused him once and didn't dare draw his attention to her again. The room was filled with ghosts. The chorus worked on Farouk, and he tried to oblige the guests by giving them his card.

It was about time we left the reception with so many persons of influence and power; my husband had disappeared into the next conversation with a tall Scandinavian in a spandex dress. I suggested we get something to eat, then, but my husband didn't hear me. I raised my voice. "Can't you hear me?" His eyes were glued to the Bambi. When I was her age, I never wore such short skirts. Now

I felt self-conscious in the middle of the room with my leather coat on. The heat must have taken the curl out of my hair, and there was Farouk standing behind me.

He had absorbed this impasse with my husband like a conduit. "Try one of these." He offered me a *mille-feuille*. He must have had his woman radar on, the way he profited from the opportunity of our failing marriage. A waiter passed with the bottle of schnapps. I stabbed at a bowl of feta dip. It had enough raw onion in it to make me cry. "How are you?" I managed to ask.

"I'm alright," he said defensively, and made me feel guilty for leaving him in jail. "I have my toys."

It was as if I had torn him from my breast and set him down in front of his choo choo. Farouk waited as I glanced again at my husband locked in conversation with the Bambi. I looked around. Nobody was dancing. "I can't be everyone's mother," I was about to say, but Farouk overpowered me: "So you were living in New York? *I* am interested in that." I found myself telling him about life in New York. I swam through the unexpected rush of empathy from Farouk. The cocktail party dissolved around us. The other people became reflections in Farouk's eyes. He seemed to understand, but was no more imposing than was water in a glass. We were comfortable on a purely emotional level. What a surprise to find such compassion. "What did you do there?" he asked.

"Oh, I hardly talked about it anymore." Or about much of anything. I mostly listened to other people's conversations. "I was a derivatives trader crashing New York society."

He waited.

"Sifting through a *crème de la crème* cocktail party, I met Charon."

"I see. And you were trading in New York?"

"Yes, buying and selling millions and billions of dollars of derivatives."

He took a sip of his schnapps, his eyes holding mine over the rim of his glass.

I took two. "It's hot in here." I was worried he would smell me sweating. I'm sure he did when he took off my coat. I blushed. He became more attentive.

"You can put your coat in here . . ." We left the embers of the party burning. He led me through a hallway to a door. ". . . on the bed." I put my shot glass on the dresser. I had to hold onto his shoulder to keep my balance. What were we doing in here? He smelled nice.

The ceiling was high, and the evening sun shone through the heavy curtains. I had to get away, and walked over to open the curtains. "Look at the swimming pool."

"Yes, these houses all have their own pools." He came up behind me. "So what does a trader in New York do?"

He turned toward me, and I toward him in syncopation.

"I was alone in the city. You have to go for walks in New York. Your apartment gets too small. You complain over a bottle of wine, and freeze all night on a lover's doorstep."

"You do! *C'est vrai?* On Charon's doorstep?"

"No!" The smell of sweat.

Farouk moved closer to me.

"Wasn't it you?" I asked.

"It's cold in New York?"

"That's right. It was February." I scolded him. He had pretended he wasn't home, but I had been determined to stay in front of his door until I found out whether or not he was there. I had to know if he was lying. Someone was playing Christmas carols. At the coldest moment of the night just before dawn, the metal lampposts contracted, chink, chink, and the sky lightened and the smell of cinnamon came from one of his neighbours' houses. "A miracle, you opened your front door. I saw your toe from under my coat. You won't repeat this to anyone? This is all Top Secret," I said.

"I wasn't Styxan, was I?" Farouk asked.

"Close enough," I said.

"I've never been to New York."

Another lie. The toes of his shoes were touching mine. The room had the same herringbone parquet as the room that morning when the ice clinked in his glass. The walls were the same beige colour, and he was drinking that black ice coffee the freezing cold morning after I'd spent the night on his doorstep. I was still vacillating like a moth between outrage and the desire to ask him to marry me. "Don't," he said. "I don't want to make it work," The room had the same glossy woodwork, the low chairs, and the same gray door, although someone had replaced the doorknob with a handle. The furniture was where we had left it. Everything was the same, even lying next to him on the bed with the coats. And that hunted look in his eyes, afraid of intimacy. I remembered not to try to touch him first. When he wanted, he would come, unless the game had changed.

"Excuse me." A woman's voice. We were lying on someone's jacket. She pulled it out from under us.

"I'm *not* going to kiss you," Farouk said into my mouth. Were we even talking? "Even though I want to

100

with all of my being, because that's what they want me to do," he said.

Who?

I whispered, "I just wish they would leave us alone."

"We have to be careful not to make them too jealous. They are mediocre, and we are —"

"Dangerous," I said.

"Listen, Mackenzie. Sometimes more is less. I don't want you to regret our friendship."

Ah well, at least you know which half of the man you are getting.

"What is your obsession with marriage?" he pressed.

I wanted to run away. His virility would make me express my needs. But he didn't let go. "Painful," I said. It was the only way. A married woman, a stable mother founding a family. Someone *men* could depend on, someone a company could invest in. "Something you can't buy." This time, *I* glared at *him*.

"Is that how it is with Charon?"

"You saw my husband. He's hunting for another woman. We don't talk anymore. I ask him a question, and I'm lucky if I get an answer. *I* want to have another baby."

He shifted back to his side of the coat pile.

"I don't know," Farouk said, "if I could do what Charon is doing. A wife for all those years, two kids. It must be heavy. I don't know! As long as I can maintain my lifestyle—."

"Father of three kids?" Because if Farouk was going to change for me, there would be another baby, right away. "That's a huge change of lifestyle."

He looked relieved, lighter. "You're probably right."

"But can you go on following your beast?" I asked. "With pleasure as the reference for everything? Never rising to anything lofty, never contemplating the magnificent or divine."

He looked at me out of the corner of his eye.

"And Niovi?" I asked.

"We never really got the chance to talk about it," he said. "I don't know if I can do the right thing."

"You *will* do the right thing."

"I have nothing to gain from you, and you have nothing to gain from me."

"Exactly," I said.

"My friend, if I may be so bold as to call you that—"

I would do whatever I could for him, and he would do whatever he could for me. "Yes." Our honourable rivalry was cemented.

"Where will I see you again?" he asked.

"Around here," I said, and looked at the coats.

The thrill of almost touching Farouk was nothing compared to the surge of power I felt when he looked me square in the eyes and said, "Around where?" He looked at the bed and pushed the coats aside, his eyes windows onto blue-sky possibility. But the windows were opened just enough to see what was really beyond, a desert so hot that nothing could survive. We knew. The dream lived only as long as it wasn't forced into reality. To see it and not reach for it! We had to be the most evolved creatures on the island.

Farouk leaned his head back and laughed. "We will be *running* this island." He took my hand. I clung to my resolve. Did his lips touch mine? I remember that vision of sand stretched out in front of me as far as the eye could see.

The party must have been over. "Mackenzie!" My husband's voice in the hallway. My body was paralyzed. Farouk stiffened. "Mackenzie!"

Farouk held my gaze. Neither of us wanted to let go, just like that day when he scooped me up and carried me up the gangplank to the boat. *Déjà vu.* I remembered that look and what came next, being carried past the enormous blue letters painted on the side of the boat. What was the name painted there? Next his eyes were going to unlock from mine. And they did unlock. I struggled to remember the name.

"What is it, Mackenzie?" Farouk asked.

"POSEIDON. The name of the ship. *Déjà vu.*"

"You get used to these glitches after living on Styxos for a while. It's a time loop. You *remember* something that is going to happen. What is it? It might be important."

"It was so clear." The hair stood up on my neck. "You were carrying me."

"Well, this time I'm not." He rolled off the bed and disappeared behind the curtains.

My mind raced to remember the boat and what was going to happen. Instinct told me to break away from the path that destiny had laid out for me.

"Mackenzie!" my husband called. "Ah, there you are."

Maybe the *déjà vu* signaled a change of path. I liked to think that I was changing direction, that I was the one in control of my destiny. I felt the urge to separate from my

103

former self, and decided to assert my freewill with a lie when Charon asked, "What are you doing in here?"

"I was just lying here admiring the view." I cringed just after saying 'view'. Charon turned to the window! I knew Farouk must be cringing behind the curtain.

My husband walked past me to the window. "Yeah, look at that pool," he said, pulling aside the curtain . . . "Farouk!"

Farouk shrank as Charon's brow bore down on him. Farouk's voice was barely a whisper. The expression on his face made him seem like he was looking into the face of death. He stammered, "Are you . . . ?"

"What are you doing, man? I've been looking all over for you!" Charon put his hand on Farouk's shoulder. I could have sworn I saw fire spark in my husband's eyes.

I could feel the heat rise to my face. I had served up Farouk on a platter. Was *this* victory? Of course I didn't *want* my husband to be jealous.

While my husband tried to engage Farouk in conversation, Farouk made a show of consulting his watch. "I'm late," he said, and disappeared through the doorway.

My husband led me out of the master bedroom. Everyone was gone, even the translucent Bambi. "We're the last to leave again," I told my husband.

"I know," he said.

The wave carried us home, and Charon, cold and pragmatic after his father's death, stirred from his grief. Maybe the ghost of his father had gone for a walk. Or maybe it was the cod-liver oil. He came back into our bedroom. He opened the shutters a crack, and the shapes in the room came alive in the moonlight. "What has gotten into you?" I said. He was such a copycat. He pulled me close for the first time in months.

I wasn't ready to give Charon up, and let him elaborate on the wave. We played out the ancient rite, and I let him fall asleep on my stomach, full of butterflies, maybe for the last time.

The cod-liver oil worked.

Chapter 17

The Game

Winter dried lickety-split and gave way to the light of spring. It set the fields and mountainsides ablaze with tapestries of wildflowers. The fragrance in the air dispelled any shadow of the gala, and it seemed that the ghost of Grushenka could no longer disrupt our relationships and would finally be forgotten. The tabloids turned their attention to reconciliation between Niovi and her 'French paramour' and spurred romantic delusions about Farouk that kept me going throughout the day, although I vowed to myself not to let him to use me like a facial tissue.

These were harmless daydreams that made the bone-gnawing anxiety of separation from Charon more bearable. I tried to channel the energy I was deriving from my feelings for Farouk back into the family. I had to make our marriage work. Pheromones only lasted a year, and I needed a father for my children, especially my son. My brother had grown up without a father, and my brother was in jail. I knew having a family that was mostly baggage, and knew that I had to keep my new family together. Dreams didn't satisfy the physical pangs, but the more I thought about it, the more I was convinced that friendship with Farouk had to be a higher love than the soured chemical reaction I'd had with Charon. I was happy to have such a friend and recognised by now that the reality of a love relationship was not the idyllic dream you imagined in the beginning. From now on, I would keep men at the distance where I could trust them.

Walking in the mountains under pine and cherry blossoms, I told my husband, "I think he needs your advice."

"They're handling it." My husband led the way down the squishy path. It had rained! The wet earth smelled like forgiveness. "The government is protecting Farouk to bring investment to Styxos. The lawyers have plenty of work schmoozing the police and politicians to keep the case out of court. They'll convince anybody of anything. They've told Niovi that she would be *spitting in her own face* if she slandered Farouk in the French papers. They advised Farouk to play along with her game asking for forgiveness and promising to make things work in order to get her to try to lift the charges they have been able to keep off the record."

"It's a small island. Everybody knows what's going on." It sufficed to pick up a British paper to find out everything about Farouk, from the fact that his aristocratic French mother had been disinherited for marrying an Egyptian, to the details of his disengagement from Niovi.

"They're in the public eye. What can *I* say to them? They do what they like."

Confrontation never worked. "OK," I said. "They'll probably break up."

"Let them. It's not my business."

"It's your island. You could explain a few things about Niovi."

"What do you want me to explain? It's hard enough explaining myself." But my husband found the energy to invite Farouk out one night, and they stayed up on Farouk's terrace until daybreak. When I asked my husband what they talked about, he said, "Nothing."

It was common knowledge that Farouk's greatest ammunition was his distance. I had heard — *not* from Charon —that Farouk's life had become a metaphor, a big reflection of a broader hypothesis. And Vanessa told me, in the embassy corridors where Farouk had been a fixture since the arrest, that Farouk absorbed the embassy staff's motivations with psychic comprehension bent on healing, and exuded positive electricity. "To him, only our problems are real. He absorbs our negative energy."

I looked at her doubtfully. But Vanessa was our 'in'. She added us to the embassy mailing list, and arranged to have us invited to a *soirée Rebettica* thrown by the French ambassador. It was at the counsellor's house, and featured "Farouk's former fiancée". On the way in, we heard the minor scales of the Ottoman Empire from the foyer, and understood the attraction Farouk must have felt for Niovi. There she was. "I'm very impressed with your singing," I told her afterward. "I didn't expect to find such a *voice* on the island."

Niovi didn't hear me. Who needed her anyway? I could make other friends on Styxos. They didn't have to be Styxan. Expatriates provided a modicum of common sense and had a stabilizing effect on our household. Vanessa sent us an invitation to a *soirée raclette* with the Ambassador, but still no Farouk. We would never be able to reciprocate for all their hospitality as long as we lived in our crowded renovation with plastic bags hanging from the trees and in-laws coming out of our ears.

More business people landed on the island, and it seemed that the collective unconscious might evolve. Springtime brought the island back to life. The newspapers buried the Grushenka scandal and ran stories on the German insurance conglomerate setting up its Middle East headquarters with a grand opening ceremony, and on a Swiss bank establishing an eastern continental headquarters to build its Jewish client base. But when the Japanese opened an embassy on Styxos, we knew we had arrived.

Chapter 18

The Lady

Many points of shimmering green rustled in the sunlight. Under the almond blossoms, a job possibility emerged. I was invited to interview a representative from a Japanese alternative energy company who had just signed the lease on a modest five-story building not far from the Presbyterian Church. One of the members of the local Ladies' Consortium was friends with the cameraman for the TV station. He was looking for a native English speaker to help him with his story on the new foreign companies on Styxos, and had heard of my knowledge of Japanese cultural anthropology. He wanted to include a scene about springtime rites. The cameraman asked me to use my anthropological knowledge to come up with a few questions.

I wore my orange jacket with the oversized buttons. We walked under the almond blossoms. The cameraman filmed me talking to the Japanese representative in front of the building. "Will you practice any rites for the worship of Osiris like those in Japan centred on a phallus?" I unearthed some interesting material, but the unfortunate events that followed would mean cutting all the footage I was in.

The feature delved into Styxos' procedural inconsistencies with the mainland. We interviewed a European Union regulator posted to Styxos tasked with ensuring that foreign offshore companies conformed to mainland norms. The regulator had formed a thorough knowledge of the company but could not tell us anything about conformity with the EU. What he did tell us was far more interesting.

He had spent a week on their premises, taking the elevator to the top floor of the alternative energy company every morning at a minute to nine. The doors opened onto the executive offices. The excellent condition of the carpet and the brand new furniture in the waiting room seemed to endorse the sound financial status of the island's newest investor. The regulator happened to know that the energy company's bank in Japan, which controlled 10% of the energy company, still had so many bad loans on its books that it should have been shut down three years ago. Instead a spider web of crossholdings supported the bank's shell. The Japanese government was assessing the meltdown and hoping for a work-around to write off the bad debt.

The regulator had practiced the routine enough to know that his real task was to find the one or two people in the organization who knew what was going on, and then the others would have to admit ignorance, or deliver hard facts.

Mr. Kato appeared immediately just as the regulator stepped out of the foyer onto the gray carpet on the first morning of the inspection. The two bowed. The regulator' bow was answered with another bow, which ended in a cascade of bows.

"*Prease* come with me, Regulatorsan." Mr. Kato led the regulator to a conference room full of executive officers apparently getting ready for their morning meeting. They all stood up and fixed on the regulator. He tried not to feel the weight of their collective regard as Mr. Kato led him around the table introducing him to each officer. "This is Mr. Shimada. If you would like to know about operations, *prease* to ask Mr. Shimada." Mr. Shimada handed the regulator his business card, which the latter took carefully in both hands as he had been told to do, turning it over again before putting it into his shirt pocket. "Thank you," he said, and bowed at Mr. Shimada.

They moved on to the 'salary man' in a gray jacket with blue pants. "This is Mr. Tanaka. If you need some technical translations, *prease* to ask Mr. Tanaka." Mr. Tanaka produced another business card. The two men bowed, and the regulator commenced turning the business card over before moving on.

At the end of the table stood a small Lady in a pink suit, next to the chief financial officer. "This is the CFO," Mr. Kato was saying. The regulator bowed very low in front of the balding CFO, and noticed that the Lady had impossibly tiny feet. When at last they came to the Lady, Mr. Kato blushed. "This is Satosan. If you would like a cup of coffee, or some photocopies, *prease* to ask Satosan." There was a small gap between her two front teeth, a sign of beauty in Japan, and she smelled like roses. She did not hand him her business card, so the regulator finished off with his bow, and walked all the way around the table to take the only empty seat, far away from the Lady.

The meeting began with a review of the company history and vision. Mr. Kato expressed his gratitude for the regulator's visit, and urged his colleagues to try their hardest to answer all of the regulator's questions to the best of their abilities. "Please to begin, Regulatorsan."

"Thank you, Katosan. I've noticed from your annual report that you have a large unrealized loss held over from the last financial year. I wondered what the current market value is, and whether you planned on closing it out before this year's annual report?" The CFO and three Japanese men rose from the table, bowed, and disappeared into the adjoining conference room, followed by the Lady. After some minutes, they returned. One of them remained standing and announced a net loss of over 85 million dollars. "We are currently undecided as to how to account for this." He sat down.

"Thank you. Well then, would I be able to get a copy of your policies and procedures?"

The CFO and his translator stood up, and followed the Lady into the conference room. In a few minutes all three came back and sat down. The translator announced, "What we have is written in Japanese, but if you have any specific questions, we would be able to provide an answer."

"Thank you." The regulator shuffled through the pile of business cards in front of him to find the translator's. "Thank you, Tanakasan. Could anybody tell me, at the end of the day you might hold a profit and a loss on your books overnight. Do you add them together to come up with a smaller position, or do you book them as two large, separate positions?"

The CFO and the Lady stood up simultaneously. "We back!" the CFO said, and walked the Lady swiftly to the adjoining conference room. The Lady briefed the CFO in a hushed voice behind the door. After a few minutes, the two returned. The CFO announced that the bank was planning to introduce netting in the coming financial year, and sat down.

The regulator struggled to hide his frustration at watching the Lady's little feet pad along the floor behind the president to the conference room. He abruptly declared, "Look, I'm sure everything is safe and sound here. If I could just have twenty minutes to talk privately with the Lady, we can clear this up and be done for the day."

There was whispering down at the other end of the table. The Lady's head sank, and she looked at her hands in her lap. Then the CFO announced, "No. I am sorry, Regulatorsan. You cannot to talk to the Lady. We back. You ask us, and we back!" the regulator continued the ritual day after day, as the CFO wore out the carpet between the conference table and the room next door. On the fifth day, the CFO confessed. "I'm sorry, Regulatorsan. Only the president know the answer."

"Maybe I should talk to the president then."

"You cannot."

"I can, and I will!" the regulator said.

The Japanese salarymen looked at the CFO, who turned and looked at the Lady. The Lady leaned forward. "I am sorry," she said. "You cannot because he is dead."

When I interviewed the regulator, I found out that he knew nothing about the company's finances. He could only report a degree of familiarity with the CFO's suits. I did learn where to find the Lady.

It took a full three weeks to gain the Lady's confidence. At last, she told me all I needed to know: The president had been found dead of a heart attack. It happened while he was in the act with a woman of ill repute.

I had my angle.

Chapter 19

Oncoming Tea Party

Nothing ever came out of the Ladies' Consortium afternoon tea at the Italian ambassador's residence, so I was surprised to have another feeling of *déjà vu* there. The house was a few meters from the wall, in the heart of the capital's fastest growing neighbourhood. The cool interior gave way to a palm-lined terrace where the ladies sat down in yellow and white striped chairs, perfect for this quiet organization with its tacit policy of never discussing politics.

I sensed another time loop when it was murmured within the shade of a palm from one of the striped chairs that, what with all the infrastructure works going on, something might be done about the human trafficking. I smelled the plate of raspberry scones that was circulating along with black tea and lemon curd and knew I had been here before.

"There is no point in pursuing this unless we are going to be professional about it," another woman said. "We have to act, before we lose momentum." What had gotten into them? My jaw dropped when the European Union women pushed to meet the next day about it. "We might invite Niovi," I suggested.

"Do you think she would come?" a Spanish woman said.

"It's up to you to invite her, Mackenzie," one of the Styxan women said. "You're the vice president of the consortium now, and since her mother lives next door to you—" The other women turned in my direction and fixed their expectations on me for the first time. How did I get dragged into this? Had I been so desperate for work? I would probably fulfil my role like a lump of clay.

The next few afternoons, I found myself watching the wall for a sign of Niovi. At last, her shadow rippled along the garden wall. Struck dumb with fascination, I went over to her. The shadows under the branches of the lemon tree played across her forehead as she looked up to see who was calling her name. The wall veiled all but her ox eye peering at me over the wall. I don't remember what I stammered and couldn't believe it when she said, "Now you're talking, Mac."

You think you make friends at cocktails, but try working on a cause. It was good to be working again. Work was real. Work gave meaning. Friends working together. It's only when you're on a mission that you can make a real friend. *Not* working was what made you depressed. Being unfaithful to your work is what caused existential crisis. There was surely a direct correlation between the unemployment rate and existential crisis — look at France.

At the next meeting, all heads followed Niovi's high derriere switching to the front of the room. She took her seat next to me and said, "Let's get to work." The women echoed her enthusiasm. Even the most docile of island wives remembered the red talons of jealousy. They spent all their energy competing with the TV. What could they do about the marriages wrecked by this vast underclass of immigrant prostitutes? Could envy and resentment be turned into peaceful revolution? I looked to Niovi for affirmation.

The German ambassador was a serious woman. When she was silent, she looked as if she was engineering a divorce. She stood up and began the meeting with a plea for our commitment. "There are more slaves today than at the height of the transatlantic slave trade. The more we ignore it, the bigger the threat to our security. We *must* devote ourselves to this cause with the level of commitment we give to our families."

"I'm divorced," a woman in heavy jewellery replied.

The ambassador raised her voice. "The European Union has issued a warning stating that it is inflexible on the admission of more slaves held against their will from the time of their capture, purchase, or birth, deprived of the right to leave, to refuse to work, or to receive compensation. Although outlawed in nearly all countries today, slavery, secretly practiced in many parts of the world, accounts today for *27 million victims* worldwide. What do you have to say to that? That's twice the number of slaves that came out of Africa during the whole trans-Atlantic slave trade. If we buy products produced by slaves and promote corrupt politicians who uphold slavery, are *we* free?"

The women looked scared. Niovi stood up. "Don't be afraid. We are not alone," she said. "This is just the situation we have to start with. It's not where we're going.

Think what you would do if you knew we couldn't lose. We believe in our cause. That makes each one of us worth ten of them. All they have is personal interests. They are cowards. They're more afraid to do the right thing than the wrong thing."

The ladies' faces brightened. This affirmation of our *raison d'être* was just what the Styxan women among us needed. Niovi had taken the helm. "Human trafficking, whether for cheap sweatshop labour or for prostitution, is a *huge issue* for the European Union right now, and I'm glad that it matters to us, too. If it were black or Jewish people being enslaved, they would stand together and fight. What is it about women that makes us look the other way?" Niovi set the date for the next meeting, and pushed harder.

The chairwoman spelled it out: "The island is on the border of the Middle East. It will have to set the standard on immigration into the European Union. The number of cabarets on Styxos compared to the rest of the European Union suggests that there is a disproportionate number of foreign *artistes* working in cabarets." This in a predominately devout Orthodox society with a population of less than a million. It was no trouble for these *artistes* to get a lengthy visa to work on Styxos.

The ambassador raised her voice. "Relative to the island's population there seems to be a lot of interest in these cabarets." Official figures showed there were 178 cabarets and 38 nightclubs employing 7,380 *artistes*, but many more foreign women worked in the island's entertainment industry. The island women confirmed that most cabarets or strip joints were centres of vice, and that many bars, pubs and nightclubs employing foreign women offered customers sex. But the intolerable clincher that made the Styxan women's eyes roll was the statistic showing one in four *artistes* married island men in order to stay legally on Styxos with around 2,000 civil weddings annually, as opposed to only 70 marriages involving island women and foreign men. Come to think of it, Niovi was the only island woman I knew with a foreign boyfriend.

"Smuggling people into the European Union is a business worth four billion dollars a year," the ambassador said. "Once Styxos accedes to the European Union, it will become an 'early warning' outpost. European Union women have called upon the island to boost her coastal defences and detection network as part of a concerted European Union effort to combat human trafficking."

The floor was opened for discussion. Some of the other countries had conducted unconventional research, setting up dummy companies that purportedly specialized in importing foreign women. One company claimed to specialize in foreign models, escorts and entertainers, complete with business cards, brochures, a telephone and a fax line to give the operation an authentic look. Under the guise of this company, investigators successfully gained entry to the shadowy operations of international trafficking networks on the mainland. They met ex-Soviet pimps who revealed their *modus operandi*. The identities of some of their financial investors and overseas partners had been revealed, but types like "Snake" continued to operate underground on Styxos.

"In other locations, interviews have been recorded by hidden camera directly inside the establishments where trafficked women worked," one of the women told us. "Why couldn't the same thing be done on Styxos?"

"It can," Niovi agreed. "Go on. What's your idea?"

The woman gathered her courage. "We need to come up with enough evidence to make arrests in the places where a lot of girls work as prostitutes." The women looked determined.

Revolution connotes a full circle, and what could be more feminine?

The meeting was a success. They had a new sense of importance. Whether this was the beginning of a new solidarity or an oncoming tea party, no one knew for sure. I hadn't spoken out in one of these meetings; any foreign woman could spark the collective anxiety. I dreaded broaching the subject since I had 'stolen' a handsome, educated island man myself.

But it was a British woman who made the next comment. "My Styxan husband had a brother who took pleasure in taunting our baby. Her in-laws came to the house one afternoon, and the brother-in-law picked up the baby's favourite doll and put it in the middle of the dining room table where she couldn't reach it. The little girl burst into tears, and the in-laws laughed. They watched her screaming. One of them asked me, 'Why is she crying like that?

" 'Well, if someone took away your favourite thing, you'd probably be pretty upset, too.'

" 'No I wouldn't. Not like that.'

" 'Let's see, I believe when the Jarmuths took away your house in the North, your whole family made quite a bit of noise.' "

There was a cold silence. I realized that most of the foreign women were sitting on one side of the table, and most of the Styxan women were on the other, with the exception of Niovi. Niovi laughed loudly. The room burst into noise. If only we could channel this anger, I thought. "Does anyone have any cousins or friends who married foreigners?" I asked the Styxan women.

"Yes," several responded.

"And raised half-breed children with strange customs," one added, "present company excepted, of course."

Everyone seemed to know a homely island girl gaining weight as the years passed with no hope of snaring a Styxan man. Some of them lost their nerve unable to fight back against the bleached-blonde assault on their fertility. The unified body of the extended family often rejected these marriages with the foreign women like skin rejecting a graft.

One spouse described an island house that looked like a little white box with metal bars sticking out of the top to be used to secure the next floor when the children got married and constructed their own apartment up above. "The American woman and her local husband built their house above the house of her parents-in-law." The grandmother did all the cooking, and kept the children with her downstairs during the day. The American mother found a job, and lost the children to the grandmother. The children preferred their *saba*, who spoiled them with candy and unlimited TV. The husband insisted that the children go to the local school, and before long, the mother couldn't help them with their homework. Slowly, the woman became estranged from her husband, and in the end he threw her out. Styxos women's territory had been violated, and the result was this general hysteria against foreigners. Of course, none of this should have happened.

Chapter 20

The Real Terrorists

I had been sending out résumés to anthropological associations for three months but got no interviews. I was happy to receive one letter from the leading authority on the Omopolis excavations — "…please excuse me if this causes you pain" — no doubt the guy's intention. In the middle of the page was a watermark of all the rejections that had stunted *his* career. That could only mean one thing: there was a market.

The mountains slept in mirage. In the furious heat, I stood under a tree and looked through the branches at the purple mountain backs in afternoon siesta. My metal watch band was burning my wrist. I took it off and put it in my pocket. Beads of sweat rolled down my sides. A cloud of dust appeared at the corner, our black Mercedes. I could just make out his mother's son masked by sunglasses behind the wheel. The waves of heat blurred Charon's dark figure. The wheels crunched to a stop on the gravel path in front of my small tree. The leaves hid my head, and my body hid the thin tree trunk.

"What are you doing?" my husband said to my tree self, barely clad in a neutral camisole and skirt.

"Is the air-conditioning on?"

"No."

"Turn it on, please."

"Get into the car!" He was swearing in Styxan. I felt dizzy. A helicopter swooped overhead. Suddenly, a cloud of dust rose from the horizon. I ducked down just as the tank appeared and collapsed into the car. My husband dodged through the city avoiding people running haphazard in the streets. "The island is being evacuated!"

A woman carrying a baby and leading five other school children raced in front of our car. Charon screeched to a halt. I braced myself against the dashboard. The children disappeared up a driveway. One had a bloody foot. There were large holes in the cobble stones. People surrounded our car. We pressed on at a crawl.

Every muscle in my body had tensed. But the air-conditioning had started to work, and soon I saw that there were no people running in the street, no tanks, just empty streets and quiet houses at siesta time. Charon took me to the American embassy to volunteer as a warden. It would be an opportunity to make some connections and build trust. Maybe it would eventually lead to a job.

The American Embassy was as imposing as I had expected. A whole city block was devoted to our Middle East spying activity. I had never seen a larger embassy anywhere. We walked around it under the covered walkway, through more security, and past more guns. To get onto U.S. soil, you had to show your passport, empty your pockets, walk though a metal detector, and undergo a search. The guards followed their procedures slowly as if it were any other day. I lowered my arms, and emptied my coins onto the counter, and in the spirit of their poker-faced security check, ventured, "Here's an opportunity to organize my change purse." The soldier did not show any sign of having heard me.

At war.

In the lobby, the TV blared news of war a few hours away in the Middle East. It was impossible to tune out the bloody pictures and the propaganda. The mood in the waiting room was solemn and tense. Charon and I sat down in the air-conditioning and listened, unable to hold a conversation over the bulletins and shots echoing from the television. A young woman with curly black hair paced up and down breathing hard and stretching her neck as if to try to find some relief. I watched her curiously. She kept her eyes to herself, and I realized she was in pain. The television was overpowering. I was unable to find anywhere to turn my eyes. I could see that it was torture for the young woman to watch the visions of war, and finally got up and walked over to the TV. "Anybody want to watch something different?" I asked, hoping to ease the woman's pain.

The people in the waiting room looked up, startled. "Can we change the channel?" said a middle-aged woman with two elderly peasants couched in black mourning attire.

We were on American soil, weren't we? "It's a free country." I surfed through the channels until a music video caught our attention. The young woman smiled at me, and asked me if I was an American. "Yes."

She was from a village that had been invaded in the North. She sat down next to me and breathed more evenly. US soil didn't feel quite the same from this perspective. Our eyes drifted up to the TV screen again, and now I saw the painted diva from next door. Niovi sang the jealousy song with passion into a wind machine. It sent a chill down my spine.

The man behind the counter called my name, and my husband and I stepped forward. I squeezed my hand under the bulletproof glass to shake his hand.

"You must be Mac," he said in an island accent. He handed me the *Booklet for US Consular Wardens* and explained that in the case of an emergency, I would be called upon to contact the American citizens on my list to give instructions for evacuation.

I looked at my husband. "And what about him?"

The man smiled. "He is your immediate family. You, your husband and your children can be evacuated. But as a commando, he would probably be required to stay and drive a tank, like he was in the last invasion." The children running in the street. *The last invasion.* That must have been forty years ago, which would explain the cobblestone streets.

I glared at Charon, and went on talking to the official. "What airline would it be, or do you have your own planes?"

"They would most likely be charter airplanes if anything like that were to happen again. That's what we used during the last invasion. We don't keep enough of our own planes on the island."

The silent mountains travelled beside us on our way back to my husband's mother's house. I had the sinking feeling that we would never escape. I didn't expect this feeling of panic. After all, Styxos wasn't a ghetto where once you fell in you could never get out.

Charon wedged our vehicle under the vine leaves, and walked through the dirt to his mother's broken kitchen door and into the crowded room with speckled tile that hid the dirt. Everywhere I tried to rest my gaze was an eyesore. The children came running into our arms, and we hugged them and fell down in the dust.

Chapter 21

The Underworld

With no job, but determined to work, I was able to use my capacity as vice president of the Ladies' Consortium to get access to the police report on Oxana, a thirty-year-old Russian. The police found her because she had managed to get her name on the title of the house owned by the president of the Japanese company.

Before going over to meet her, I went to the clinic and got an AIDS test, just to be sure of the consequences of Charon's philandering. To distract myself while I was waiting for the results, I called my former boss at the wire service to tell him about Oxana. For once he was delighted. "You can work on it freelance. See if she knows anything about Grushenka."

I sat down across from him. There was a catalogue with a full range of spyware on his desk. "Mind if I look at this?" I asked. There were all kinds of listening devices. There was a SIM card reader to keep track of unfaithful spouses and criminals. It was able to recover deleted telephone messages. Maybe a gadget like this was just what

I needed. "Do these work?" I was already writing down the address.

"Of course they work, but our criminal is already caught. These would be more useful." He handed me a pack of cigarettes and dismissed me with his profile.

The next morning, I woke up again to the shock of sleeping alone. Memory came rushing back. I could hear Charon in his mother's room. I needed a way out, and there was none. I had to continue to hope. If only I could change my thoughts about being trapped here to the work at hand. Then I could change my world. I grasped at the nearest available strands.

It seemed to me that solving the Grushenka puzzle would help a lot more than just me. I took a taxi to the prison. After waiting for a half an hour in a room full of women and children visitors, I was shown to a small building for female prisoners. The police officer led me to the room where Oxana was waiting for deportation. I asked him to leave us alone, and he went and stood outside the door. "My name is Mackenzie," I said.

"Mackenzie? Ah, Mac! Niovi's friend, right?"

No one had ever given me a nickname before, and even though 'Mac' reminded me of a truck or a hamburger, I warmed to the masculine nomenclature. It made me feel like I belonged, however feeble the hand that had lifted me up. "Yes. I think that telling your story might help warn other women in danger."

"What women?"

"Well, there's one in particular, but she's dead. Did you know the woman named Grushenka?"

She nodded, but said, "Maybe."

"Did you ever meet Grushenka?"

"What to you?"

I offered her a cigarette. Oxana took it eagerly. I lit it, and she began to talk. "I know about her long time ago. Some men were looking in her village, saying, who needs job? She was suspicious, but her family was sick. They needed some medicine, and she must to do everything she could for them. She climbed in truck and found herself in dirty place 1000 miles from home. After few weeks, she decided to quit. When she tried to walk away, the whip came down. She discovered she was slave. They sold her for ninety shekels."

Oxana's own debut was similar, but her career had lasted a little longer. Her favourite job had been as a party starter jumping off a yacht and swimming up and down to lure the passengers into the water. She had been engaged to the president of the Japanese company, but he met Grushenka, and that was the end of that dream. Now Oxana, who liked to think of herself as an ex-underwear model, was in the public eye, and had to leave Styxos.

"She only liked him because he was rich," Oxana said.

I had to smile at her pragmatism.

"Grushenka have no idea how old he is, or even that he was having heart condition. She no speak a his language . . ." The president had taken to Grushenka immediately precisely because neither of them spoke any language the other could understand. Together they explored a realm where no regulator could go and discovered that they understood each other completely. "I walked in one day. He showing her what he wanted, and she obeying as she was just beginning to see. I had to pretend I didn't know anything."

Oxana explained how the president would come home after his morning meetings and spend languid afternoons entangled with Grushenka under the whirr of the air conditioner. He took her white body in his arms, barely stopping for breath. He forgot about his medicine. Grushenka didn't know his title or his real name. Ah, he gave his undeniable orders ever so gently. I'm sure she could not refuse when he demanded to take her *derrière*. But his entire body stiffened. He fell backward off of the bed.

It was a shame. He had been good to them, "real sweetheart," Oxana said. "He was maybe little peevish toward end, but generous to settle our bills."

"Was she in business for herself?" I asked.

"Who?"

"Grushenka."

"Give me another cigarette."

I lit it for her.

"None of us is," Oxana said. "There are always debts."

I stifled a laugh. The idea of a sex slave incurring debts was mindboggling. "Where are the other girls?"

"In the centre near checkpoint. On both sides of wall. Places like 'Tropical Hotdog' and 'Dervish House'.

"Is that where Grushenka worked?"

"Yes. In Tropical Hotdog."

"Who runs it?"

"A guy with a tattoo."

"Snake?" The name on my tongue gave me a chill.

"You know about Snake?"

"Oh yes," I lied. "I know *all* about him,"

"Well there are others above him."

"Who are the others above him?"

"I only know Snake."

131

The AIDS test was negative. That revived my will to survive and its shadow, the hope that Charon could be faithful.

The Grushenka story made a comeback on the wire with my new background as the lead. It got picked up everywhere. Articles came out, and the human trafficking outrage grew. A *bona fide* businessman from a first-world country had died in the cradle of the underworld — and during Styxos' accession negotiations with the continent. The human trafficking outrage had blossomed into an issue. Apologies would have to be made, laws changed, responsibility denied. It was rumoured that someone might have to step down.

The Interior Minister of Vice defended himself. Human trafficking was certainly no cause for *his* resignation. "Come, come now! This rash of family breakdowns has taken everyone by surprise. The Vice and Virtue Department maintains the highest standards for upholding morality. This is a petty crime. It had nothing to do with the squandering of public funds. Even the intellectuals had based their theories on the assumption that communism was permanent. Everyone is still struggling with the unexpected crumbling of the Iron Curtain. How could they have estimated this family fallout in bordering countries? Can I help it if those fungi arms dealers used women's bodies as their front line?"

It took the Special Forces months to trace females handing out invitations on Styxos beaches to arms deals in underworld bars, but there was never enough evidence to keep anyone in jail. The Chief of Police, Special Forces apologised to our Ladies' Consortium. "The chance of catching the Big Boss only happens once a year, in a brief window of opportunity with the arrival of a large haul of 'formula'." We learned that that was cocaine. I pointed to the evidence we'd gathered, but several of the government official gala invitees tried to ruin my investigation by denying being present at the scene of the crime.

"I would investigate those lying government officials if I still had my job here," I told the bureau chief at the wire service. I had avoided another kick in the butt.

"Really? Write their names down here."

I did it without thinking twice, just knowing that there was that evil monster lurking in the depths of the underworld selling human beings by weight into misery, only worrying when he would get the next shipment to satisfy some new Egyptian client. I regretted composing that useless list later on when I felt not only Grushenka but also the government breathing down my neck.

Chapter 22

Democrisy

One day, my husband got a phone call that changed my life. He was pacing up and down talking excitedly on the phone in Styxan. He smiled and hung up. "They liked the footage at the Japanese company and want you to come work for the TV station."

I stood up. "But they cut me out of all of it."

"I know, and they were sorry they had to do that. The Japanese company story would have been bad for the country's image, considering that it ended in a sex scandal. They probably liked the fact that you didn't complain. It's the government TV station. They don't want whiners working there."

"Do I have your permission?" I teased Charon.

"This could propel you to small-time celebrityhood."

"I could probably make more driving a taxi." I slipped into a daydream about merging into the public eye, with middle-age closing in fast from behind — another one of life's little jokes.

The American embassy had just asked all the wardens to circulate a warning in my community raising the national threat level from elevated to high risk of terrorist attack or 'Level Orange'. This meant that I was supposed to get in touch with my list of American citizens, cautioning them against any public display that could precipitate violence against American citizens. The thought of terrorists looking for symbolic targets increased the tension of my upcoming interview at the TV station.

I stared at the freshly painted living room wall for a long time. It looked brand new. A sense of accomplishment crept over me as I flipped the job at the TV station over in my mind. It would be no good to be a victim with two babies at home. But the American embassy diffused these threatening messages so often, I began to wonder if they weren't the ones fomenting terrorism. Inciting fear was one way of keeping weapons of missing destruction from undermining our *democrisy*. The messages seemed more like an attempted justification for further war. Was it up to me to kick-start the US economy and get the Republicans re-elected?

At the TV station, I went into the small office that looked like it hadn't been renovated since it was built in the 1950s and shook the hand of the head of broadcasting, a man in a T-shirt and black jeans. He explained in a perfect London accent that they had received my résumé months ago, but hadn't had time to interview me. "Now that summer vacation has come around, we have a severe shortage of staff. I will have to show you how to write the outcue myself." He had me edit a news story and practice reading the final script out loud. He took me down to the changing room. I picked out a purple jacket with the tag still on. He pinned it behind my back. "The shop that furnishes the garments gets a percentage exceeding the newscasters' pay every time the jacket appeared on TV."

"Glad to be a part of it."

The makeup room in the basement was just an aisle with a mirror. The Styxan makeup artist had spent thirty years of her life there among the ashtrays creating the illusion of beauty. She covered my jacket with paper towel, and began to dab my face with cover-up. She opened her pots of eye shadow. "Any requests?"

"People keep telling me I look better with my glasses on."

"That's not good. I'll use a charcoal colour to make your eyes look really big." Styxans did have big eyes, but the makeup artist seemed confident that she could correct my deficiency. She opened a pot of black theatrical eyeliner and painted a streak across my eyelid. "Look this way," she said, and I faced her cleavage. Stylists were always wearing the darndest tops. There was something reassuring about her smell, pungent lilac mixed with sweat. "Do you have any kids?" she asked.

"Two."

"That's wonderful! Me, too. They are everything."

As I watched my eyes grow, a newscaster with a microphone attached to her Muslim scarf walked past in the mirror behind me.

"Have they already hired newscasters from the North?" I asked.

"Yes, it's at five o'clock, for the first time in years."

"Did they have it in the old days?"

"Yes, but then it was stopped." She took a deep breath. "We used to get along with the Muslims. We didn't have any problems. The Muslims were modest people. They

136

worked well, and didn't ask for a lot of money, and we loved them. It was because of outside influences that Styxos was divided. You know, divide and conquer. I remember we had a Muslim neighbour in my village. He had a lot of land that he cultivated. He raised many animals, and he was the richest man in the village. During the invasion, his wife and children hid in the cellar."

I looked up at the peeling walls and the small windows near the ceiling.

"They told him to pack his things, leave his house, and come to the North. He said, 'I'm sorry, but I don't want to go to the North. I am staying here.' So they took his daughter. He waited without any word about her, and then he sent his wife and his two-year-old son to the North to fetch her. They didn't come back. Finally, the troops came and killed all his animals, with knives. He came to us crying, telling us how he could hear the cows screaming all night."

I heard the sound of footsteps running outside. The air smelled of gunpowder and cigarettes. The scream of the cattle made me cringe, and I didn't dare to open my eyes.

"He asked my father to keep the key to his house. 'I know they are going to kill me, but what can I do? They have my family. I have to go.'

"He went away, and we never heard from him since. I believe that if any of them were alive, they would have sent word. After that, Christians started to do terrible things in anger. They would take a saw to the old grape vines that were a foot wide at the Muslims' houses, and cut them down. They killed the animals, and cut down the trees. Now if anyone does any such thing —" A black tear had broken through her mascara and rolled down her cheek.

I watched her open a cake of pink eye shadow, and wondered why people insisted on race and nation as the ultimate source of legitimacy. She dabbed a tiny sponge into it and brushed it on a piece of tissue on the counter. "We were all manipulated. Where did the will come from to create a 'master race' of Christians to rule over the Muslims?" She applied it to the corner of my eyes, where it seemed to completely disappear. "The mainland, that's where."

It was hard to imagine either community taking up arms. "Both sides seem docile now," I said.

"We *are* docile. Our biggest fault is our fear. You would be shocked to see what we are all capable of when we let outsiders manipulate us. They are only starting to tell about the suffering under the occupation. For years they said nothing for fear of being punished. They all seemed to support it. Now that it is over, more stories are coming out."

The makeup lady was nice. I only saw her a few times after that. They say she ran off and left her children behind. It didn't fit. She didn't seem like the type who would leave her kids.

Chapter 23

Newscast

After an hour of brushing and applying powder of all colours, I was done. I looked like someone else. Someone ten years younger on her way to a nightclub.

I walked up and down the hallway looking for the way back to the studio. If I could pull this off, I could get a grip on my life again and maybe get us out of Styxos.

A well-built man appeared at my side. "Are you looking for the news studio?"

"Yes."

"It's just through here. Follow me." He turned around to catch me looking at him. "Where are you from?"

"America."

"What are you doing here?"

"The news in English."

"I'm from Greece," he said. "My name is Adonis. You are very nice. Sweet face. What sport you do?"

"I run."

"Very nice. I teach aerobics. The studio is just through there. Good luck."

A talk show was just ending. The producer changed the background to a blue screen with a globe on it and came out. "Where have you been? We have one and a half minutes to get you in the room and plug you in!" He sat me down in front of the globe and scurried about plugging wires into the console. He adjusted my earphones. There was my new face on the floor monitor. I looked like a doll in my purple jacket with a string of pearls around my neck. The producer had just enough time to clip the microphone to my lapel and press a button to bring the prompter back to the start. Our text appeared on a screen above the camera. The producer's voice in my ear said, "The key is to relax and just keep talking. And remember, keep your head moving so they can't tell you are reading from the monitor. Lights, camera, ready...cue!"

I struggled to control my voice and looked directly into the lens with as convincing an expression as I could muster. I tried not to think about the implications of the sentences I was pronouncing. "Good evening." I bobbed my head from side to side. "You're watching the news in English, live from Styxos. American troops came under fire despite UN efforts to mediate the situation..." I watched my face disappear from the screen out of the corner of my eye, as the producer switched to a clip of battlefield footage. That was it; I was a newscaster. "In Israel, American tanks rolled into town as residents looked on in apprehension."

I just had time to straighten my jacket. Then, the microphone in my ear buzzed, "Ready . . . cue!"

"An estimated 30 million humans are slaves today worldwide, mostly women and children." I paused to catch my breath and then quickly went on. "The UN

Secretary General estimated that worldwide, more than 700,000 people are trafficked each year for sexual exploitation." Amnesty International claims that the judicial system in Montenegro has failed victims of forced trafficking. A 28-year-old mother of two from Moldova had come to Serbia looking for work. She became a slave and was sold like an animal to different 'owners'. A major ring of traffickers routinely beat, drugged, burned and raped her."

I was short of breath, and tried to ignore the subject so I could steady my voice. It was easier to actually breathe out before starting another long sentence about bombing *sorties* by mainland jets destroying what international officials claimed was the biggest narcotics discovery in history. I tilted my head downward and then looked directly ahead. "Anti-narcotics commandos made their discovery on Monday after being tipped off about the presence of what were described as underground warehouses by a convict indicted on 15 charges of trafficking including kidnapping, facilitating the entry of illegal immigrants into the European Union, incitement to rape, procuring a teenager to have unlawful sex, and drug smuggling. He was alleged to have run a lucrative racket that was the biggest of its kind ever seen in the European Union." *Keep going, keep going.* "The convict was arrested a day after he bought himself a black Ferrari. His boss, operating under the code name, Snake, is believed to be at large on Styxos." I gulped a mouthful of air. "The covered trenches dug by bulldozers contained what is believed to be the largest ever seizure of cocaine stockpiles." The Boss of the underworld would have surfaced on Styxos for a piece of that. I knew he was watching.

"Insurgents stood to gain about € 50 million from the sale of the drugs, officials said. The quantity of cocaine, which was allocated into 100kg sacks, was so great that it would have required 80 trucks to transport it over the nearby border crossing. Eager to destroy the haul before any of it could be siphoned away, Harrier jets dropped one 1,000 lb bomb and two 500 lb bombs on the cocaine trenches, a spokesman said."

It's almost over.

"Ready, cue!"

"And now for a look at the weather forecast for tomorrow, which will bring fine conditions in the morning with slight sea breezes. Temperatures will reach 34 on the coast…" I imagined the children at home watching me on TV, and smiled, "…until then, have a goodnight!"

I did it! My hands were shaking as I unplugged my earphones. I collected my papers. The music came up with a computer generated globe spinning on the monitor at my feet.

Chapter 24

The Interview

"For your first time, it was good," the producer said. "Don't worry. Next time you will be much more relaxed."

I repeated the Styxan pleasantry, "Time travels in loops," as to remain humble.

Adonis was waiting for me in the hallway. "Very nice. You do it better than the girl they fired. You want to come to my house?"

"Your house!"

"It's on the beach."

"I'm married with two children."

"My brother met German woman, married, one child. When they together, he say, 'I love your child like our own, and you love our child.' They have new baby. Think about." His expression implored me for an answer, but when he saw he would get none, he went on. "I like I not meet you again because if I do, danger." Adonis slipped away.

I turned down another hallway. A man with a camera was standing talking with Niovi. She grabbed my arm. "Mac! Are you working here now?" She seemed to be reappraising me. "Good for you. Believe in yourself! I know you can do it, Mac. I'm going to have a cup of coffee in the cafeteria." She led me down the hallway to the smoke-filled room and installed herself at a table in the middle.

I sat down, or rather, my knees crumbled under me at the prospect of being friends with Niovi, and I fell into a chair. I asked, "So what's it like being a star?" and watched her chiselled nose and naturally big eyes.

"You would think it would be like driving down a highway, but it's mostly fighting with zealots like any other job on Styxos. I have all these people who have nothing better to do than come and make problems for me. They are jealous, you know 'zealous' is 'jealous', so I spend most of my time fighting over petty things that they are not worthy of a second thought. Everyone talks about me, and I read about myself in the papers. What do you call that? An occupational hazard. That's what it is reading the newspaper."

She sipped her coffee. "If I had to do it over, I'd say, don't fall into the role they hand you. It's not going to be a big one, and the more you conform, the smaller it will become. You carve out your own plan, Mac. My dreams are coming true, but they are worn-out dreams from childhood. Getting is not so hard, but getting what? A lot of people dream of becoming a millionaire. A million's not that much anymore, and now that I've made my million, I realise I'm not the type to want to spend it. I'd rather make another million."

"Poor millionaire." My voice trailed off as I noticed a familiar face approaching the counter.

She followed my eyes. "You've met Adonis?"

"Yes."

"We went to high school together."

"Him? The Greek Adonis?"

She nodded hello to him as he picked up his coffee and left, then whispered to me. "Adonis is Styxan, not Greek. What did he tell you?"

"He said he has a house on the beach."

"A house on the beach! Really! So Adonis is going to try to seduce the new girl. And what are they saying about *me* these days?"

I couldn't help smiling. "Besides that you're a witch and can give people the evil eye?"

Niovi cringed. "Stay away from whoever said that! It exists and someone can do it to you without your knowing it. Don't be surprised. It's one of the most widespread superstitions mankind has known, especially along the Mediterranean."

"You don't believe that old superstition."

"You believe that love emanates from the eyes, don't you? Then why wouldn't you believe that humans have the power to transmit evil with their eyes? Because you have a block there. The evil eye is the name for a sickness transmitted by a person who is envious, usually without knowing it. I'm serious. It's existed since the time of prehistoric man."

I left off telling her that I was a scientist, since I could barely get a word in edgewise. I had finished my coffee, but Niovi hadn't started hers. "The origins of the belief are obscure, but the superstition carried forward through the period when witchcraft was more important than science." I was curious to know what she thought about the evil eye, so I set down my cup and let her talk. "Amulets to protect against the evil eye have been found on every continent of the world. It appears in Egyptian hieroglyphics, the Bible and ancient Greek and Roman literature. All these which say that envious or evil people could induce sickness and death by casting their eye on someone else. The evil eye's piercing force is so powerful it could infect those around it. It is bad enough when someone casts the evil eye bringing about an action created in the mind, but what is even more terrible is someone whose power of the evil eye is natural and unconscious. Then their look can produce truly destructive effects."

"Maybe an academic journal would be interested in that. I'm an anthropologist, you know."

"You are! Well, you should write it! It would be nice to read about something else for a change. We have to see how are we going to do that. Let's meet again here at the same time on Monday to talk about it."

Excited about my new friend, I stepped outside of the TV station into the late afternoon heat. I didn't mind that Charon was late to pick me up. Standing there thinking about Niovi's big eyes, I watched a black government car swing into the parking lot at full speed. It careened toward me. I realized that the driver had no intention of stopping. I dove into the rhododendrons. The car sped away before I could get a glimpse of the license plate.

Chapter 25

Fascinatio

I was afraid to go back to the TV station and regretted having insisted on pressuring the government officials who had denied attending the gala. But when the time came for my coffee with Niovi, I ventured back to the café there. Unsure whether I'd mistaken the time, I checked my wristwatch. The bands of rhinestones gleamed up at me: *On time!* I twisted the pink leather band in place and noticed in the mirror on the wall that the people behind me were watching. The windows opened onto a marvellous autumn evening. A breeze scented with barbecue wafted in through the window, and a pair of green-breasted humming birds with shiny red necks buzzed around a bougainvillea and landed on a rock in the garden outside the window. One flew away, and the other called out in lonely song.

I grabbed a fashion magazine from the rack and flipped through the pages. Niovi would come soon, and I would laugh and say, 'Don't worry!' like one of the glossy models in the magazine. I know Styxans have a different conception of time, but as it got later, I thought I might mention to her that I had a busy schedule, too, and two children waiting at home. *If you couldn't make it, you could have sent someone to tell me so I could be home with my children by now instead of risking my life sitting in a café alone.* I would show her I was angry at her for making herself scarce, but the next moment, I started to get up, regretting it immediately. She might not invite me for coffee again. I could leave a message for her with someone so she at least knew I'd waited the full fifteen minutes. I paid the waiter and asked if he knew Niovi. He didn't seem to understand. "Never mind."

Suddenly, her voice filled the hallway, and I screwed my lips into a grimace to let her know how I felt. The only trouble was that her absence had made me want to see her more, and in such relief, I couldn't pretend to be angry. Niovi's wild silhouette filled the doorway. "Mac!" She threw her arms out wide exuding the odour of department store gift wrap. My heart leapt for joy. Her outfit was put together with the utmost taste. Her smile was shining. Heads turned to see as I tried to hide my relief. The Styxan beauty kissed me. The room came to life in her presence. Did I love Niovi so much, too? Before I could make any of my speeches, I was following her wide hips to her favourite table. She made me forget her slight with an indomitable *parole*, punctuated with guttural h's, which I scribbled down on my notepad. "What do you *cxhave* there, Mac? You know those fashion models aren't real. And we have to compete with them! The best we can do is convince the men that *we're* not real."

I was in the spotlight when Niovi was talking to me. Heads turned and the other tables in the mirror animated to her rhythm. "I will tell you the symptoms of the evil eye." Her hair brushed my cheek. "Headache and heavy eyes; nausea; and everything seems to go wrong." I wrote as fast as I could in my own shorthand.

She was so enthusiastic, I forgot to tell her about the car that tried to run me over or any of the things I had rehearsed. "There are several ways to defend against the evil eye," she went on. "The most harmless is to pass a raw egg in its shell over the face of the victim. Then, you break the egg in a saucer, and put it under his bed. Me, I did this once, but it was in the heat of the summer, and I wasn't sure how long the egg had to stay under the bed."

"My goodness. And what is the least harmless?"

"That would be human sacrifice."

"Uh—" I saw Grushenka's body again at the poolside streaked with blood, her hair matted, face frozen in livid panic. They said it was a superfluous crime, but then why did that malignant cult of a chorus press against the window to get a better look? It *was* a sacrifice. "Let's stick to the present. What *is* the evil eye?"

"Sometimes it is God, the devastating, omnipotent eye of providence who knows all, and sometimes, it's just a 'jinx'. Mac, you have to understand that envious people have the ability to destroy your sexual power. Try to notice how do chaotic things, anything outside of the norm of society, affect you. People are afraid of chaos because it upsets the reproductive balance between men and women. Symbols of chaos are unmarried or widowed women, lesbians, gays, in your country, the Salem witches, hunched backs, club-foots, the infertile, women like Grushenka. Even the blue eyes of the foreigners. You have to be careful with your blue eyes, Mac! That's why

149

Styxans try so hard to fit in. Anyone different might be accused of being a jinx. Differences antagonize the group. Outcasts risk imprisonment and murder."

It was refreshing to find this nimble intelligence in the Styxan singer. She was an exceptional woman, strong and cultured with unbeatable faith in herself. "What do you think happened to Grushenka?" I asked.

Niovi brushed her hair back. "It's not what I think; everyone knows. You want to understand why did everyone look the other way. Remember the Greek theatre. The chorus needs a scapegoat. The mob accuses one of its members of being responsible for the disorder. Grushenka was a human sacrifice. I don't know to what god, but a clash of the power of the male versus the power of the female made her an unfortunate victim. Because she was different from the Styxans, she was held guilty of the problems of society."

"That seems a bit ridiculous, sorry! Which problems?"

"Mac, you are an anthropologist. Do you think we have changed so much since ancient times? Think about it. The problems you are having with your Styxan husband. Marriage problems."

"What marriage problems?"

"Mac! Do you know why God made woman weaker than man? On the third day of creation, woman tricked man into marrying her and God pitied man and scooped up some clay and gave him muscles. When God was done forming the wet clay, he rolled man in the sand to make his skin tough to defend himself for the rest of his life in his struggle with woman. Every time woman outsmarts man, he has to find new ways to destabilise her so she doesn't get her balance.

"Remember that only a generation ago, housework was long and hard labour and the Styxan women had a dozen children. There was a train of camels tied together carrying water from village to village. Some houses didn't have electricity. Maybe you had a wringer for the laundry, but no appliances. You had to have a wife with rough, red hands to beat the wet clothes with a stick — there were no rubber gloves — and she had to finish before dark. Women were keeping chickens, growing the food they cooked for large families because some of the children would die. They were sewing clothing for everyone, cleaning the dust coming into the house from the desert, and digging outhouses.

"Now a woman comes home from the office and doesn't know why is her husband in bed with a prostitute from abroad. The twenty-first century is painful."

Styxos will never be modern.

The voice sent a rash of goose bumps all over my body. I broke out in a cold sweat. I'm sure Niovi heard it, too. Her gaze hardened, fixed on something behind my right shoulder, but I could see in the mirror that there was nothing there. I turned around anyway, in time to see the girl's pretty face dissolve in the air.

I was amazed that Niovi was able to go on talking as if nothing had happened. ". . . If you stay in Styxos longer, you will begin to understand ruins. In the final act the scapegoat was murdered, the source of the chaos was purged and natural order restored. Nature starts over from chaos. If the chaos continues afterward, another person will be persecuted." I looked around the cafeteria. Everyone else was Styxan.

"The death of Grushenka sanctified her. After the murder, we were united to venerate her, where before, she was held responsible. Now that she's dead, she gets the credit for the resolution of the crisis." Niovi was showing me a book on ancient rituals.

The repetition of purging forms the basis of ritual. The ritual becomes less and less violent with animals and plants replacing the human victims. The victimization moving increasingly toward the goal of eradicating the violence.

Strings of silver charm bracelets adorned her arms and marked her as a perpetrator of the ancient belief, *baskania* in Greek, in Latin, *fascinatio*. Spanish-speaking countries of South America call it *mal de ojo*. In France, *mauvais oeil*, in Haiti, *mauvais jé*, in Germany, *böse Blick*, in Ireland, *droch-shuil*; in Scotland, *bad Ee*, in Arabic, *'ayn*, in Hebrew, *ayin hara*, in China, *ok ngan*, in Tuscany *jettatura*. In the USA, they're calling it *psychosis*.

Chapter 26

Act of Jealousy

Niovi wore a blue eye bracelet to confound anyone who might cast the evil eye on her. One of her aunts had bought it on the mainland where they made glass charms in the providential eye-in-hand patterns. I touched the little blue eyes dangling from her olive wrists. "These are pretty."

"Shhhh. On Styxos you have to be careful when you say things like that."

"Like what?"

"People say if anyone admires even your shoes, the envy of that person can put a spell on you."

"They're ugly, then."

"It's not just me. The Jews wondered what did they have to do to safeguard against *ayin ha'ra,* so rather than taking a census and exposing some families to jealousy because of their larger number of children, each person had to pay a shekel and let the coins be counted rather than people. The best month for taking a coin-census was the month of Adar, the month of fish and the Zodiacal sign Pisces because fish are immune to *ayin ha'ra*. Farouk is a Pisces, one of the people who don't suffer from the afflictions of the evil eye. Fishes cannot be overlooked because they are covered with water, and are not jealous."

I was relieved to hear it, and put aside my worries that her eyes would devour him. "OK, for the record, why are you wearing all these eyes?"

"Spiritual protection." The scented pomegranate amulet at her throat was also meant to invoke good spirits and to protect her from evil ones. "Now you know why do they have almonds at weddings. The shape symbolizes sexual power." Niovi's own eyes were outlined in heavy black, and it occurred to me that, although women everywhere wore eye make-up, its original purpose may have been protective.

Niovi noticed I was inspecting her eyes. "In India, women line the eyes of their children with dark kohl as a form of protection against the evil eye. Your eyes are suspect, Mac. In our culture, people believe that the blue eyes of foreigners cast the evil eye on others. After three thousand years of invasions with foreigners coveting island soil, the brown-eyed islanders have become suspicious of blue-eyed foreigners. Romans, Goths, Slavs, Ottomans, and not long ago the blue-eyed Germans had invaded. Back then, the taboo against inviting strangers into your home might have really kept livestock and children from dying."

"That's interesting, but it's old. We should go to a school and find examples of the first representational thing little children draw, this circle with sticks coming out, with a dot for a pupil in the middle, in the skies of their paper, and on the ground as heads in masses like animals, this spiked eye. This sun. You see, I need something living." Now that I was talking and she was listening, Niovi looked smaller.

Niovi pursed her brown lips. Her elegant hands folded over the book. "You're a good woman, Mac, a really nice lady. And humble. You don't even know the positive effect you have on people's lives. If you found a cockroach in your kitchen, you would let it outside so it could escape the heat. I know it must sound silly to you, but the people on this island are jealous with a negative force you can't imagine. You can find a lot of examples around here."

"That's more like it." I tried to get her to describe this mass psychosis in detail.

"People who have never had anything of their own before suddenly have so many material things that you take for granted. They get caught up in materialism and don't know what to do with themselves. Just look at the ghost town in the occupied area. Why would they take it over and leave it to rot? It was the jewel of the Mediterranean."

"That's what Charon said."

"Charon!" She mumbled under her breath in Styxan. "Maybe that's what Charon would like to do to you, Mac. Me, I don't think it is Christian or Muslim. It's just another example of the evil eye. You see, because I am a singer whose fame has spread throughout the island, I also *cxhave* the misfortune of attracting the evil eye."

She led me with her hard h's into her private life, and I felt the room slipping away. "You need the story of someone," she said. "Do you *cxhave* the possibility to get a

155

person's perspective? Or it could be how are you yourself adjusting to your mixed marriage."

'Mixed!' It was the first time I heard our marriage referred to as 'mixed'. "Well, I'm *not* a collectivist, but where I come from, 'mixed' means black and white."

"Sometimes it seems that way to me," she said, brushing back her black mane. Tears filled her eyes.

I wasn't accustomed to her effusiveness, and put my pen and notebook away to indicate that the interview was over, but this only prompted a subtle lowering of her voice, and she began down another vicissitude.

"Chemically, Farouk is simple. Pheromones are easy to understand. But when we get back to civilisation, we are different animals." She choked back the tears. "What was so easy is now so hard. He is my sweetest enemy."

"Farouk? — I mean, off the record."

"Yes, Farouk."

"Great," I said. "No, um, that's really touching."

Niovi's voice shook. "I know how you feel about him, Mac."

I felt the heat rise to my face.

"I know what you are thinking because I'm thinking it, too," Niovi went on. "We are free to think what we like, aren't we? As long as we don't *do* it. How I wish *I* could go back to the days before Farouk and I ever touched. But after what *he's* done, they say he is not good enough for me. You can tell me what you really think, Mac."

"No man is good enough for you, Niovi. You just go ahead and pick whichever one you want."

Chapter 27

Energy Descends

"How did I become involved in his childish game?" Niovi confessed, "There was a big private party at the prime minister's palace, and that is where we met. He wanted to meet again. I didn't give him my telephone number, but he found me and called a few times. I was terribly busy. He must have thought I was playing hard to get. When we finally went out, he didn't understand why did I want to meet his friends, and I didn't listen when he said he wanted to come to my house. Me, I know I have different expectations from the French, and even if I was worried he would lose interest, I didn't want to be used. I made him wait for me, and he made me wait for him. Mac, I have never spent so much time waiting for a man.

"How silly I was to think that I loved him. And to let him romance me. Ridiculous illusion! Usually men are there for me. But if I let go of Farouk, he would disappear for weeks at a time. What kind of creature wishes for the minutes to pass quickly and the years to pass slowly? I don't have that kind of time! This year flew by. It was a smaller fraction of my life than last year, when I was still a child, and I barely noticed it fly by. I moved out of my mother's house and became somnambulant waiting for Farouk every day at my new house. I looked out at the street for his car, and expected the phone to ring every minute.

"I caused the river to swell with jealous tears over the Grushenka 'incident' and drove his love away. The farther downstream he drifted the more real my dream of him became. The expectation of his arriving left me riveted. The waiting was dizzying. I put my house in order and stocked the refrigerator, but he did not come. When I went to sleep, I dreamt of him, and I was filled with fire and ice. I lay awake turning the dream over in my head. It could mean that he had not left me, or it could mean that he had. Gods are ambiguous, and layer every truth in lies.

"I hired a detective to follow Farouk. The detective worked on contingency. He confirmed that Farouk was meeting a woman. It cost two thousand for three black-and-white photos that showed Farouk turning his key in the door of a rundown apartment. In the next picture a blonde was getting into his car. In the third, they were sitting in a café. The detective overheard them talking. She said to Farouk, 'You are so kind!' or, 'Oh, Farouk, I have never met anyone so gentle. If all men were like you, I would never quit my job!'

"Me, I felt like I had been hit by a truck."

"I know the feeling."

"That's not a good feeling, Mac. I started talking to the walls. 'Oh whore! You don't love me.' I couldn't stop walking back and forth like an animal. 'You are feeding me lies, and then satisfying someone else.' I paid the detective and threw the photos in the garbage.

"Why are the past six months still echoing? Because I want them to. I let them. What a waste of time! He came to help me set up my new house. He held the paintings in place and I told him, 'Up a little, to the left, there.' He looked so good that I believed all his lies! I was afraid a goddess might swoop down and take him up with her.

"He was good at moving boxes. I liked to watch him carry them around. He was tall and strong. He started to show off and hurt his back. I had to move the books so he could lie down on my new white couch. I walked around him unpacking my statue of Leda and the swan. The power Farouk possessed lying there helpless was more than I could resist. If Zeus could descend in the form of a swan, then he must also descend in the form of a man sometimes, and it was one of those times. I was kneeling beside him. I gave him his glass of mint tea. He set it down and reached for me. Even without his strong arms, I was drawn to him like a magnet, but the kiss was so soft! I almost died of a kiss. He noticed my nipples were hard, and my shirt, it fell off by itself. He had me half-clothed on top of him. There. I have seen God." Niovi's big eyelids closed half way remembering the vision.

"What was he like?"

"It's like a kind of energy that descends when things are harmonious. It's finally safe to take off our masks, and there is God. God is love."

"Some people are blessed."

"If you can recognize the god behind the mask, you have lived forever. And to think, this can happen more than once. But to love Farouk — misplaced illusion.

Becoming a singer hasn't won me more love from my friends and family. If anything, it's come between us. They get angry about it sometimes, but me, I have to go on. I don't *cxhave* time to go to the movies with them or cook for them. I have a more general recognition in their place. But that's more visual than heartfelt. It's not a job; it's a calling. It's consuming, I have to do what I love to do until I'm an instrument, and there's God in that. It's another kind of love, vocation, a way of reaching people generally, and there's some point there, although now that Farouk is gone, I can't remember what it was."

A man at a nearby table lit a match. "I'm sick. Every time I see fire I think of him. I remember he brought a bottle of cognac to my house, and set it down on the kitchen counter. Then he put a portrait of himself on the mantelpiece for me to look at when he was gone, which was often. It was a wonderful picture. He was looking far away, and his nose looked very nice. He would stay for a little while in my house. I can still see him climbing the staircase or standing in the window next to the urn in my living room under the colonnades when I close my eyes, there, his arm raised, illustrating a point that he was trying to make. And then he would be overwhelmed and leave.

"My mother went around talking about him. 'A man who can find a little something to say to everybody is better brought up than one who converses with only a select few.' She thought he was a snob. I had to see how could I keep my family from getting into my love life. I made sure they left Farouk alone. I told my mother to stop bringing food to the house and hired a maid. Up until the scandal hit the papers, they had only met him on two occasions. Everyone had been polite.

"My Sri Lankan liked Farouk immediately. Her dishes from Sri Lanka came to life with new flavours. I told her, 'This is so good! If you keep on cooking like this, I will give my Egyptian arm band to you!' She walked a little taller. I know she began to think of my armband as hers. In the beginning, I just laughed when the woman brought Farouk coffee and forgot mine. 'Would Monsieur like sugar?' It was funny, and Farouk laughed, too.

"But me, I could feel things slipping out of control, and *that* is *not* my style. I was on a tight schedule, the studio, photo shoots. When things didn't go according to the plan, I ran the risk of having a nervous breakdown. I had the feeling that time was running out, and that there was a certain way that things had to be done. My father had very high expectations of me, before he gave up on our family and left. I felt like I had to show him I could do something great. I had to prove that I wasn't a typical island girl who was satisfied with watching Brazilian soap operas. What do I have in common with Farouk is that we both read constantly. We need answers to the questions that bother us. One day, I made a list for the maid — wash and iron the draperies; dust the icons; wash the windows, you know.

"Farouk and I left the house to satisfy his caprice. He had a way of asking that you could not refuse, so I put on my sunglasses in controlled panic, and went out into the heat with Farouk. He wanted to take a stroll down the empty street at siesta time. Nobody does this, so we were the only ones out, looking at the buildings that were going up around the neighbourhood. All the shutters on the houses were closed at this hot hour of the day. 'Everyone is building an apartment block,' Farouk said.

" 'Yes.'

" '*Mon dieu*, Niovi. What is this frenzy of construction? They are building towers and bizarre extensions with complete freedom to do as they like — look at all the styles! — a *veritable soupe d'architecture*. But what they realised is the cheapest solution, without any learning from the past. Look at this one. The land is lower than the street, so they built a pedestal and put the building on top.' The building was sitting on a solid block of cement to bring the ground floor of the apartment building up to the level of the street. 'All that cement must have been very expensive. For even less, they could have built a hollowed out parking structure underneath. Instead the cars are double parked on the sidewalk. Look at that Mercedes. The paint is cracking in the sun.'

" 'Yes.' I glanced at his profile fixed on some vision of an orderly neighbourhood. Ah, looking into his blue eyes was like trying to look into the sun, and I looked down. 'You are right, Farouk.' I was melting in the heat. He reached for my hand, and I was suddenly happy again." Niovi's face relaxed as she decanted the memory.

I, too, like to remember them like that, tranquil eye at its zenith reflecting the couple's happiness all over the world: They come to a small church with an octagonal roof and walk past. The church's stone courtyard has been swept clean, and butterflies dance above the wildflowers there. He is holding her hand, watching the saffron blossoms and the little fluttering souls in the breeze.

Chapter 28

Skin Trade

The iron gate of the courthouse rolled open. Its afternoon shadow rippled across the concrete as Niovi and I stepped inside. A cloud of perfume wafted above the maelstrom of female lawyers at the colloquy. The security guard wheeled in a cart of juice and snacks. In denial of their real purpose there, the ladies reached for the refreshments and exchanged glances of complicit innocence.

It occurred to me to urge the diplomats to leave the 'ladies' alone in their blindness. Many had already been manipulated out of their husbands and their money. TV had convinced their daughters that they didn't need families, or that it was safe to take drugs. Their husbands had bet their houses in the stock market, and almost everybody was renting without a single regret. At least they'd managed to have grandchildren renters too. There were public statistics proving that women had not stopped acting like commodities. They had failed to meet the challenges of securing a respectable place for themselves in the economy. I wasn't sure whether we'd have phoenixes or Cornish hens once they were let in on the secret of their own misery. I did manage to say, "Women are just as bad as men sometimes."

"Just as bad as men?" The German woman ambassador, in her role as president of the Ladies' Consortium, barked. "More than ninety-four percent of the people in jail are men. Less than six percent are women. How are women just as bad as men?"

"Sometimes," I whispered and cringed in my seat. I could feel my face turning red. Ninety-four percent. How could I not know that? That seemed like an important figure to know.

The door opened, and a police officer stepped into the room dispelling any question of a tea party. He was followed by a bleach-blonde swaying from side to side in a black pleather skirt, a low-cut bodice that showed off her deep cleavage and fishnet stockings. The whore took the seat next to me.

The German woman ambassador, also president of the Ladies' Consortium, raised her voice and spoke to the group. "Good morning, everyone. You all know why we're here today. We thought we could shame the 'merchants' into giving up their profits. We showed the damages these brothels were doing, the breakdown in the social fabric, the divorce rate, drug-related crime. How naïve we were, thinking we were talking to modern politicians about some kind of 'accident'. Well, we're smarter now. Now we know the ruling class here actually wants to create this chaos. They want to keep the Styxans down so they can run the country like the colony it was in the past."

This news made the Styxan women angry. The idea of sinking back into colonialism was intolerable. There was no breaking from the past in the heat of Styxos. It was soldered to the present.

"We're here today because we're fed up. Everyone, this is Oxana. She has agreed to come and talk to us in exchange for deportation from Styxos. Many of you undoubtedly recognize her from the news story about the Japanese businessman who died a short time ago, but what you don't know is that Oxana is HIV positive. She is a prostitute, with a message: in the age of AIDS, prostitution is tantamount to murder. Please feel free to ask her any questions you might have."

The ladies clad in tailored jackets and designer jewellery stifled their shock and leaned haughtily back in their chairs. The denial of responsibility was complete. They clung to their status. Recognition was the motor of history, not something to be scoffed at. The trick was to replace their selfish desire to be recognised as being greater than others such as Oxana with an appreciation for recognition as being equal.

"Very well, then. I'll start," the German diplomat said. "Oxana, how many men did you have sex with on a normal work day?"

"Usually five. Five is good. I used to do 20 to 30 men in day."

The ladies gasped. Niovi gripped the arms of the chair next to me.

"My worst day, they locked me up in a flat for five days, handcuffed and no water in August heat. There were no cigarettes. When I asked for water, they dumped it over my head. They did it to make me suffer during… work. I lost count after 49."

The ladies leaned forward. "Did you know you had AIDS?"

"No."

"Do they use condoms?"

"Ha," she scoffed. "You have unrealistic view of men. How do you explain a married man with three children who goes out and kills people, and then comes home and plays with his children? Some men are animals."

"How did you come here?" I asked.

"I came to Styxos when I was eleven to learn a foreign language and live in a Styxan family, but when I arrived, man who met me at the boat was trafficker. He beat me and raped me and cut my hands and feet. He forced me into prostitution for five month. Police raided the cabaret. I told police I was travelling on fake passport to get help. Policeman raped me. I was sent to refugee camp where social worker released me back to trafficker. After six years more of forced prostitution, they made me have six abortions. Now I am in jail after another police raid."

After an uncomfortable silence, Niovi, in her plaid suit and hoop earrings asked, "Would you say you were kidnapped?"

Oxana's breasts heaved as she shook her head. "No. I had idea of the kind of restaurant it would be. Most of girls do. I can think of only two women I have ever met who didn't know what they were coming for. If they don't know what requirements are, they can guess. Maybe they hide it from themselves. Women in poor countries make a contract. Traffickers exploit poor women. Sometimes they kidnap, usually they rape them, and live off prostitution and smuggling. I was ordinary girl in my country, and I couldn't get job there. There is horrible. I

166

knew girls who came back from abroad with big money, so they must have been properly treated. Everybody thinks of doing something proper. But it's money that seduces you."

"How *organized* is it?" asked another island woman, covering her long fingernails painted red.

"Very. How do you get someone into the country with no passport and no residence permit? — because many are drug dealers using structured violence." Oxana furrowed her painted eyebrows.

A Spanish woman in a smart orange suit with a scarf tied around her neck asked, "What happens if they try to run away?"

"They usually don't." Oxana lit a cigarette. "They don't know the language and in their own countries there is a mistrust of police, so such women are at mercy of pimps who control them. And where would they go? Home? In Saint Petersburg most of young women would like to leave country to find work abroad. You can run off to the Styxos police station. Please do. They will arrest you as illegal immigrant, and you will be deported. And everyone will look forward to seeing you back home? You have to tell them, especially young ones. They don't know anything. Pimps are trying to get younger and younger children because they think they are AIDS-free. But children catch disease more easily. Their bodies are more likely to tear and get infected."

There was a hush. One of the ladies excused herself and left the room.

A Dutchwoman spoke up. "This is serious. It is our responsibility. We need strict but compassionate legislation. In the Netherlands, you get six years in prison for human trafficking. If you want to get your case into court, you, of course, need witnesses, and the most important witnesses are the victims themselves. They give them a residence permit for the duration of the proceedings — and sometimes, if it's thought to be inhuman to send them back to their own countries, they will get a permanent residence permit. Now, how do you assimilate them into your society? What do you do when your children play with their children, or when they come to you for a job?"

The women argued. "That would never work on Styxos. We don't even have anything for women who are badly treated by their husbands, and you want to put traffickers in jail?"

"Everyone comes up with rubbish to avoid responsibility!" said a French woman with translucent skin.

A small Styxan woman stood up, showing her long torso and short legs. "We must find out who is responsible for this!"

"Styxans never take responsibility for their own problems."

"It's up to the government," said a Styxan. Her olive skin shone with sweat.

"Who is the government if it's not us?" said the president of the Ladies' Consortium. "This is supposed to be a democracy. Government agencies have failed at using technology and modern practices to stop human trafficking on Styxos. This only happens when the people responsible get the information on the effects of their decisions. We're going to give them the information."

The Styxan woman leaned over the table and barked dissent. "You foreigners don't know how to live!" Black hair flew over her eyes. Her spit fell on the table. The other women tried to calm her down, but she didn't want to stop.

She and the president of the Ladies' Consortium both repeated the same arguments *ad nauseam*. "You are too insecure to accept anybody different into your society!" the president said.

The scornful expression on the Styxan woman's face showed that she would never accept these blond 'noodles'. She stalked out of the room.

Who would thank us if we lifted them up from their misery? If our disparate forces could bond long enough to accomplish eradication of slavery, some people would still say, "Nothing has changed."

Chapter 29

In My Day

The president of the Ladies' Consortium stood up. "Freedom comes from acts of bravery. Don't be afraid of each other just because you are different. We are proud to have different kinds of people here, and we have some excellent Styxans." She looked at Niovi, slouching in her chair in the back of the room. She straightened her back and flashed a magazine smile.

"That's true," another Styxan woman ventured. The hysterical woman calmed down. "We should make *Jealousy* our theme song. We could run an ad on —"

The Frenchwoman in purple Chanel who emitted a suffocating perfume said, "What a stupid idea."

"Why not have it as theme song?" Oxana said. "It's like Argentine tango; it's my favourite song."

"Thank you." Niovi lit up, and the women around her began to take courage.

"Let's get down to business," the ambassador said. "Leniency encourages women to claim 'sex slavery' as a way of gaining residence permits. Look at Belgium's human trafficking law: up to 15 years of hard labour for convicted traffickers. That's the example we have to follow."

"What are the traffickers like?" someone asked.

"Not what you think," said Oxana. "It's not necessarily mobster with Mercedes and gold ring on every finger. Sometimes it's organized criminal gangs, but sometimes it might be husband and wife who saw gaps in law and exploited their contacts. They get about $300 for each woman they deliver to brothel. Or, they might run VIP 'escort' agencies with educated women from poorer countries who can talk to educated men."

"Can they be reintegrated into their societies back home?"

"I think it would be possible from ten girls to get maybe three girls back into society. Here, Czech women are less educated than Ukrainian women, who can be university graduates, and are aggressive, and self-confident. That helps. But really they have no self-confidence. They are isolated."

"At least the continental prostitutes are usually educated," the German president said. "Just imagine the problem in poorer countries. Sixty five million girls worldwide never go to school at all, which results in low self-esteem, low earning power, disease, and poverty."

Niovi stood up. "No more!" She pounded her fist on the table. It had an astounding effect on all of us. "The island is on the verge of acceptance into the European Union NOW. Why aren't the laws enforced?"

The diplomatic ladies' blood had begun to boil. That day, Styxos ladies, native and foreign, vowed, No more! Human trafficking would stop before any tenders for any infrastructure projects were accepted. There were no further questions. They thanked Oxana and wished her a smooth transition back home. When the door closed behind her, there was a communal sigh of relief, and a Styxan lady chuckled to herself quietly.

Our heads turned to the island woman. She looked up at us and surmised, "Times have changed on Styxos since the days when miracles would occur because the women believed in and obeyed God. In the villages, you didn't have sex until you were married." There was a general murmur. The woman kept talking through the din, and her voice was eventually heard. "When I was a child, we were poor. We made our own clothes, and sometimes we would go hungry. The prettiest girl in my village ran away for the big city and got tricked into working in a brothel. They raped her and forced her to have sex with the clients. The camel-driver knew her and stowed her away on his camel train under a rug. She managed to escape back up to her mountain village. The next day two Mafiosos came in a black Mercedes to take her back. In those days, if a woman was raped, it was *her* fault. Some people could remember women being stoned to death for similar things. The two men got out of the Mercedes and went to the doorstep of the house where she lived. There was a struggle and one of the men pushed into the house and dragged the girl out.

"One by one all the doors in the village opened. The villagers came out of their houses. One of them had a can of petrol. They surrounded the men. They took bricks and threw them at the men. The girl broke free as the men retreated into their car. They locked the doors, but the villagers had piled stones around the tires. They poured petrol on the Mercedes and lit it on fire." We gagged on the acrid petrol fumes. Foul, black smoke blocked out the women in front of me. The only thing everyone agreed on was killing the Mafiosos. We watched the two men burn.

There was no police investigation. Who could they put in jail? The whole village was responsible. We had passed our judgment. The woman folded her wrinkled hands on the table. "Life went on. But no one would marry the girl."

The woman who told this story was nice enough to give me a ride back. Her name was Heqet, and she lived in our neighbourhood with her family. "Nowadays, they just cut off their fingers if they're caught pimping. Two, sometimes three."

"That way they won't be able to count the prostitutes," I muttered.

At home with the children, I shook off the memory of the burning Mercedes when my husband's Mercedes came around the corner.

"Papa!" The children cried.

Chapter 30

Playing the Man's Game

My job prospects had improved with Niovi's friendship. Sitting at the bar in the TV station café, she would come in, "Mac!" and order us a cup of coffee. She insisted on paying for it.

She straddled the barstool and dispelled what was left of the diva image I'd had of her. She was a wounded creature who looked dolefully into the mirror and then leaned closer to me. "Since the failure of our relationship, I feel lonely."

"Ah well. At least you have a lot of people around you."

"That just makes it worse. They are not him! In misfortune, you don't want to see your neighbours. Let them be victorious over me at a distance. It is harder to justify a breakup in the public eye. Fans see it as an obsession, the kind of caprice stars are known for: easy in easy out. Stars are supposed to be about sex appeal. Why else would they keep on getting married and living painfully ever after? But a real relationship is more than romance and attraction, and stars often don't have what it takes. They work on their image and let their other qualities fall by the wayside.

"Me, I feel like I had a husband. Now I'm experiencing life as a half of a couple. Even though he was selfish and manipulated by events, *I* was *his*. I know what it feels like to be divorced."

I was going to say I doubted that she had any idea, but she cut me off. "Farouk talked to me so sweetly." I placed the recorder on the counter in front of us, and she let me turn it on. "He said he was drawn to my warmth and my honesty, but I can't take credit for that. It wasn't me, it was us. When we were together, the truth was just there, between us, as long as we didn't try to hide it. The energy that descended all around us! Farouk's heart was open. It was just a matter of planning our escape. But there were obstacles, and Farouk is not a planner."

"He seems noncommittal."

"Exactly. We *cxhave* to face reality." It was time for Niovi's talk show, and she rose from the bar. "I'll be here tomorrow at this time."

"Sure."

We met again. She'd had too much time to think about her position and poured her suffering into my recorder. "Oh grand prize! To be first lady of Olympus, always enraged by Zeus's infidelity. A Hera seeking revenge, full of hatred and jealousy of the lovers of her mate. I have also left Olympus and returned to my island, but it would take a Zeus to coax me back spreading the rumour of a new woman to take my place. Eternal trickster. And if I let him live with his rumour — some replacement! — and if not, what kind of Olympus to return to?

"My new house is close to the office of Farouk. He would come 'home' for lunch. My maid would bring dishes from her own country out to the terrace, usually stir-fried rice, which Farouk preferred to my attempts at the cooking of my mother. One day, the maid was waiting in the doorway until he had taken his first bite. The spring air was cool enough for a glass of white wine with lunch, and we settled into our routine on the terrace with our view of the mountains. Farouk uncorked the wine. It had gone bad from the heat. I could tell just by looking at the orange colour, but he insisted on trying it. We poured bottle after bottle down the sink until we found a good one. Life is too short to be drinking bad wine, Mac.

"I asked him, 'Have you ever been close to getting married before?'

" 'I never had the time, always transferring.' "

I couldn't help smiling.

"I know," Niovi said. "He told me, 'Frenchmen don't necessarily marry these days.' He had lived together with a Czech woman. A model in Paris. He said she was always showing off her legs in Gucci skirts with matching hand bags. She was some kind of dominatrix. She lied when he asked her if she bought the clothes with his credit card. He managed to live through three years of torture before she'd spent all of his money and left. The ironic thing was that the whore was a *noble* —"

I had to talk over Niovi's monologue to make any observation. "Nobility derives from the warrior class: people ready to die for a cause rather than submit to a system. Farouk must have been rebelling heavily if it took three years to spend all his money. Assuming he doesn't have any children."

"Children! No. At least he *said*, 'If we'd had children, I'd have taken out loans! No children. How could I have had children with a woman who never read books?' When people first get married, they don't realize what kind of compromises are ahead. They think they just live happily ever after, but sometimes there isn't very much of that. If I marry, it will be to have children. Then he asked me, 'Do you date?'

" 'Date! That is something that I don't understand. *Date* — that means seeing several people at the same time. Is it supposed to be free? For the women? Me, I don't see how a *woman* can accept such a trap. That's playing the man's game. Even female animals are almost always monogamous. It is in their interest to find a mate who will help look after the young, while the males are always trying to spread their seed around to as many females as possible. Dating is a male construct. Your society is more *macho* than ours in that way. So, no, I don't date. I go out with groups of friends.'

"He came for lunch almost every day. One day, my Sri Lankan put the food on the table before we came to sit down, and when I slid into the chair of Farouk, the maid was surprised. 'That is Monsieur's lunch! Madam's is that one!' Farouk and I looked at each other, then at our lunches. The two plates were identical with equal portions of vegetables and rice. The maid left the terrace in a fluster. Monsieur ate Madame's lunch without conversation, and then went back to work.

"Did he get sick?"

"Maybe, Mac. That would explain the way he disappeared. I sat there in doubt with the empty plates. Farouk didn't come the next day or the next. Had he really said he needed me? I wondered what was this neglect, now that we had confessed our feelings. A cunning silence from an ex-noble versed in the art of war. That's when I decided to fight back."

She reached for my arm, but I instinctively pulled away. "Are you holding a grudge against Farouk? You realise how much compromise it takes to make a marriage?"

"Mac, do you think I'm not sorry about the way things turned out? I was true. I acted according to my nature. I know that if I had to do it again, I would have done the same thing. Mac, do you know what it's like when your man cheats on you? I'd put everything into Farouk, and he was lying all along. I was alone the whole time like some kind of dummy. What could I do? Submit? No one does that to me. I don't like violence! But he *wasted my time.* I'm not getting younger. It's time to have a baby, not turn into a black hole. I've developed this negative power, like an outcast. I had to turn the tables. I couldn't have done anything else! I would do it again!"

"Do what?" I asked. Niovi looked flustered. "Tell me," I said. "What?"

"Nothing. Everything. There was more. He finally called a week later. We talked about the maid and decided that I would do the cooking myself. I called my mother for her *psito* recipe. She wanted to know why I was cooking. '*Umma*! It's nothing. It's for a potluck. I have to bring a dish.' Farouk and I watched the dark maid brood over the ironing board out of the corners of our eyes. Me, I would let the maid cook lunch, since I was still paying her the same wages. We talked over a glass of wine while I dished out the potatoes. But sometimes Farouk had a lot of work and didn't come.

"In the morning, I opened the bedroom shutters and let the light in. It was delicious to lounge around the house in the morning in my pyjamas. The sky was clear and the birds sang. Down below in the garden, I saw the brown arms of the maid, digging for something, which was strange. I didn't have any vegetables growing in the garden, and I got a funny feeling in my stomach.

"I tiptoed down the stairs and hid behind the kitchen door. I saw Amanthi, the maid, come into the house with a handful of weeds from the garden. She washed them, cut them up, and put them in a pot of water to boil on the stove. Then she went back outside to hang up the laundry. I went to the pot on the stove and lifted the lid. The pot reeked of a foul vapour, and I put the lid back to lessen the stench, with an open slit at the side the same way she had done, and went back to the living room to practice. I hurried to finish singing my scales, and told Amanthi that Farouk was coming for lunch, and that I was going upstairs to take a shower, and I was not to be disturbed until lunch, which we would take on the terrace.

" 'Yes, Madam.'

"I went upstairs and turned on the shower. Then I tiptoed back downstairs and watched her through the window. Her cracked hands that never came clean worked at the cooked plant cutting it into smaller bits. She mashed the bits into half of the ground beef. I watched her make a separate dish without the plant, and put it at Farouk's place at the table.

"I stood there, paralyzed, eyes wide, trying not to make a sound. Then, I managed to sneak out of the house, and walk through the garden toward my car. The minty smell of the eucalyptus tree made me pause for a moment, and suddenly I saw hanging from one of the branches were strange trinkets sewn with the buttons from one of my blouses. I looked up in the tree and saw a little doll with long black hair like mine. Pins were stuck in its back. I yanked the doll out of the tree and plunged it into my bag. A strange feeling came over me. I must have been moving very quickly, but it seemed like everything was happening in slow motion. I started to run, but time had slowed down.

"I don't remember getting into my car, but soon I was pulling out of the driveway and scolding myself. 'What did you expect? With all these poor women from everywhere coming onto your island to do your dirty work for you!' Niovi looked in the rear-view mirror. 'What does that make you? Clean?'

"I found Farouk in his office. He wasn't surprised at all. In fact, he was ready to handle everything. He made me sit down and called for a cup of coffee. He said, 'This sort of thing happens more often than you think. It will be over soon. Don't tell Amanthi anything. You don't want her to leave and find work at the house of someone else.' He picked up the phone and dialled a number. I was alarmed at his familiarity with the police. You can never get a ticket out of here unless you book a few weeks ahead, but it seemed like his travel agent was doing it for him. I wondered if he could disappear so easily. Then he hung up the phone and announced that together we would pack the bags of the maid and send her away on a flight at two a.m.

"Amanthi cried in the lobby of the airport. 'Only Monsieur is good. Madam is bad.' She had made herself quite comfortable in *my* house! I stuffed my Egyptian armband into the hand of the maid and shoved her toward the gate.

"Monsieur was good! Monsieur was *too* good! I had emptied everyone out of my life for him. Now there was no one left to come between us.

"He drove me back to the house. I felt only felicity and could not contradict him. He opened the car door for me and picked me up in the street. He carried me like a baby into the house and up the winding staircase. I held onto his neck and breathed the smell of sweat and cologne. He laid me on the bed. I felt like I was floating. *'Je t'aime.'* He motioned the words with his lips, but no sound came out.

"At dawn, I watched him walk across the garden path from my bedroom window. The sky was streaked with red. He must have felt my eyes on his back because he turned around, and our eyes let go once more. If I knew then that he wouldn't be back soon!

"And now all this quiet. Did Farouk ever really come here? Even when his ear was close to my lips, he never *cxheard* what did I dare to whisper. His hair lay on my new pillow as undeniably as sand slipping through my fingers."

"Ah, Niovi. That is sad. I hope you win him back, although he doesn't deserve you." I packed up my tape recorder, hugged her, and left the café. We wouldn't be seeing each other for a while. I had been fired from the TV station. They gave no reason, and I didn't ask for one. I knew the decision came from the government, and that no one would ever admit it. Never mind, as my mother-in-law would say. I had children to take care of.

Chapter 31

The Cult of the House

The Styxan home, however modest, is imbued with mystical importance as the ultimate medium for one-upmanship, and must be kept cleaner than other houses. In Styxan, the expression for 'How do you feel?' is the same as 'What do you want?' No doubt the cause of this rampant materialism. There are always neighbours coming around to see the new statue in the garden or the wide-screen TV. If a Styxan invites you to their house, you are under obligation. Not going would be like quitting a poker game after winning the first hand. I had recently become aware that we were in last place in the house competition among our friends.

At home, reflecting on a new colour for the exterior, I toured the house with the babies in their double stroller. My husband's mother had said 'white', but meant beige, which I considered a rip-off. Beige looks old as soon as you put it on. It fixes buildings in the communist era. On the other hand, we already had plenty of white inside. I thought the outside of a house should look quaint, perhaps in a very light, almost white … yellow. Most of the family had walked around it with us by now expressing differing opinions. Heqet from the Ladies' Consortium dropped by with her children and suggested painting the pillars orange in the style of the day, which I couldn't stand. Another suggestion was to only paint the porch — but not yellow! — and let the rest go to hell. The beige lovers came next, all from the older generation.

Charon came up the driveway with a small package in his hand. Could it be the SIM card reader I'd ordered from the spy catalogue? I tried to see the words written on the front. His fingers covered all but the '–zie'. It had to be for me. I put down the paint roller a minute after he'd gone into the house, and followed him. It was sitting on the kitchen table. I quickly grabbed it and threw it into the cupboard behind the pot lids. I would get it later on when his mother went off to do the grocery shopping.

The house seemed beyond repair. We had already overhauled the plumbing, paved the dirt driveway, made a terrace outside of the kitchen door in back and set up a plaid umbrella. It looked a little less miserable. We had carpeted, insulated, exterminated, and mopped and mopped and mopped for months. One day, the floor cast off its dusty aspect and shone. I knew it was time to walk down the hill and buy the can of outdoor paint.

The man in the paint shop told me, "On Styxos, the only thing people agree on is that you have to wait. Just go ahead and do it your way, and when they see it happening, they will love it. They will even copy it. You'll see. I better order more. Half of the neighbourhood will soon be painted 'gardenia'."

I handed him twenty shekels and lugged the can of 'gardenia' up the hill. A man named Hercules, who had done some work on the house, passed me in his diesel pick-up truck. I struggled with the can of paint, as he drove by without waving. "You are the worst villain I've ever met," I muttered to myself.

He was at the house when I arrived. He'd come to fix the hole in the bottom of the kitchen door ostensibly to keep cat-sized cockroaches from strolling in. I did not comment that our little friends were just as likely to be strolling *out*, but got sucked into the debate anyway. There was always something stopping me from painting.

Hercules took the door away with him and brought it back repaired at the end of the day. My husband's mother went to work painting it brown. That night, we tried to air the paint fumes, and found that we could no longer open the window in the upper half of the door because he had put on an industrial-looking door handle that stuck out and blocked the window. The imp came back the next day to fix that. He cut a golf-ball-sized hole in the window frame to allow the handle to pass. "This is fixed?" I demanded. The hole was too low, so Charon's mother showed me how to pull the handle down to the hole to let the window pass. The handle pinched her fingers as it passed. "Never mind," she said.

"Why not put on a doorknob that won't stick out at all?" I insisted on sending the door back to Hercules so he could put on a doorknob.

"OK," Charon said.

The light in the kitchen went off by itself. "That's the third time that's happened," I said, and went to turn it back on. As my finger touched the switch, a chill ran down my spine. "I think I got a shock!"

"It's nothing," Charon's mother said.

"We need to get someone to look at the electricity," I insisted.

The light went off again. The temperature in the room seemed to drop to an ectoplasmic chill. It was the ghost of Charon's father. When he was alive, he had always been turning off the lights to save electricity.

"Never mind," Charon said. "It's just the way it *is*."

I got the paint ready and started on the outside of the house. Charon complained about the thickness of the paint. I added some water, thinking I had to make this work. They say that if one person in a relationship puts all their effort into it, they can overcome any obstacle. Now the paint would seep into the porous exterior. The wall soaked up an enormous amount of paint like a sponge, and I only succeeded in painting a small area. This job was going to be a much bigger job than I'd imagined. Charon's mother came by with the children. "How's this?" I asked.

"Good!" she said. She signalled that she had the children under control, and I went on painting the patch bigger.

Niovi came to the wall and laughed at me. "Mac! Is that you?"

"Niovi. There you are!"

"Seriously, Mac, let the workers do that. No one will thank you for it. They're taking advantage of you."

"I can't stand to look at the house like this anymore."

Next, my husband rolled his Mercedes into the driveway. "It's really yellow." Followed by his great-aunt coming to see how I was doing. "Well, *I* couldn't do it."

I had just finished a large square of the front wall when an uncle stopped by and said, "Yellow. It's a big improvement. When are you going to finish it?"

"Not soon." I filled the tray with water, dunked the roller in, and walked to the kitchen door to wash up. I reached for the handle, and froze. Villain! Once upon a time, villains were just villagers, or uninformed characters who came out of the villages to plague city folk. This one had survived. I had underestimated Hercules' ignorance. My husband's mother followed my gaze and tried to justify the villain's handiwork. He couldn't find a doorknob, so he cut a hole the size of a doorknob where the handle had been.

"Never mind," my husband's mother said. "It's hard enough to get someone to come and fix things at all."

Everyone had gone off to take a siesta. I reached in back of the pots and found the SIM card reader. I was glad that I would finally be able to put my misgivings about Charon to rest. Just a brief check once in a while to make sure that things were moving in the right general direction . . . I could feel Pandora running through my veins as I opened one of Charon's phones and removed his SIM card. I slipped it into the SIM card reader. I selected 'deleted messages' and scanned the long list.

Something was not right. Something was very wrong.

Chapter 32

Romantic Love

There were many women's names on the list. After selecting a few, I found:

> yes i heard you. thank you. you have phone-sexed before but I won't think about that
>   You can hear and tell me what you would want me to do, like the last time you were here . . .

I was shaking all over. It was hard to breathe. There must be some misunderstanding.

Charon's betrayal hit me like a train. It was impossible that he could just throw away all the love and investment I'd been putting into our relationship for so long. But there it was. We had come to his island, and he had turned into a jackass. My heart wrestled with my brain. *Maybe he's sick. Maybe I can win him back. What will the children do without their father!*

I couldn't let them find out about it. They might copy his behaviour and learn to act in this horrible way. My mind tried to play tricks on me. It made me think there must be some explanation, but when I asked for explanations in the past, Charon just tried to find out how much I knew so he could tailor his lies. The only way out was to keep quiet. It wasn't enough to beat him at *his* own game. I had to outsmart him at *mine*. At the same time, the woman in me tried to play tricks on my rational mind. She tried to rationalize away his misdeeds and make allowances for stress and the loss of his father. It was hard to argue with the prevalent opinion that women are dumb. I had believed Charon was buried under grief at his father's death, but now I saw it was more than that. He *was* his father. I re-read the SMS messages; there it was again, the bald truth. There were messages to several women, and there was talk of an abortion. I felt sick thinking what that could be about.

The shock continued. It smacked me first thing in the morning. At night, I watched Charon's tall, dark figure as he passed me in the hallway and closed the door to his mother's bedroom. I went into our old bedroom and pounded my pillow with both fists until I was exhausted. My mind never stopped playing tricks on me, letting me believe what I wanted to believe and deny what was really happening to me. Sleep was the only way out of this nightmare. I heard the voice of that woman in army fatigues who used to yell at passersby outside of the Public Library in New York. Her blond crew cut shone in the sun. Her voice got louder as I approached the library steps, and filled my ears as I passed her — "Fight back! Women, fight back!" — and then faded into the distance. I could hear faintly now. *Fight back!* I must not let him *find out* that I am fighting back. That's how *hard* I would fight back.

In the morning, Charon tied his own tie with his back turned to me. I swallowed my spite and went on putting the children's toys away. But one of his phones was on the floor, and before I could stop myself from bringing it up, I said, "Why do you need so many phones, anyway? It would be much cheaper to just have one."

"Hmph," he answered. "One is for the mainland, and this one hardly works."

He didn't bother to account for the fourth phone.

"What happened to us? We need to talk."

"There's nothing to talk about. You get what you deserve."

"What about the children?"

"The children are fine. My mother can take care of them."

During the day, I went on painting the house. I didn't know what else to do. Niovi came over and helped paint the south wall. "How's it going, Mac?"

"Good enough."

"You've lost weight."

"Well, it just dropped off."

"You look good. See that. You don't have to get there; you just have to be going in the right direction."

"I might look better, but I feel worse. I have a big problem, Niovi."

"If *you* have a big problem, Mac, what are the rest of us going to do? Come on, Mac, don't cry." She put her arms around me. "That can't be easy. I'm counting on you. I need you. I have a hard time making friends. I divulge private things to my friends and they run away embarrassed."

On the sixth day, I felt a little better, and actually thought of the children first thing in the morning instead of the nightmare we were in. My mind wandered back into my dream of Farouk picking me up and carrying me onto a boat. But forgetting came at a price. On the seventh day, I woke up paralyzed. Every bone in my body hurt. The joints in my hands ached. I must have internalized the shock. I could barely walk. I would have to get to a doctor without Charon noticing.

There was no meaning in the things I was doing. No reason to keep on doing them. The only way to keep going was to believe that on some level, it couldn't be true about Charon. There must be something left of the man I loved. I became an easy target for all the self-help junk they sell to housewives trying to learn the secrets of being a modern Aphrodite, 'secrets so powerful he will find you irresistible and do anything to be with you and only you.' They claimed to be able to make men *fall in love with their wives again*. What I wouldn't give to believe in such crap. Pay and 'learn how to inspire a man to sacrifice everything for you.' Ha! I wasted about a thousand shekels on this fluff. What I learned: being married helps men live 1.7 years longer, but married women live about 1.4 years less than unmarried women.

I had thought that my sweetness would convince him that I was made for him, but it didn't. When did I give up standing up for myself the way a high-maintenance woman would. When he tried to seduce women right in front of me, I just didn't look until it was over. I tried to be smarter, more curious about the things he was interested in, better in bed, anything to get closer to my husband. I thought the feelings I had for him were real, and assumed he must feel them, too. I thought he was endeared to me, a caring woman with a spiritual side. He was not. I'd married a player, passing through on his way to more phantom relationships. Maybe I was too smart, too intimidating. I had never really touched him. I had never moved him. He never felt like he was about to lose control of himself and fall in love with me. Sex turned out to be just a small part of his needs.

I'm sure he didn't want to hurt me or take advantage of me at the outset. The abuse had just gradually slipped up on us. I had stopped receiving and ended up doing all the giving. I had to become high-maintenance. I had to make him work harder to be with me. Was it too late to refuse to put up with bad behaviour from Charon? The risk was that he could divorce me, and the courts on Styxos would award him and his mother custody of the kids.

I was so upset all day everyday that I pushed it out of my mind to avoid the shock. I convinced myself that I had to go through this ordeal so that Farouk would scoop me up and carry me onto the boat that I could see so clearly in my dreams. And I had no business with Farouk, at least not on a personal level. Still, it didn't add up. It made me so mad, the way women's hopes, dreams and energy were being thrown away. It was too much to waste. No wonder I wasn't nervous wandering into Farouk's office before lunch. "He's busy," his secretary said.

"Not too busy to see me." I pushed past her and closed his office door behind me.

"You came to *my* office? What will my secretary think?"

"That's not my problem. *I'm* clean. I'm here officially."

"How so?"

"Make the skintrade your business."

He perused my pink suit buttoned at the breast. It was too hot to wear a shirt underneath.

"Put a social plan into your infrastructure bid. That's the way to win the bid and heal Styxos."

Farouk's eyebrows rose. "I can't, Mackenzie."

"Then what *can* you do?" There was a stack of folders on his desk. "I guess you won't be needing these." I swept the folders onto the floor.

"*Mon dieu!*" He rushed around the desk.

I left him picking them up. It was noon. The street outside was deserted. Nobody walked in Styxos, especially at this hour. A black government car rolled out of a side street and stopped a block away. A silhouette got out and walked toward me. The car pulled away. As the silhouette approached, I saw that it was a man in black. He didn't step aside, but came directly at me, eyes boring down on me. He meant to attack.

I saw red. Time seemed to slow down as I dropped my bag on the ground. He raised his hands over his head into one fist. I raised my palms to his chest in one swift motion I'd learned so long ago in karate and struck as hard as I could. A look of surprise froze on his face as he fell. His skull hit a piece of metal sticking out of the broken pavement.

Cars were parked on the sidewalk around us. The ambulance arrived, but the police had already hoisted the man into a taxi. They sent him to the hospital. Two witnesses had explained what had happened to the police, who had given up on questioning me, and offered to drive me back to the house. "I'll drive her." It was Farouk.

"It's OK. I can walk."

"I insist Mackenzie. You're in shock."

"No really. You just focus on the skintrade. Then it won't be so hard to take care of myself."

I shook all afternoon. Someone wanted me out of the way. It was all I could do to stop myself from hitting Charon when he came up behind me that afternoon and handed me a letter from *Living Anthropology*. Against all hopes, they were interested in my 'Theory of Light', an idea I had been developing since the dig off the coast of Alexandria. They wanted to commission me to write an article. This was an honour beyond my dreams. I tried to remember what I had been thinking about when I first queried them. I think I proposed fieldwork using a variety of methods: curating materials, participant interviews, the crafting of ethnographies. I wandered through the house, trying to feel the joy I should experience holding a letter like this.

I couldn't let Charon drag me down. I had been isolated at Charon's mother's house for a long time now. I had to get to work collecting data for my article. I decided to ask my neighbour, Heqet, if I could use her stories of life in the village, and walked over to her house.

Her husband answered the door. "Heqet is not here." There was something final in his voice. Her forlorn children peeked out at me from behind him.

"Where did she go?"

He avoided eye contact. "Their birthmother has left us. *My* mother is taking care of the children now."

My jaw hung loose. I didn't know what to say. I think I just turned around and walked away.

That night I let the kids sleep in the bed with me. What if my husband gave the kids to his mother and sister and discarded their 'birthmother'? In the morning, the children and I marched into the kitchen, and looked at the tidy breakfast his mother had set out on the table for Charon: one cup of tea made with herbs grown in her own garden and dried in the sun, one dried piece of toast with butter and honey, and one slice of the wonderful, salty goat cheese of Styxos. A basket of lemons on the counter filled the room with their smell. I rummaged around in the cupboards for something for the rest of us to eat, and then left for the studio.

I needed to talk to Niovi, not only about Heqet. The week I'd spent away from Niovi had fed my curiosity about her. Did she have proof that Farouk had betrayed her? I would find her in the studio and get her to finish her story.

"There you are!" I was glad to see her, and ready to be transported by the life of a star.

"Mac! You didn't paint the whole house. I told you be careful not to give too much, Mac. They will take advantage of you." She dragged me into the café and arranged her belongings on the table.

"*Living Anthropology* wants the article," I said.

"Congratulations, Mac!" She threw her arms around me. "You have to show me the article before you publish it. A lot of people believe in this superstition. It's true. The first time I heard Grushenka's name I felt drowsy, and I went to hang my horseshoe up in the kitchen. I looked at it while I did my own cooking, and waited. That's all I could do. I lost a record contract. My band started fighting. Things seemed to be going all wrong. I had a constant headache. I went to see my mother, who said a prayer and then yawned, which meant someone with the evil eye had over-looked me. When my mother had absorbed the curse and yawned it away, she said she was sure it was a foreigner with blue eyes.

"Styxos is small. Farouk would have to come and save me. So many nobles are hypocrites, but Farouk, precisely because his mother didn't marry a third cousin, possessed new blood, and still had access to the ways of the aristocracy. Me, I strove for the highest, and look, my envy over a hopeless call girl has destroyed me. If he saw the depths I have sunk to since I left him. I thought I was taking back my freedom, ha! I'm the most manipulated of all — I'm enslaved! My soul needs a way out. I wanted to change things with my music, and now I've lost hope. I never used to think the successes of *others* were blocking *my* way, but now I'm tempted to undermine other people. My own dreams have fallen away.

"Deep down, I know that whore has put a curse on me. I think of Farouk more often now that it's impossible, and throw myself into a thousand different imaginary chance meetings. If only I could forgive him, but I come up against my pride. The Grushenka scandal is always there in the back of my thoughts. My love for Farouk was a mistake, my reason for living, a delusion. My mother found a glass vase with balls in it in my garbage and said, 'Is this broken?' She saw it wasn't even cracked, and suddenly understood: I was keeping myself from throwing it against the wall! She put it back in the garbage! I lived on nothing, no food, no sleep, like a flame. I'm sure my muse would laugh at me if he knew."

"Your muse."

"Yes. With Farouk as an inspiration, I have enough music for a whole CD, all authentic. He is such a faithful engine, never there in the flesh, always leaving me hungry. Look how I have gnawed my fingernails! I mistakenly recorded an evasive musical score about him one night when I left the tape recorder running — a divine accident from my desire to touch his soul, this longing sound, begging for life, to transform me from black to white. I wish I could play it for him, but something is blocking me. There is that crippling whore. The heaviness is more than I can bear. I tell myself, things could always be worse, but I know I can't stand any more. I should be sending out my cavalry, but my cruel streak has dissolved into gentleness. People have stopped calling me conceited and ask if I am sick. They say, 'You *cx-have* lost your edge.' The chance of breathing the softest words into his ear seems remote now."

"Niovi, I'm on *your* side. You're such a talented and strong woman. You *are* too good for him. I don't like to see this guy who just got out of jail dragging you down. What's going to happen when you're sixty, and he leaves for a younger woman?"

I reached for her hand, but this time, *she* pulled away. "Slaves cannot be friends." She had collapsed inward.

"No one wins by weeping over them," I said.

"Your advice is no relief." She hung her head, an imploded star threatening to pull me in after her.

I remember those torrents of romantic love and how it used to seem that there was nothing else to live for. But the truth is, there are many kinds of love to live for once you've put the romance in its place. How lucky I was to be married with children. It would be impossible to share it with Niovi, yet I heard myself saying, "Why don't you come out to my husband's great-grandmother's beach house sometime? The seaside would do you good."

"It could. Nature reminds us of our duty to God."

Niovi was nice now that I knew her better, and I needed a friend. I thought about Niovi and Farouk all the way in the car. My love for Farouk was deepening into friendship when suddenly, I found myself on the wrong road heading for the outskirts of town. The dunes were in sight, and the roof of the cabaret with its neon sign, 'Tropical Hotdog', beyond. I parked the car on the side of the road, took off my shoes and plunged into the sand. I scaled a dune and ran down its back far away from everyone, then another with thoughts of Farouk to keep me company. Feeling him with me floating over the dunes took the anxiety out of being alone. My memory was so full of him that I couldn't wait to steal off by myself. I didn't have to trust him on a dune. Our friendship could endure from a safe distance. I felt sorry for Niovi, only hoping to be bogged down in marriage to him. Our souls travelled together over the sand dunes avoiding all the utility that pervades marriage and the changes in personality that come with age.

My subconscious delivered me to the wooden door. I heard voices inside and scurried back behind a sand dune just as the door opened. I heard some men come out. All was silent again. I thought about leaving, but I had to find out what made Farouk tick. I waited ten minutes until it was quiet and opened the door. The bartender was behind the bar, alone. "You back!" He had already drawn a beer and placed it on the counter. "Come in! Nobody come here since the investigation. How's the job search?"

"Hopeless."

"I thought it might go tits up."

I sat down in front of him and raised my glass. "So what else do you know about Farouk?"

"Why you want to know about him?" he said. "Now that they let the foreigner out of jail, everybody asking about the other man she was with, Snake, the colonel in the Russian army."

"Who?" That's where I'd heard that name before. The man pushing her down the street before the gala. That was the name she had cried out. The same person involved in the cocaine run on the news.

"Snake. After a few months on Styxos, he want to retire in the Mediterranean. Here is quiet, slow life he's looking for. The capital is the best place in the region, but if he drives a short distance outside, it is back centuries to the days when 'simple pleasures' are allowed." The bartender laughed in a cloud of bad breath at his own joke. His teeth were rotten.

"Snake has his favourite country *tavernas,* and know the people at the market in town where the way of life is same for a thousand years. He is in good company with the emperors who marched through history to enjoy the pleasures of Styxos. He is having such a good time that he thinks about having children. We on Styxos live for our children, and this affects him. He watches the large Styxan families when they go out to eat and drink, and begin to feel at home loving life on the island. It is easy to meet people, and he sometimes get invited back to simple Styxan home for dinner.

"The warm climate and so many different cultures are the playground he was enjoying by then with his new woman, Grushenka. He is more comfortable with her, and she in his apartment waiting for him."

"Waiting for him?" The bartender made it sound like it was her choice to stay with him. "How could anyone sink so low?" I immediately thought of what my marriage with Charon had become, and wondered how low I could sink. "What was she doing with him?"

"I don't know. Maybe she trying to get to the Big Boss."

"Who's that?"

"You don't want to know. No one ever see him. Sometimes she talked to him when she answer Snake's phone. She chat him up and try to arrange a meeting. Or maybe she stay because she become a stump."

That was it. It crept up on you slowly. You were in love with them, and at first they were just a little bit mean. Relations with men were a gradual stupefying process.

"The closest they come to happiness is stopping to expect anything," the bartender said. "Grushenka's friends are drugs and alcohol. She protecting herself against losing love by loving men with her body, you know, in general. These girls are like that. They not put themselves in a position to feel real pleasure or pain. When she had the possibility of extreme suffering, to defend herself, she . . . switch off!"

Chapter 33

My Real Job

My memory was playing tricks on me. It had me picturing Charon the way he was before. Maybe it was true, women were like machines. They just switched the present off and thought of life in the past. Wasn't I comfortable enough? I was even thinking, *I wouldn't trade my married life for the torture Niovi and Farouk were inflicting on each other*, as I walked into the backyard.

Justin was trying a new stunt: skateboarding on his wagon. That didn't look like a good idea. "Justin! What are you doing?"

Suddenly, he pitched off the terrace, and his face hit the cement step. I ran to him. My adrenaline was flowing. Time slowed to a deliberate march. His face was covered with blood. I watched my arms scoop him up in slow motion and my hands wash his face in the sink. His mouth kept bleeding. He was in shock. My husband came running into the kitchen. "Oh no! Oh no!" He tried to help me wash Justin's face. Justin had stopped crying and curled around my arm.

"Hand me a towel to stop the bleeding," I said. "We've got to go to the hospital. Do you have your keys?"

"Yes."

"Your wallet?"

"Yes."

"Let's go."

We piled into the Mercedes with one mind. It took a crisis to get our family working like a team. But the bond was there, intact. A stronger kind of love than any other reminded me of my real job: protecting my children, then myself, then my family. The dusty city flew by. It took a long time to get Justin to the hospital. At least he didn't have his big teeth yet. I held the towels up to Justin's mouth as my husband drove.

The doctor was a friend of the family's, and he was waiting for us when we got there. "O.K., there was a lot of blood, but the cut isn't bad. He'll be O.K. I called a plastic surgeon to make sure he was ready, but now that I see Justin, I know that we don't need him." I stroked Justin's hair as he lay on the hospital table. He was shaking. "Are you cold?" I asked.

"Yes," Justin said, looking up at me with his deep brown eyes. He was still in shock. Suddenly the room was a flurry with everyone hunting around for a blanket. His face was pale. Face red, raise the head; face pale, raise the tail, I remembered. I lifted his feet and put a pillow under them.

My husband covered Justin up. Alex settled into a chair and watched the doctor administering the bandages, and then throwing them soaking red into a garbage pail. "It's *biyud*."

I was holding my stomach, and sank into a chair next to Alex. "I forgot that I faint at the sight of blood," I said. My husband looked down at me and scoffed. He watched the doctor clean Justin's cut. A few minutes later my husband moaned. His face was white.

"Papa!" Alex said.

In no time, the doctor was rushing Papa out of the room and stretching him out on a table in the hallway.

"Papa!" Alex screamed. Her long curls bounced like a lion's mane. She burst into tears and ran after them into the hallway. She held onto Papa's ankles. The doctor waved a vial of smelling salts under my husband's nose. When Papa came to, another doctor was preparing to give Justin a shot in his lip to numb the area before the stitches. My husband and I wanted to stay by Justin, so we both dragged ourselves up and held onto him. Alex peered over the side of his bed. The doctors put Justin's hands under the blanket. "You are a brave boy," Papa said. Everyone said how brave Justin was. I got ready as the needle approached the cut in Justin's lip.

"Now, this is going to sting a bit," the doctor said. "Just look up at the ceiling."

Justin looked up at the ceiling, and didn't even flinch as the doctor injected the anaesthesia into his purple wound. Alex was impressed. There was a general sigh of relief.

"You're the bravest four-year-old I've ever seen," the doctor said.

After the stitches, they told us to put Betadine on the cut, and have Justin use mouthwash rather than trying to brush his teeth until the stitches came out.

"I was so scared," I said, hugging Justin. "Papa and I almost fainted."

"Papa did faint!" Alex said.

"Shhh. Were you scared, Justin?"

"Yes." He could barely talk.

The children were distracted by two kittens playing outside the hospital window, while my husband paid the bill. "O.K., let's go home and try to relax," he said. "We have to keep an eye on you. It's our fault, obviously. We should have been there."

"Oh well," the doctor said, "Boys will be boys. Justin is athletic. At least he's never broken any bones."

Oh! Is that what we had to get ready for? I knocked on wood. We all piled back into the car. I got in the front seat this time. I folded up the bloody towels and put them on the floor. I reached into the back seat and held Justin's hand. Alex looked disgruntled. "Are you jealous, little two-year-old?"

"I'm *jeawiss*," Alex said.

Everyone laughed. "Why would you be jealous?" my husband said.

She turned away and looked out the window.

"Did *you* want to go to the doctor, Alex? You didn't mind Justin spurting blood, lying on the table, getting a shot and getting sewn up, but Papa fainting!" I said. Even Justin was laughing. It took a crisis to get our family working as a team.

Back at the house, my husband went to his mother complaining of headache and drowsiness. I thought it was more likely a hangover. Charon's drinking was getting out of control. I found the receipt for the beer Charon had recently bought, and I returned it to the grocery store. I didn't want so much alcohol in the house. Something bad might happen. We needed to live to take care of the kids. His mother was lighting a charcoal disk and burning on it the seeds of a plant called Aspand, while reciting an ancient Zoroastrian prayer against evil spirits. She spread the smoke around the house, and the children gagged. She took this prophylactic measure every time she suspected that the children had been given the eye. The evil eye was one of the reasons a man needed his mother. His mother had taught him that she could cure him.

The first day of Justin's recovery, his *saba* brought the children a baby chick from a farmer at the market. Justin and Alex took the box with excitement and opened it to find the fuzzy golden creature peeping and hopping about. It fluttered its little cream coloured wings and looked at the children.

The chick immediately adopted Justin as its Papa, saying, *peep, peep,* until Justin picked him up and held the little chick against his chest. Everyone was amused. "You're going to be a great Papa when you grow up, Justin. Whoever gets you as a Papa will be very lucky, won't they?" Justin managed to stay still enough taking care of the fragile chick while his lip healed. Alex played doctor, helping administer Betadine to Justin's lip. "Here are some books." She piled a stack of books next to his chair for him to read and said, "Now keep still. Don't wiggle," in her best Mommy voice. Alex babysat the chick with *saba* while Justin and I went for a walk in the stroller to get some children's mouthwash at the pharmacy. I spotted an old birdcage in a neighbour's garbage. "Look at this, Justin," I said holding up the wreck, full of old newspapers and shavings.

"So?"

"So, we can use this for your chick."

"We can't put Justin in that dirty, rusted . . . jail!"

"It's not broken. We'll clean it out and paint it white. It'll look beautiful."

Justin looked at me sceptically, but carried off the birdcage with pride. At home, we dug around in the closet for some house paint and some brushes.

"What?" asked Alex. The chick chirped from its nest.

"We're going to paint this old bird cage," Justin said.

"That junk?" Alex wrinkled her nose.

"Yeah," I said.

Pretty soon Alex had found a third paintbrush and some red, yellow, and blue finger paint, and was decorating the water dish and the tiny perch.

As they painted, our next-door neighbour walked past. She peeked over the wall and saw the children splattered with a rainbow of paint. "Look at you," the neighbour said. She stared down at me.

"Your children just do whatever they want, don't they?"

"Taking care of an animal is a good way to build children's confidence and help them learn to take care of others." Why did I bother? The children had painted the birdcage red, blue, yellow and white, but they kept on painting anyway. It changed colours several times and finally took on a new lemon-green scheme.

Charon had invited a young diplomat, a Greek named Bambos to the house. Bambos played with the kids a lot, especially Alex. He swung her around and carried her around the yard.

On Sunday, I took the kids to the zoo. This would get them excited about birds, taking care of animals and having our chick at the house. We had a wonderful day walking for at least four hours. We saw animal shows and an amazing bird show. When we got back to the house, Charon and Bambos were drunk on whisky — because I had returned the beer, they brought out the hard liquor. We never drank it, so I hadn't thought of getting rid of it. There was an empty bottle of Scotch on the table and the two of them were lying in the grass in the backyard. When Alex walked up, Bambos was all over her, hugging her and calling her 'his doll'.

I went into the bedroom to get my key so I could get our backpack out of the car, and left Alex sitting together with Bambos on the terrace for fifteen seconds. When I came back, Bambos jumped up, saying, "I didn't do anything!"

I called Alex away from Bambos. "Charon, Bambos is drunk and has to leave."

"No he's not!" Charon said.

"I don't want him near Alex."

"What are you saying? I'm *very* protective of Alex."

"Aren't you watching what's going on?" I *had* to get the family off of Styxos. It was becoming a matter of life and death.

"OK," Charon said. "It's time to take Bambos back."

Bambos made a big show of saying goodbye to Alex in front of Charon, who did nothing. "Bambos!" I yelled, "Get in the car." Bambos wanted another hug from 'his doll'. I glared at Charon.

He put his hand on Bambos' shoulder and said, "OK, let's go."

I talked to Alex afterward to find out if Bambos had touched her anywhere sexually. She said he just patted her on her back. I talked more with her to try to explain to her about the dangers of playing with men.

Charon drove Bambos home and came back. As soon as we sat down for dinner, the phone rang. It was Bambos' sister saying they were taking Bambos to the hospital for alcohol poisoning.

"Oh no!" Charon left for the hospital. At 10 p.m., we called Charon to ask when he was coming home. He said he was walking Bambos around and they were giving him a lot of water.

Justin had let the chick out in his room, and couldn't get it back into its cage. In the morning, the chick was still out, standing on top of his cage. It was the day of the nursery school trip from which Justin was banned for not listening, a result of Charon's yelling at him. Justin was already sad about that when Charon, hung-over, came out of his mother's bedroom, and started yelling at Justin about the chick.

My husband had become another man: his father, who had drunk himself to death. If you think about it, after seven years all the cells in your body have changed. Charon was literally no longer the man I'd married. I threw the covers off, mind racing to think of what I should do to stop the monster. I got in between Justin and Charon and yelled back, "Don't you dare dump your hangover on my son!"

Chapter 34

Divine Eye

I announced to my extended family that we needed a vacation on our own. With much coaxing, I was able to get my husband and children packed and into the car. We left the city melting in the heat and drove to a peninsula on the sea. Justin had a small scar on his lip, but he looked happy. We walked past rows of yellow bungalows with their shutters closed tight and put our cares behind us. Roof tiles baked in the sun. Splashes of red anemones dotted the bushes lining the pathway. Inside each was a tentacle with a crown of five fuzzy balls. They opened their large blossoms in the sun and were kept alive in the heat with desalinated sea water. I breathed in the healing sea air. The children hopped barefoot on the burning tiles from one patch of shade to the next. A lizard crossed Justin's path, and he bounded off after it into the bush. Soon he came back, its wiggling tail broken off in his little fist.

In the morning, a gleaming expanse of white light crept out of the sea and cast long morning shadows on the field between the house and the beach. Flocks of small birds filled the quiet. The waves rolled into the shore, answering each other. The hushed caress of summer breeze welcomed travellers to Styxos.

A litter of puppies lived in the dunes nearby. To the children's delight, a sandy puppy wandered into our kitchen and began licking our plates. They chased the fur ball around the kitchen. "Puppy!" Justin squealed, "This is a dishwasher that already licks our plates for us."

One morning walking out of time down the mirror shore, I thought I saw the silhouette of a swimmer coming out of the sea. Blue sky faded to white at the horizon. I saw the woman's figure in a white tunic waving in the distance. I turned around to see if there was anyone behind me to answer her. No one. The rolling sea beat the shore. She waved again. The woman's hair blew in the breeze. She had high hips. Niovi? We walked toward each other. Yes! There was Niovi's fierce profile. We flung ourselves into each other's arms. My conflicting feeling for her and Farouk had subsided with my recent discoveries as to his true nature. It was good to be hugging her. Still, I felt Grushenka coming between us and hoped that Niovi could help investigate the murder.

"I was early and had to go swimming right away," she said, apologising for the salt on her body. "It's been so hot!" The children followed behind me to where the red sand beaches are. All their fussing and arguing melted away when our feet touched the water. Our toes squeezed the red sand, soaked with so much iron. Schools of little fish jumped out of the water. The children frolicked behind us, pointing at the arches of little fish. We walked along the shore and skirted around the rocks at the tip of the peninsula under the lighthouse. We waded into the orange sunset, turquoise waves crashing onto the red sand. Ethereal colours! The foam shone as if under a black light.

"I know how Farouk affects people, Mac. You don't have to feel bad. We're all human. But don't forget, he is as guilty as the rest of us."

"You think so?"

We swam down along the coast, our heads out of the water to take in the view and watch the children running along the beach. Niovi made me wash my mouth out with sea water for its curative properties. There was one puff of cloud in the clear blue sky. The land was a strip of red between the blue sea and sky. We came to a sand bar where you could go quite a ways out and still lift your feet out of the water and run. I was sure I was going to feel this exercise in my thighs the next day. This would become our daily workout.

We came to a cliff. The beach ended in a pile of rocks. "I wish we could keep walking," I said to Niovi. She scooped up Justin and picked her way around the rocks.

"Niovi!"

"It's OK, Mac. We can get around this cliff."

I picked up Alex and followed her, the waves crashing around the rocks, my feet picking out the sandy spots. Then we were on the other side of the cliff! Back on luxurious red sand, a mixture of iron ore, copper and volcanic ash, we veered along the peninsula to the right and found a whole new beach with bigger waves. We walked toward the sunset into the orange reflection on purple crashing waves. The children jumped into the waves. The lighthouse on the point above blinked in the twilight.

"I don't need a lot of friends," Niovi was saying. She only needed a handful of people who could handle the power of her passion and reflect some of it back to her. She tried to impress me with a new song.

"Don't you know that I already love you?" I asked. We walked back to the house to the rhythm of the sea crashing all over the shore. A roll of foam broke and lapped our feet. The beach was strewn with blond seaweed. Cicadas hummed in the shrubbery. We went through the white umbrellas and climbed the dune with the weight of the sea on our backs.

The wind blew the sand off of a buried ruin, the house. From the terrace, we watched the sun set on the placid sea. The tree shadows grew longer in the dusk. A family of skinny cats battled each other in front of the terrace. The wind carried distant shouts up from the beach. The sun still lit the treetops. A pink blossom floated down onto the terrace next to me. A bird careened through my picture of the sea. A slight breeze rocked the leaves of the olive trees, their trunks painted white. A whole flock of sparrows swooped down from an olive tree, as if out of nowhere like leaves falling on the ground. Then they leapt back into the tree.

The sea sparkled behind the trees. A pair of yachts had moored on the slab of blue between the dusty olive leaves. The moonlight on the night water kept me awake for hours that night, another glimpse of Farouk.

The batteries in our watches died in the heat. Now we kept time by the sea with her placid face in the morning, desert colours at noon, and secretive dusks. What a luxury to be able to see to the end of the earth! One morning, the sea and sky were the same white. You couldn't see the horizon line for the humidity. Charon's car moved silently down the beach, headlights shining on the gnarled olive trunks. Then, no one. A bird settled in the olive tree. The branch bounced.

A cloud of dust rose from a jeep driving through the baked earth one siesta time. A friend of Vanessa's was the first to arrive. I handed her a wine spritzer. She looked through the bougainvillea flowers to the brazen sea. "The view here is magnificent," she said. "I can't believe more people don't know about this place!"

As I was telling her how much I admired Vanessa, she screwed up her nose mischievously. "She's leaving soon, I'm afraid," Vanessa's friend said. "Don't mention it to anyone, though. It's a secret."

Some secret. Why was it so hard for women to stick together? I would have to remember to keep my own secrets. I watched the 'friend' smile and decided to find out from Vanessa herself.

Vanessa came down the walkway through the red anemones, without her husband. She was wearing an African print wrap-around skirt. She introduced a new friend, Giuseppe, a small man with a bald spot, a little pot belly, and a very prominent nose. Niovi successfully avoided the others, sighing and pacing the terrace where faded pink tri-petals of bougainvillea wafted along the floor. The children scrambled out onto the terrace to get a better view of Giuseppe. "LOOK at his nose!" Justin said.

"Shhhh!"

"But LOOK, mommy!" I hushed him and scooted them into the house.

Niovi set her pelican beach bag down. "When I came to this beach with Farouk, we decided this is the loveliest place on our side of the island so close to the city."

"I haven't heard from Farouk," I said, hinting at the unaskable.

Niovi mumbled through her long hair. "How could I let that trivial detail spoil my plan? It's become the focus of my life. I overreacted and that made me noticeable. Nobody becomes so adamant over such a lost cause, and that's what drove him away. How could he let months go by without calling even to see if I am fine? He has found some other distraction. A work, or another love interest. Ha! I should have been more inconspicuous instead of leaving this trail of grotesque clues."

Giuseppe came and sat down next to me on the terrace wall. "Farouk again. Look how sad he made her. He's not an easy man to get along with, a typical French *directeur général*. He flits around like a mosquito, never here, never anywhere! He knows nothing about the business. I don't know how he got where he is today. His office is the biggest one in the building with mahogany furniture and a nice view, but he's never in it. There's no computer on his desk. The biggest part of the budget is his salary, but there are no results. Niovi, you can do better than that. He will find out when he's fifty that he's a dildo."

The sea glistened up to the horizon line beyond the row of olive trees in our garden, a tangle of dirt and rocks with hoses running through it to water the trees.

The wedding band on Giuseppe's plump finger gleamed. "How detestable," I agreed, watching that indisputable line of reason where blue sea met infinite sky.

There's something so relaxing about that horizon line. Maybe it's because it's not vertical. It annuls all ambition.

"It's a waste of the money of the shareholders. People like Farouk cost millions when you see how they do to loot the companies."

The triangles of orange and pink bougainvillea flowers wafted onto the terrace. I swept them into a blanket in the corner of the terrace.

"We have to water the bougainvillea. It's drying out. Soon there won't be any flowers left on the branches." I looked up at the thinning branches with more green showing through the lipstick orange and pink blossoms than usual. The children and I went to the kitchen sink to fill up water bottles and went back and forth pouring water on the thick bougainvillea trunk.

I made ice coffee, and our guests came into the cool shade of the kitchen to drink it. Giuseppe contrived to sit next to me again. "Have you been able to return the wedding dress?" I asked Niovi.

"Oh yes. The return policy of Taylord's is excellent. I couldn't get my mother to return her dress, though."

"Is she still hoping things will turn around?"

"Maybe. I've been trying to get her to return the dress since before the scandal, but she won't hear any of it."

"Why before?"

"I had gone shopping one morning before the gala with my mother at Taylord's. We found a classical wedding dress with a high waist and a white, satin ribbon that wrapped around under the breast and tied in front. Back then, nothing could damage my excitement about the wedding, not even the memory of the divorce of my parents. My mother found the perfect dress, rust-colour, on the designer level three and decided to be the best-dressed mother-of-the-bride ever." Niovi sipped her *café frappé*. "The next week, I went in for alterations and was shocked to hear from the sales clerk that the new, young wife of my father bought the same rust-coloured dress for the wedding."

"They have the same taste, in more than just men!" Giuseppe said.

"It's uncanny. I called my 'stepmother' up and gently asked her to exchange it. I explained what had happened, but she refused. Niovi mimicked a spoiled child, 'There's no way I'm returning this dress. I look like a million shekels in it, and I'm wearing it.'"

"How awful," I said.

Justin held up a baby lizard. I gasped and the lizard jumped onto his tummy.

Niovi tickled him. He laughed as Niovi went on talking. "Me, I didn't know how to tell my mother that the new woman was planning on wearing the same rust-coloured dress. But my mother had her own way of understanding what I was telling her. 'Don't worry, my love. We'll go back and buy another dress tomorrow when we go in for your fitting. Really, it's a small thing. The most important thing is that nothing spoils your special day.' The wedding plans had lifted the spirits of my mother more than anyone could believe. She stopped her crying over my father, you know. We went shopping and did find another gorgeous dress. A silver-blue metallic cloth that was just as flattering to the figure of my mother. We bought it, and I started back up to level three to return the first dress.

"But my mother refused to set foot on the escalator. I couldn't get her to return that rust-colour dress. She wouldn't listen, even when the saleswoman assured us that they would exchange it. I tried to reason with her and told her she didn't have another occasion to wear such an expensive dress to."

"Strange," I said. Our neighbour, Niovi's mother, was not rich.

Niovi had brought her guitar. She sat at my kitchen table strumming her new song, and translating in a wistful melody. *Oh man, you looked after me, and kissed my hand, of all things! I can still feel it in my toes.* Niovi paced the terrace as she had done so often alone at her house, waiting. We took in the aroma of the sea. Waiting. There was something I knew about. I was also waiting for my man, for an end to his grief, for the chance to take his hand and escape. I had loved in vain. I felt sorry for her spending her nights alone. I was already with Farouk in the afterlife. But she went on, heart exposed, in a suspended state of readiness, telling herself they were eternal here, at the threshold of unrequited possibility. "I could wait forever for that man."

Ah Niovi. That is how a real woman loves! She thrashes and sings.

I followed her gaze to the branches of the four olive trees in front of the terrace and behind them, my little boy in his blue shirt. He was looking for lizards under a stripe of turquoise sea that faded at the horizon line. Stalks of cut hay crunched under his sandals. Justin could spend the whole of siesta time hunting for lizards. Alex was spread-eagled in her bathing suit asleep on the couch with one arm hanging over the side.

Chapter 35

Baptized Capitalist

The sea was flat except for a rolling wave that had appeared in the deep. I watched it move slowly toward the shore. A sliver of white appeared in the middle of the eddy. Our boat. It came closer.

We skipped down to the beach toward Papa. Justin was like a little cat, chasing all the critters at the waterside. The water eroded the red sand under our feet. We waded into the water in our uniforms. We all scrambled into the boat. My husband ferried us along the bombed-out coast past the wall to the North. We cruised along the ghost town of hotels with apprehension. The patrols had just been suspended. My husband knitted his brow and said, "There are no mines in the sea." The silhouette of degraded hotels and bombed-out restaurants was an eyesore. We looked away from the dangling wires and graffiti.

A crime that continues to be committed.

The heat welded us to the seats. Decades of waves crashed on the sides of the boat rhythmically. The incessant bombing grated my nerves. Charon fitted the rack at the back of the boat with machine guns. Laden with bodies, the boat rode low in the water. A bomb exploded behind one of the hotels. Another shell met with screams. The building wall crumbled. I ducked down in the boat and begged Charon to move us away from the shore. My body cooled with the spray of the waves.

Charon laughed and stopped the motor. He stood there in his bathing suit recalibrating the rods at the back of the boat with three baited hooks on each fishing rod. I peeked out of the boat. The shore was peaceful after all, just a ghost town where a battlefield used to be. "You see, Mac, these old hotels prove that all is illusion. When they take your house away, chemistry doesn't matter. I danced on that terrace right there on a summer night until two in the morning. Our interest was the magic of each other's company. All an illusion, including your romance, Mac. Anything can dissolve into torture."

"Jackass," Niovi said.

Charon pretended he didn't hear her.

We threw our lines over the side. The weights sank fifty meters to the bottom of the sea. Justin moved his rod back and forth. "Fishing is good! You don't know what's going to come out, or how long you'll have to wait."

"The sea is beautiful," I ventured.

"It's a taker," Charon said. But the sea had a relaxing effect on my husband. In the sun and the warm breeze, Justin reeled in the first keeper, a kind of fish that died as soon as it was caught. Niovi looked at the bulging eyes. "I envy its mechanism to avoid pain." We put all the fish in a bucket and moved to another spot where Niovi tried the octopus bait, a curled white ribbon wrapped around a large hook. We let the spool of fishing line out, and the current carried the bait away from the boat.

Charon dropped anchor near a crowded beach and climbed off the boat into the water. Here the sand was golden. A hundred children were screaming and laughing at play on the sand. People swam in front of the ghost town as if nothing had happened there. Women in veils floated like clown fish in the turquoise water. I dove into a warm current coming from the mainland. The water in this fenced off area was the cleanest we'd seen on Styxos. Alex squealed with fright when a big sea turtle swam under her mommy. I saw it as it dovetailed under my thigh. I scrambled away, startled. My husband swam out with his harpoon.

You never saw sea turtles on our side of the island! The South had been growing in the wrong ways. I swam underwater with my snorkel and mask. It was a paradise of marine life. What foolishness, to pollute the free world. Man had evolved to the point where we could only think in derivatives. It took calculus to show that growth in Gross Domestic Product was cancerous. There are fish that die of over-consumption, why not us? GDP had supplanted evolution. What were we succeeding at? If it was only wealth, one person's success could be society's failure. Swimming along the beach we marvelled at the effect of rampant inactivity on nature. Bombed-out hotels were a heavy price to pay, but the water was pristine! This water was teeming with life. In the North, where doing nothing is good, you have time to think, for example, of a realistic measure. How will the next generation advance if it can't breathe? What we needed was an indicator that measured not cancerous growth, but evolution — sustainable, environmental, educational, cultural, ethical — the rate of change in Gross Domestic Evolution in competing countries. Then there might be something realistic to succeed at.

We dried on the shore and ate our sandwiches. Niovi watched my tanned children bobbing in the sea, placid mirror with goggles and flippers flapping under pink sky. "Mommy, look!"

"Sweet children. You are lucky, Mac."

Charon came back triumphant with a handful of jelly. The frogman waded up to the children holding up two writhing octopuses in his hand. The suction cups formed neat diminishing rows down each looping tentacle. "When do octopuses have 16 legs?" He waved them in front of the children, then separated them and held one in each hand.

"When there are two!" the children squealed, in horror and delight. These monsters were their favourite dish.

Niovi waded out in her tiger-striped bikini, and we admired the dimples on her back above her high derriere and the languid way she moved her hips. She dove in and flipped over on her back, buoyant on the salty bed, her shadow skirting along the little sand dunes on the sea floor. Above Niovi in the blue sky was God's eye shining through her melancholy. We followed. Our troubles melted into the turquoise sea. The sand on the seabed exploded around our toes. We floated under the infinite blue sky on our salty sea-beds and watched the children play in the sand on the beach. Alex was eating the juiciest peach she'd ever had. She waded into the turquoise, juice dripping, electric hair silhouette flying behind her in the sun. I washed that peach in saltwater. It must taste wonderful after all that swimming.

The sea. The sun. The sky. I floated on my back listening to the sound of the waves. Lying on top of the water, divine eye penetrating from the blue sky — I remember it like it was tomorrow. I lay my head back looking into the whitest part of the sky, and closed my eyes, watching the unforgiving sunspots through closed lids, and began to understand how complex molecules on dust flying past a star could organize themselves into life. How did energy *know* to change into matter?

It was fitting to have suns as gods. I could feel the gravitational pull of the heavenly bodies in my bones. How could astrology have lost ground in a neopagan age? Were we too busy with freedom to notice destiny? Astrological archetypes imposed themselves on our weaknesses whenever we gave up responsibility for our actions. Lying on the water, the sunspots danced on my eyelids in dark celebration of Sol.

The shadow of camels harnessed together rippled across the sand and shifted down the beach. Against the laze of the camel train, the Styxan sea turned to silver and the sky faded to rose. The sea never stopped moving. The dark undersides of waves flourished and died. Tomorrow I would lie on her seabed again without moving listening to my breath count out life under that bright deity. The heavy taste of the salt water, laughing sun, jealous moon. And every morning that horizon line.

There's nothing like the first time.

It's a mystery how much cold beer you can drink when you're living at the beach. My orange flowered skirt open to the sea, I soaked it up like water and it had no effect.

If the stuffed grape leaves needed salt and it was too hot to move, I licked the salt from my lips. Salt, sun and the rush of the waves, the arc of God's eye across our terrace, plenty of couches for siesta time. The Styxans have contrived to sleep after every meal. They take a siesta after lunch and eat dinner at ten at night. They top this off by skipping breakfast.

I don't know how many days we stayed at the beach — long enough to find a bronze coin from the ancient city of Amisos with my metal detector. I reached down and dug among the stubborn plants trying to live in the rock and sand near the shore. On the way back to the house, the red anemones were folding their large blossoms in the evening breeze. Some were still open to bees. I stuck my foot into the swarm of drone bees under the water faucet and washed off the sand. I went into the house and found everyone on the terrace, a bottle of cold beer sweating on the table. Niovi's laugh was loud and deep under the starry night.

One day our friends had gone. Justin's silhouette stood on the barricade of rocks holding the fishing rod up to the twinkling sea. His sister sat on the cove kneading the sand into a castle hidden from view by her little body. The wind carried away an orca float. It turned over and over away down the beach. The summer heat had subsided, and we were able to go outside at midday. Many drip castles later, it was time for the children to go back to the French school. We packed our suitcases and drove to Styxos, also the name of the capital city, where you could *see* the social fabric, a ragged piece of cloth with people sewn in. The nights had grown mellow, and the streets and cafés were full of people of all ages: machos, little children, old people, middle-aged couples — everybody was out. Walking down the street, I could still feel our boat rocking.

Chapter 36

The Trick in Life

I was dusting off my shoes on the roof of the Robinson Crusoe. We'd come here for a view of the old city under consoling palm tree tops. I was trying to forget the shock of my sudden dismissal from the TV station. It helped that my ex-boss hadn't bothered to fabricate an excuse for firing me. In the US they would have found a reason and degraded my professionalism. At least on Styxos, you knew it wasn't your fault. And I wasn't going to wait around for them to *tell* me it was because of that list I'd given the press with the names of the suspect government officials who'd denied attending the gala.

My article had just come out, and they were happy to have me back at the old amphitheatre. We had unearthed several specimens of pottery shards providing extraordinarily detailed insight into the life of the city at the height of the Persian Empire and were fencing off the excavation to keep developers away.

The view from the Robinson Crusoe rooftop was comforting. Traditional dancing had started in the square below us. Dervishes twirled in their long sleeves. They looked overheated. If the sleeves were to ward off the sun, then why didn't they have different clothing for night time which was still so hot? I was thinking, it must be to ward off the evil eye, when I spotted Farouk brooding on the other side of the terrace. I knew one of the Italians he was with, a Jewess who called to me. "Mac! My God, look at that tan. You look like a movie star." She was in a cocktail dress with cognac tresses. They must have just come from an event. We installed ourselves around their table laden with handbags. Farouk and I sat down on a sofa together. His eyes held mine, and time just slipped away as we sank into the cushions. I was falling, again.

Farouk's body tensed. Niovi stepped off the elevator, alone, in a fashionable sweater dress. A photographer was following her. I waved to her, but she hesitated when she saw that we were with Farouk. Heads turned in the restaurant and the chorus whispered, *Wasn't that the singer, Niovi?* The photographer snapped her picture as she approached the table. *Are they back together?* Everyone knew her latest hit song and the story behind it. We all stood up. *Flash*, another shot for the press. The Italian, Giuseppe, in snakeskin shoes welcomed Niovi. "Join us."

She recovered immediately. "Your wife's not here?" Niovi teased Giuseppe, "OK, then I can kiss you." She looked venomously at Farouk as the Italian kissed her cheek. But Farouk was elated. He didn't take his eyes off her. It was as if he thought she might disappear. I ceded my place next to Farouk.

Farouk had been trying to comment on a newspaper clipping he had taken out of his pocket. "I read your article," Farouk said.

I cringed. "Is that from the magazine?"

"Is that an academic journal?" Niovi asked softly, as if she were arranging a piece of crystal in a china cabinet.

Farouk unfolded my article on the evil eye, 'A Theory of Light'. "*Intéressant.* I admire anyone who can sustain an effort," he said.

Effort. There was that "e" word. I was having trouble breathing, but stammered, "Anthropologists are supposed to contribute to the knowledge of our collective human history. The only problem is that if I'd published in an academic journal no one would have read it. *Living Anthropology* wanted to hear about ancient modes of living in Styxos, and after I started looking into superstition, the article wrote itself."

"See!" The conversation shattered. "She lied! She didn't even write it herself," Niovi said, haughtier than ever. Her eyes locked onto mine.

I got a clear image of a magnifying glass training the sun's rays to burn a hole in something or someone. I had underestimated the power of Niovi's mind when it wanted to concentrate. Was she the reason that the TV station fired me? Words got stuck in my throat. I wanted to answer that she was the one who suggested the interview, but she had lost her temper. "I didn't lie," I managed to say to no one in particular. I'd tried not to look at the people who had congratulated me on the story's success, but now I was being 'overlooked' anyway.

"They all lie," Niovi said. "You go to a magazine rack and you don't find anything written in blood."

Why argue with her? She was going to change her mind anyway. I wasn't used to such harsh criticism from anyone but Charon, and struggled to see things objectively. "The article tracks my Theory of Light across spatial and temporal boundaries: I used multi-sited ethnography to follow the evil eye through global networks." At least I had left out the *graphic* details of her relationship with Farouk. But delirium had gripped her. I was at the heart of her nightmare, and Niovi was determined to save the pond of journalism from stagnation, as if there would be no more room for thinking soon. Or, who knows, maybe she was angry at someone who just reminded her of me.

"And look at this! It says, 'by Dr. Mac'. "

"It was the editor's idea." I avoided catching any malignant influence that might be darting from her eyes.

Niovi spread her poison. "You are too gullible, all of you. Especially you, Farouk. Did you think your Russian girlfriend was going to change into a housewife because you asked her to marry you?"

Farouk dropped all pretences and pleaded, "*Écoute, chérie.*"

"No, *you* listen." It was clear that whatever he said would be taken as fresh dissent.

"Sit down, everybody," Giuseppe said.

"And you expected me to believe that her father was a colleague of yours! That you were trying to help them out!"

"Yes. That's a good idea. Let's all sit down," said Farouk. Everybody sat down, except Niovi.

My husband and I ordered crêpes, and Farouk invited Niovi to sit next to him on the couch. They talked to each other in hushed tones while we ate.

They quarrelled on. "And you don't understand why I don't sleep with you!" she said. "I'm not as dumb as I look." She had given up on living in her house, too, and had effectively moved back with her mother.

Farouk was gaunt with fatigue, cheeks sunken like a desert creature. The lines carved in his face deepened in the twilight, and the moonlight shone in his hair. It was hard to see him destitute. He didn't seem to hear her nagging. He negotiated.

I was hoping Farouk would get Niovi to agree to retract all of her accusations in a written letter to the judge. My husband had said the court had taken it up, and Farouk would have to appear, since the case had been filed. Everyone hoped it would be quick and discreet.

"We all know about it anyway," my husband said.

"But the newspapers in France don't," I said.

"At least he wasn't married."

Niovi went on arguing.

"Look, here come the musicians," Farouk said.

The saxophonist strapped her instrument on. I looked at the men and tried to guess their next moves. The 'Grushenka mishap' hung in the air. "Things were simple in the beginning," Niovi confided to my husband. Farouk pretended not to watch. "I have to admit that I changed when I moved back in with my mother. We are so spoiled here with the extended family. Our parents never stop giving us whatever we want, a car, a house, breakfast, lunch and dinner brought over to the house. It's too hot to think sometimes," she sighed.

"The trick in life is to appreciate what you have," I said.

Niovi whirled around. "In *your* life, Mac."

In the line of fire.

She sneered, "Hold off condescending until I get a chance to tell *my* side. In *my* life, the trick is to watch a man with a roving eye." She would invent her own reasons, and nobody was going to be allowed to agree with her.

"Maybe if I went blind," said Farouk.

"Relax," said Giuseppe. "It doesn't matter where your appetite comes from, as long as you bring it home for dinner!"

"There is no dinner at home," Niovi sneered. She reached for her glass and toppled my husband's beer drenching his shoes and socks.

"Oh whore!" Charon jumped up.

There was a general rumble of disapproval. Heads turned.

Charon knocked over another glass trying to grab a napkin, and yelled, "That's enough now! You remind me of my two-year-old, except that she is much more reasonable!"

Niovi grabbed a napkin and tried to dry off Charon's beer-soaked shoes.

"You have to learn not to want more and more," Charon gasped, teeth clenched. "Life is not a zero-sum game. These days, more is usually worse. We all like you. No one's trying to trick you. We want you to win, but how can you be so self-destructive? Couples are made up of separate people, too. We have a duty to respect each other and make each other comfortable. There is no use in complaining ALL THE TIME. It doesn't work! That's not how you get what you want. That's how you get punished." He was taking off his socks. "We have been waiting thirty years for you to grow up, and *if* you do you're going to look back and wish for our childhood. I don't know where you get your stubbornness from, but it's not from our side of the family."

Our side of the family! I looked at the two of them as if for the first time. Only then did I register the resemblance not just in their nose and eyebrows, but in their temperaments, that went beyond shared nationality to kinship.

"You have a lot going for you right now: your voice, your social standing, a fiancé who — excuse me — but who comes from a civilisation much more advanced than ours, even if he believes whatever he reads." Charon grabbed my anthropology article away from Farouk and shredded it to pieces in front of me.

"Stop!" Farouk said.

I burst into tears.

But Charon continued his tantrum. "There is no need to make so much noise all the time," Charon yelled. "Sometimes it's better to listen. In your place, little sister!"

Niovi sat back down. Then she looked slyly back at Charon. "At least I *am* a woman," she said.

He glared at her. "*All* of this is your fault!"

Farouk looked at Niovi with fury and desire in his eyes. My heart raced as he said to her, "You can't escape from yourself, Niovi."

"Did you learn that in jail?" Niovi said.

Farouk looked at the palm trees. "Since we're among family, I didn't go to jail."

Chapter 37

Round-Trip Ticket

Farouk's frame was a scaffolding of bones. "You can play for all of us, Mac," he said under his breath. We were all leaning forward with our hands on the table, as if we were conjuring up spirits in a séance, and I knew the others were thinking about what I was thinking about: Charon and Niovi; Farouk and the ghost of Grushenka.

I let my thoughts wander. By now the court must have taken her up, and it was too late for Niovi to retract her accusations against Farouk. The temperature seemed to drop. I could make out Grushenka's limp body travelling light above the coffee table.

"*Chérie*," Farouk said to Niovi, "I was never in love with that woman. You mustn't believe the rumours. It's not what you think. Her father did ask me to look out for her, and for that, I lost everything: everyone's respect, my fiancée . . ."

"You have to get up and brush yourself off," I said. "Try again. That's what people respect. The rest will follow. Whoever said it would be easy? And if it were, would you want it? The goal is the struggle."

"I am struggling." He hung his head. "Maybe I would not go through it, except he was a colleague, *un ami*, an old friend, my mother's gardener. He's dead now. He was only sixty-two."

There *was* something fishy about Farouk's story. If her father was Farouk's colleague, they must have had enough money to keep their daughter out of white slavery. And how convenient that he was 'dead now'.

But Farouk went on. "My gardener, he believed that his daughter had been kidnapped. The police had given up hope, so I agreed to investigate. There was a French company already working on the island to prepare the way for the infrastructure bid —"

"Investigate?" Niovi said.

"I found her working in a cabaret. I went to her apartment behind the club. The key was in the lock, on the outside of the door. She was locked in. There was a window in the stairwell overlooking the street, and I made sure that no one was watching me."

Niovi had pictures of that. She stifled the smile that threatened to peel across her face.

"I turned the key," Farouk said, "and let myself into the apartment. Gru opened her eyes and sat up on the sofa. There was no one else in the room. She was just a girl, nothing special without any makeup or costume. But she had a nice proportion, and was a blonde *naturelle*. I explained that it was her father who had sent me."

"Gru! Is that all? You mean she wasn't chained to the bed?" Niovi demanded.

"*Chérie*. Don't believe everything you hear. Of course she wasn't chained to the bed. She cried, though, from relief and shame. She said, 'I can't leave. They will kill me.' I convinced her to meet me at the Tropical Hotdog where she worked. I thought that if I could just get her to trust me a little, she would be able to leave.

"We met the next day. She recognized me from the newspaper pictures, and asked me if I was Niovi's fiancé. When I said I was, she decided to tell me her story."

A look of triumph seized Niovi. She tossed her head.

"She was on the 'closed system', which meant that she could go out of the room for two hours a day. It could be worse; she had heard they sold girls in Germany. There was nothing like that on Styxos.

"Then we met in the café again. I started to worry that there was no helping her, but I felt I couldn't abandon her, at the same time. That was the start of my confusion. I knew she was helpless and in danger. The line between my motivations and her needs blurred. I continued in this destabilised state. I was standing next to death. It was no longer possible to continue trying to convince her. I decided to bring the situation to a close and hoped she would go along."

Niovi stifled a look of incredulity, still working to deny what we all knew was the truth, until it burst out on its own. "So you *were* meeting a prostitute while you were engaged to me!"

Chapter 38

Personal Commerce

Farouk mopped his forehead with a white handkerchief. He insisted on explaining himself. "I orchestrated the girl's smooth transition into the free world, arranged for her passport and plane ticket. All I had to do was point her in the right direction and let her sail. I had chosen a night flight, and pretended that I was her customer to get her out of the cabaret. She had no baggage. At the airport, we said goodbye. But it didn't go as I had planned. I had read her wrong. It's difficult to understand her way of thinking. The streetlamp on us was like lightning when we moved. She would never see me again, so she kissed me on both cheeks, for the last time, and as our noses crossed, I said, '*Bon voyage*' into her mouth."

Niovi tried to contain her rage. "Did you kiss her?"

"Not really. I don't know how I let that gesture escape me. Gru turned around and glanced at me over her shoulder. I smiled and waved goodbye from behind my car. She said it was with the look of a man who suddenly discovered he was happy. I watched her eyes open wide.

A glimpse of eternity.

"She walked into the airport, got her seat assignment, and made it through security. There couldn't be any love in all of this, but she had seen it, *l'éternité.* It was an ocean. She felt dizzy, and sat down in a chair on the other side of the gate. And, regardless of my rejection of her every illusion *romantique,* she was convinced I had seen it, too. Gru sat there reliving our goodbye, wondering whether the life of freedom I was sending her to was another trick.

"For me, freedom meant human rights and stamping out injustice. She had agreed when I explained it, but now that she thought about being on her own, for her, freedom was an incontrollable desire erupting from her personality. 'You talk about free speech when there's not even free thinking.' The only way to attain it seemed to be through destruction. Even if she could become a *grande dame,* she doubted she would be satisfied. She longed to see for herself, just once, if society women were free. Maybe the personal commerce of their lives was just another form of prostitution. She had to see for herself.

"She was determined to see just how much middle-class women were really free to feel happiness and had an idea. She went back through security, waited in the ticket line again, and asked if her flight could be postponed a few days. She was overjoyed at her cleverness when the ticket agent told her the ticket could be changed.

"When I discovered that Gru was still on the island, I felt a curious mix of desire and frustration. I was touched that she had fallen in love with me, but there was no way, no matter how hard I tried to rationalize it, turning it over in my mind *comme si et comme ça,* that I could let myself be tempted to pick that apple. Still she continued to appear here and there.

"The more I tried to ignore her, the deeper in love she fell. One day, she called the house. We had passed the point of going back: that's when you answered her phone call, Niovi. Gru hung up, *n'est-ce pas?* Gru knew everything there was to know about requited love. There was nothing that hadn't been done to her. If I *had* reached for her, she would have known her bearings. But the kind of love that lives in dreams and meanings *double* seized her. 'Tell me.' We were sitting in the café window looking down onto the street. 'I want to hear you talk. When you talk, it feels like you're making love to me.'

" 'Stop.' I thought of you, Niovi. I could feel you with me.

" 'Ah. Let's be quiet, then.' She was ready to jump out of the window. But instead, her disappointment festered and turned into a frustration. I wouldn't go to see her, and she succumbed to malady. She was more than obsessed. She was possessed. Her anger would turn into loud wailing sobs. She called your house, Niovi, again and again, and finally found a way to call me.

"She insisted on seeing me. A demand *impossible.* She looked into my eyes imploringly. 'I am getting sick here. What you call civilisation is making me miserable.' Her eyes filled up with tears. Gru was attached to life by only a thread and was no longer, shall we say, her own best friend. She was sweating, and we were both in danger. Her boss had taken to victimizing her. She put up no protest. It seemed to her that they were on the same side.

" 'Since they took my plane ticket away, I am unhappier than before I ever had it. I don't believe you. Show me your upper-class freedom.' She pleaded with me. A girl with ripe cheeks who knew too much about the wrong things. She needed someone to show her the beginnings of culture, to show a relationship that was not subject to authority *arbitraire*. Someone else. 'I cannot,' I said.

"She cried. 'You can play for both of us.' Because I could not allow her instinct to be satisfied, some kind of serious disorder threatened to arise. I didn't know what it was, but I felt it. Her condition begged for some kind of compensation. So I paid her." Farouk avoided our eyes.

"How much?" Giuseppe asked.

"One hundred shekels."

"That sounds about right."

"I was compensating *her*, for damages that had been done. In my mind, I couldn't have done anything less egotistical, but people wanted to know if I had got anything in return. The ironic thing is that the ones who claim to represent the law never believed for a moment in the remote *possibilité* of a man sublimating his drives into a civil act. The hypocrites. They have no use for the dictates of civilisation. But what choice is there in life? If you choose to do the wrong thing, there is a prison waiting in your head. You are only free if you choose to do what you must. I thought at least you would understand, Mackenzie, after all the work your group of women has done on human trafficking. Do you condemn me for helping a girl? The underworld network does create problems for all business attempting to develop infrastructure across central Asia. You understand the need to fight it.

"I'm sorry if I took a risk with our relationship, Niovi. I know you were angry listening to the breathing of Grushenka on the telephone. And I knew if I did what I thought was right, I would lose you. So I tried to convince you to be polite with her. Gru could feel your anger, and every day, she sank deeper into her illness. Now when she dreamed of love, her mood turned sullen, and she stayed in morose thought that began to affect me. I watched her face change and darken. Gru said, 'I am loving you constantly and you think only of this low tramp.' The voice was not hers! Even the expressions on the face, the mannerisms were not hers. They were yours, Niovi. I knew they were yours. Or she would say, 'How can you look at her and leave me alone for all these hours? My soul has wandered into the woods. I never wanted to come to you in this way.' I knew it was you.

"I've never believed in this sort of thing. I always laughed at people who talked about the spirits of the vengeful dead clinging to the living. But I was repulsed. A dead thing had taken Gru into its grip. It wouldn't let go. Now you understand for your part, *chérie*, the reason why I've stayed away."

"You knew," I heard Niovi say under her breath.

We looked at each other. Giuseppe tried to ease their pain. "It was bad luck."

"Is that all there is?" Niovi's voice softened with a note of clemency, but she was merely gathering her strength. "That doesn't explain Grushenka's death."

Giuseppe leaned forward. "Explain what? In order to have a mystery, you have to have somebody who wants to solve it, isn't it? If *you* had died, we would get out our magnifying glasses. But everybody who is concerned says there *was* no Grushenka. The bottom line — sorry, I can't control myself! — there *is* no mystery."

Niovi lowered her head muttering words that set her on fire. "Good for you. I'm glad you are satisfied. But how can I live with myself? *I* will tell you how she died."

Chapter 39

Cat Fight

Niovi breathed deeply. "I hired a detective." She waited for the surprise to register on Farouk's face. "I was lucky that Gru had so many clients. She was a popular girl, a portal to the underworld. I might have gone out of my mind if I hadn't found out more about her. That's all. The detective said he couldn't go further with the case because Gru was involved in an international human trafficking ring that was over his head. He barely understood it, but Gru had become involved with a man named Snake."

Farouk sat up. "You know about Snake?"

"Only his name," Niovi said.

"He's held a lot of odd jobs, most recently assassin," Farouk said. "Snake tried to play the authorities off each other. He went too far when he offered the police his services as a spy against the Jarmuth. The special forces investigated him on suspicions that he had approached the other side with the same offer."

"And?" I said. "You can tell us, now that the crime has been solved, as you said yourself." We all urged Farouk to go on.

"Snake is insane. To give you an idea, when he was in prison, he cut himself with the silverware in the prison canteen and watched the blood swell to the surface of his tattoo where it was written 'Hell on Earth'. A picture of a vulture eating a woman alive.

"As usually happens in this kind of case, it was his own stupidity that got him caught. Snake marched into the fortified defence ministry building with his spy offer. They accepted. Gru was excited when he entered the bar with the news that he was on the payroll, and Snake recruited her saying, 'Baby, all you have to do is sell whatever documents we get our hands on.'

" 'Who will I sell them to?' she asked.

" 'Buyers. Arabs mostly. I'll tell you what you need to know when it's time.' The expectation of deals with the Arabs aroused his senses. We are talking about a dirty animal. He had felt cleansed lately, living under the island sun, but when he could feel the violence of his past erupting in his veins, he pulled her upstairs to celebrate.

"There was talk of selling information to an intelligence unit regarding a secret delivery of tanks. Then, she overheard some talk of 'marketing' an Islamic bomb to Muslim nations, and that's when Snake stopped talking. Gru tried to piece together the schizophrenic explanations of her friend. He laid the money on the table as if to justify his secretiveness. She leaned over, her hand grasping the bills. His big hands locked around her waist. Gru's share of the embassy payroll fell through her fingers like a sieve. He looked like a reptile to her. She tried to hide her fear.

"Snake was contemptuous of the girl. She might need him, but she didn't want him. Now that the money was in front of her, she was faking it. The only real thing about her was her terror. He knew that they were both being watched. There would be no retirement. He had become a mere assassin.

"They put a bug on him and followed him in Taylords," Farouk said. "They have the whole thing on tape. Immediately the salesman came to him and said the code words, 'It's windy today.'

"Snake hesitated, then remembered the response: 'A nice day for sailing.'

"The salesman's eyes widened. 'Give me the map.'

" 'There's also a key.' Snake held up an envelope. 'Give me the money first.'

" 'That's not the deal. I see the map first.'

The assassin handed the shopkeeper the envelope. The shopkeeper's fat fist trembled as he opened it. The assassin smiled with satisfaction as the fingers glided over the deadly powder on the opening of the envelope. 'And everything's here?'

" 'Everything: the missile kit and forty kilos of chemicals.'

"He didn't know the value of the substance he was trying to sell, just that it was a rare product of an ex-Soviet laboratory. He was giving it away for only € 800,000. What he did know was that there was money in the cash registers. He pointed a gun at the salesman's head and had him scoop up the money. People all over the ground floor stopped what they were doing and watched him go from cash register to cash register grunting. He unfolded a canvas bag. He herded people out of the way, knocking over racks of Gucci summer wear, and filled up the canvas bag. When the police cars arrived, his gun was nowhere in sight. The officers simply surrounded him and slapped the handcuffs on his wrists.

"During questioning, they emptied the canvas bag and found that he had put the gun in the bottom of it under all the money. The dope. Unfortunately, they didn't know about the chemical on the envelope. The salesman died later that day.

"Then, after Gru's ticket was gone, everything else started to slip away. Certain friends tried to give her money, the friends responsible for firing you from the TV station, Mackenzie. She was not thinking straight anymore, and it just disappeared. The only hope Gru had left was me."

"And you had stopped answering your phone," Niovi said.

Farouk slid down in his chair. "A second opportunity came along. Gru made another attempt at escape as a runner in a drug haul. But it was another ex-Soviet national who was the one to wait in the airport lounge with Gru's ticket to leave: Snake.

"They arrested Snake and found a kit with chemical agents and a kilo of enriched uranium wrapped in newspaper. But they didn't want him. Snake was just the surface of the cesspool. They wanted the Boss of the underworld. It is a shame that they weren't able to use Snake to get to the person behind the arms deals."

"Who do you think it could be?" I asked.

"The serpent starts to smell from the head."

"Someone in the government, then."

"Including their mediocre offspring. We are talking about a hundred billion shekels worth of criminal infra-structure that is ready and in place to do every kind of sinister business from daily human trafficking to an annual uranium deal."

"I wish I could have helped," Niovi said.

"It wasn't your responsibility," Farouk said.

"I wish I had done things differently," she insisted.

"*Chérie,* forget about it. The authorities are handling it."

"I shouldn't have lost my temper." Niovi leaned forward so we all could hear. "When Grushenka called my house the night before the gala, I shouldn't have flown into a rage. I could hear her breathing into the receiver. Me, I don't like strange phone calls. I was about to scream, burning to see with my own eyes this girl who was the source of all my pain. I said, 'Who are you!' The silence made my head spin. I managed to say, 'I think we should meet.'

" 'I don't think.' Her voice was ragged.

" 'I *need* to talk to you,' I told her, as nicely as possible. 'I have a problem. Maybe you can help.'

"The phone line crackled. 'All right.'

" 'What do you look like?'

"There was no answer."

Chapter 40

All Those Hours

"Me, I went into the Tropical Hotdog, and my heart stopped when I saw the foreign doll," Niovi said. "Her beauty was an insult. Her angel-face glowed from a group of men. Her long, straight, blonde hair made my blood run cold. She moved her pack of cigarettes closer to her chest as I sat down. As if I was going to take one! Ha! I'm a singer. I don't smoke. She had drunk to the bottom of a glass of beer. I said, 'I thought I was early.'

" 'I have been here whole time.'

"We smiled at each other. I looked away. 'I came here to talk about Farouk.'

" 'Of course.'

" 'I don't know why we haven't met before. He could have introduced us, since I know all his other friends. Or at least he says I do.'

" 'Us? Friends! Does he do this in front of you?'

"There it was. I knew it. I felt the heat in my face. I tried to look for information to explain it away, but there it was. He was after a whore decades younger than me. We exchanged a hopeless look.

" 'I should have never talked to him in first place,' the girl said. 'I know you won't believe me, but he was always *correct* with me. We didn't even share kiss.'

"I could imagine how tired I must look sitting there. My eyes were bulging. Her pack of cigarettes sat half-opened on the table. She didn't offer me one. Her blue eyes were outlined in a minimum of black liner and a touch of mascara. She looked like a professional girl in her white blouse. She brushed back her long, blonde hair, and I knew what effect this must have had on you, Farouk. I said, 'But you have been meeting for a long time, secretly.'

" 'I know, and it was wrong. I am in trouble here, and he tried to help. We just met to talk, and never for more than hour.'

"An hour! My back stiffened. 'How many hours?' *I* was alone all those hours.

" 'We met six times.'

" 'I think I know when you met for the first time. In July That's when he changed. He stopped all our conversations short, and seemed angry if I asked him what he was thinking about.'

" 'Yes, it was July. I knew we liked being together, but I thought about and decided not become mistress.'

" '*You* decided? Did he proposition you?' How silly, to be asking this of a prostitute. But I was determined to find out as much as possible before tearing the girl to pieces.

" 'Not in so many words, but we had been talking and talking. I said if I were fiancée, I would have thrown him out. But he said you did not like come to this kind of place, and it was relaxing just to sit with me and have beer. Normally by now, man and woman sitting across from other like we are sitting now would have gone to bed together.'

"There was no comfortable position on that chair, and I asked for a drink. The bartender brought a glass of whisky and demanded to be paid right away. The girl sat frozen. I paid and drank.

" 'Can I help you?' the girl finally asked. 'It was brave of you to meet me. I don't think many people would do it. I won't talk him anymore. You like?'

" 'That would be nice. Thank you.' It hadn't occurred to me that she would offer this of her own self, and suddenly, I didn't think I could be very convincing yelling at her. To tell the truth, I didn't feel jealous anymore. If I were jealous, I would be angry. Instead, I felt like I was late for something, and had to go away. It was sickening to think that I had wasted all this time on Farouk and his mess. I had to devote myself to something that mattered, someone true. I left the bar with no intention of seeing either of you again, ever. You deserved her. I was *lucky* to get away.

"A week later, I was relieved not to hear from either one of you. I went to the studio, came home and did my exercises. In a way, I had let myself down by not fighting her as I had set out to do, but I felt like maybe I had learned something. Maybe he wasn't worth it in the first place. I should have chosen more carefully to begin with.

"Then one day, at dusk, I noticed an old blue Toyota parked on the street, down the block from my house. It was such a piece of junk, I knew immediately that it

247

didn't belong on my street. I don't know how she got her hands on it, but I did know she lied! She exploited my weakness. Such an enemy is a formidable training partner. Grushenka had no idea how to find you. You had always found her. But everybody knows *my* address. I could just barely make out the skinny silhouette and the straight hair of the prostitute. She had come looking for *my* man at my house. I had to recover from the insult. She was starting her car. My muscles tightened, and I could barely breathe as I grabbed my keys and followed the car through the back alley, and onto the main road. My thoughts were concentrated on cleaning this abomination from my life at any price. I was not going to stop until I found out where she came from, who had put her there, and how to send her back. However long it took, I *was* going to take her apart.

"I put my foot to the floor just as the traffic light was about to turn red. My engine revved. Another car screeched to a stop, and I sailed through the intersection. Grushenka was three cars ahead, and didn't seem to know she was being followed until she had crossed one of the gates of the Venetian walls and led me into the circular labyrinth of the old city.

"Grushenka passed the old houses. She just missed an old woman carrying bags from the market. The street thickened with tourists crossing back and forth to visit the souvenir shops. One of the cars in between us turned off onto another road, honking. Grushenka looked into her rear view mirror and saw me. Grushenka flicked her headlights and accelerated through a tunnel of double-parked cars. She turned the wrong way down a one-way street.

248

I held my breath glancing both ways and banked to the right. I nearly knocked over a moped. The little blue Toyota swung to the side of the road barely avoiding a head-on collision and screeched and then stopped. I managed to get my car onto the sidewalk. The whore ran through a courtyard and then disappeared. I stared at the house with a wooden balcony on the upper floor. There was a sign that said, 'Dervish House'.

"As soon as she was inside, Grushenka melted into the arms of a Russian, and looked over her shoulder at me. Suddenly, the cabaret quieted down. Me, I felt self-conscious of my big purse and wild hair in the doorway. I walked across the room to Grushenka, in the arms of the Russian man. 'Liar! What right do you have to bother me at *my* house?'

" 'How dare *you* come here," she yelled. "Next *I* will come *into* your house.' She was not meek, and not pretty, either.

" 'I'll take out a restraining order on you. If you set one foot on my property, I'll have you arrested.'

" 'What do you know about being arrested? Ridiculous snob.'

" 'Ha! You don't respect the law or anything else. Watch out you little slut. I'll have you arrested!' I screamed the same thing again and again.

" 'You are ridiculous,' Grushenka echoed, and we both repeated these things. Customers crowded around us and tried to pull us apart, but the presence of men enraged us. Grushenka spit into my eyes. I grabbed the hair of Grushenka and tore a clump out.

"The men placed bets. I reached up and sunk my fingernails into the neck of the whore. It was a terrible fight. We rolled down steps. At the sight of blood, her Russian stepped into the circle around us and lifted me off the blonde. The other men shouted at him to get away, threatening to kill him. Grushenka looked up through her hair. Her shoulders were streaked with blood, and she was panting. The bartender hopped over the bar, seized me, and dragged me out the door. 'I'll have you arrested!' I screamed. 'All of you!' The bartender picked me up and thrust me into a cab. 'Turn around!' I yelled at the driver. 'I left my car there!' But the driver had his instructions. He was already driving. All he wanted to know was where I lived. As the taxi drove away, I saw the fight begin between the men from the club and the Russian. The Russian tried to break away. There were gunshots. I sank into my seat and watched the house tops glide past. I got an icy feeling, as if someone were there with me. I turned and saw pretty foreign face of Grushenka next to me, but we weren't in the backseat. I don't know where we were. I think we were floating next to each other under the water. I could taste the chorine. I was holding my breath, and it affected me like a dream where you can't scream. I could feel myself under her dark power. Grushenka hissed, *He came to rescue me. Now you let go of him.* I held onto her neck and didn't let go. She tried to leave. Those bruises on her neck were from *my* fingers. I struggled with her, *and I wished she was dead.*"

"*Chérie!*" Farouk said.

"You can go home and sleep at night, but *I wished her dead.*"

Chapter 41

How to Love a Woman

"The next day, Grushenka was dead," Niovi said.

"Indeed," Farouk said. "The autopsy found €120,000 of cocaine in thirty-three plastic bags in her stomach," Farouk said. "One of the bags had fused to her organs and saturated her body with the drug. She fell into the swimming pool and took your wish to the grave, Niovi. I should have cleared up my reputation and explained the situation to you, *chérie*, but I thought I had lost you, and . . . I wanted to get to the Boss of the underworld."

Niovi's face was flushed with excitement. "I was fighting her right up until the end. Now you know why I am angry. Because I *am* a monster!" Her black curls glistened in the moonlight as she sobbed into her hands. "She was sensitive! Could a dumb woman die of such an affliction?"

We looked at each other. "Life is short. *Everybody* has a round-trip ticket," I ventured.

"That is true, Mac," Giuseppe offered. "We all die. The future is no snob there."

Niovi went on crying. Farouk reached for her wet hand. She turned away from him, but did not let go of his hand.

The band launched into a Cuban salsa. Farouk leaned his slender frame forward in the lounge chair. "Are you ready to hear plan B?" he said.

My husband's eyes brightened. "Yes, what is plan B?"

"The lawyers will take it from here."

"You're leaving," my husband said.

"Yes," Farouk said. It was time to take positive action.

"And you'll go home?"

Leave home!

Niovi sat in the crook of Farouk's arm. If Farouk went away, there would be no one left to blame, and her life still wouldn't work. "Have they decided not to invest in Styxos?" I asked.

"They aren't satisfied that the risk factors are under control," Farouk said. "But they're negotiating investing with caveats involving increased police forces to deal with the corruption."

Nice answer. Farouk had a motorcycle, too. I had to laugh at the dumbfounded expression on my husband's face. Farouk's plan must have sounded reckless to my husband, who did not easily sail beyond native shores. Even living on the verge of Arabia, my husband thrived on stability. "But the country is united now. All the action is on the mainland," my husband argued. He watched Niovi flounder. Now Farouk would find out about island wives. It hardly mattered that she was stunning, or that she had street smarts. Why had we tried to understand this woman who had almost everything? Charon's socks and shoes were still wet with beer. He looked like he was on the verge of exploding. I'm sure he would have liked to tell her again what a peasant she was.

The waitress brought us another round on the house. We made the most of Farouk's company that evening, knowing that it might be the last time we would see him. "Tell him that story about your dad and your motorcycle," I said to my husband.

Charon smiled. "You want to hear that story again? O.K. I had a motorcycle, too, when I was seventeen. I crashed it, and almost killed myself. I was in the hospital, and my father came to visit. After a while, I asked him, 'Where is the motorcycle?'"

" 'Don't worry,' my father said, 'It's being fixed.'

"Then he came to the hospital again. I asked him, 'Is it fixed yet?'

" 'No, another week.'

"He kept coming and saying it wasn't fixed yet. Finally I confronted him and said, 'You keep on telling me next week!'

" 'Boy, are you crazy? You almost died. I don't have the money for a tombstone, and you think I'm going to fix your motorcycle?' They all laughed at Charon's story.

"The moral is, buy Paris stone," I said. "An apartment, or better yet, a whole *pierre de taille* building."

Niovi had perked up listening.

"You can live off the rents, and if you really must travel, you can always rent yours out, and pay for the trip. When it comes time to buy another one, mortgage out. Just don't sell the Paris stone! We'll come and visit."

Chapter 42

Che

Giuseppe started laughing first. The people at the other tables turned around and watched us laughing. We wanted to savour Farouk and Niovi before they pulled up roots and left Styxos. The night had been too short. The threat of scandal was finally blowing over. When we were about to say goodbye, the Cuban singers came to our table. Niovi sat on the edge of her seat.

"Can you play 'Che Guevara'?" I asked.

A big woman started to sing the heroic folk song.

My husband said, "We remember Che who spread the overthrow of dictatorships across Latin America."

I put my arm around him. "My husband identifies with Che Guevara because I am so oppressive." My jacket opened onto a tight red camisole.

Farouk's blue eyes swept down my body. His hair had grown wild, sticking straight up over his sunken cheekbones.

"It's a popular song," I told Niovi. "A lot of bands play it, even French bands."

They sang, *Che-che* — *il-lus-tri-ous Leader.* They swayed from side to side in syncopated steps to the bongo and said *Che-che* to the sax and the reincarnation of Che, the accused. The singer's voice was deep.

First of all I don't regard only Argentina as my native country but the whole of America.

They sang, *Che-che*, and stepped from side to the side, smiling widely.

Besides, you can't call it interference if I want to give myself — up to my blood — to a cause, "Che-che," of a people seeking liberation from a tyranny that ON ITSELF brings armoured interference of a foreign power with AEROPLANES, weapons and military advisors.

The song finished, and Niovi looked around in glee. The suggestion of an outside threat had quelled our own little battle. "That was good," she said.

"We are going in the other direction," Charon said. "We can be proud that Styxos is on the verge of reuniting with the European Union peacefully. If Che were alive today, he might have to try something more civilised to change things around here."

"Today it's more shocking to do something emotional-ly intelligent," Niovi said, "like expressing our feelings." Niovi hadn't moved from the crook of Farouk's arm. She laid her hand on Farouk's knee. A Grecian smile crept across her lips. Life was short again. Time would devour them both soon enough, but for now it was a question of rebuilding.

The conversation became animated. "Farouk and Niovi will probably end up owning all the stone in Paris," said Giuseppe, "and Charon and Mac will drift around the Orient humming *Che Che!*"

We said goodbye and pretended to ignore our two friends as they looked at each other in the elevator. "I'll bet that's not her real hair—," Niovi was saying when Farouk disarmed her with a kiss so soft that she must have forgotten where she was. The doors closed.

"I'm going to miss them," I said to my husband.

Chapter 43

Gross Domestic Evolution

I played in the yard with our big-tummied children, fed and bathed them noisily, and put them to bed. Life had fallen into a familiar pattern at home.

The children slept like angels. Then, Charon came home and started yelling and woke them up. "Get ready! We're late. All eyes will be on us, now that we were all over the tabloids as Niovi's 'extended family'."

"Should I wear this neutral outfit, or the red dress?"

"Give them what they want. It's their national day, so wear the dress. You're keeping my options open in that dress," he said without looking at me.

"It does look like a flag," I said. I tied the bow at the side. "I could even be German in a pinch." I turned my back to my husband so he could fasten my gold necklace. He didn't get the hint. "Can you help me out with this?"

He fastened the gold chain around my neck. "There," he said.

"Now everyone will know I'm taken."

He didn't smile.

"You didn't tell me I look nice," I prodded.

He looked cowed, and I discovered that naming what I saw him doing slowed him up. It made his back straighten, his tone soften. The reason he was able to carry out his evil at all was because he thought it was covert — no one would notice anyway. This logic hid from him his point of departure from normal society.

"Strange man," the women at the Ladies' Consortium had commented about Charon, but he didn't notice and probably thought, They can't tell what I'm really doing. He was what he thought we couldn't see.

Oh if only he were working on some pleasant surprise for us all! But a diabolical snake had woven itself into the bottom of his identity. He was just the holes where it wasn't. I could hear that short-haired woman in front of the library, "Fight back! Women, fight back!" I wonder how many lives she's changed.

When Charon was in the shower, I put his SIM card in the SIM card reader again. There were more women than the last time I had looked. He was operating fulltime. One name looked familiar, and I selected the message.

cannot pay for shoes for our daughter. can you come to the shoe store at 11?

Our daughter! The room spun. I sank to the floor, and everything went black.

The first thing I heard when I came to was the shower turning off. I awoke lying on the floor at the foot of the bed just as Charon came out of the bathroom door. The SIM card reader was next to my hand. I pushed it under the bed at the same time as he pushed the bedroom door open.

He stood over me and demanded, "What are you doing?"

"Looking at the ceiling."

"For Christ's sake, you'll get your dress dirty lying on the floor."

"I think we need to paint the ceiling."

"Not now!" It was time to show off his trophy wife in her red dress.

Summer was coming to an end. We drove along the jagged mountains in silence, past the fragrant orange groves. The plains were in bloom leading to the port. This time, I wasn't confronting him with it. All he ever did was try to find out what I knew so he could tailor his lies. This time I would keep it to myself. I wanted to scream! I would handle it alone. I didn't expect to be seeing Farouk and Niovi again.

The houses in the formerly occupied territory looked familiar in the twilight, with architecture similar to the other side's, although there were fewer of them. Less economic activity, less consumerism. Less people.

When we arrived, we took off our shoes and walked on the pebble beach along the seaside. The waves lapped at our feet in the clean water, with its thousand little fish swimming up to the shore. It was good. It was priceless. *How would the next generation advance if it couldn't breathe?* Enough of GDP. I would mention having another measure of progress tonight to anyone who would listen. GDP had become such a Christmas tree contest. I pondered

GDE as a new indicator of environmental, intellectual, educational, and spiritual evolution as we approached the tower, a perfect place for a reception. After a glass of Santorini white and a solo from *La Traviata*, I noticed the sound of whispering coming from a group of women behind us.

"What are those women talking about?" I asked my husband, who was bringing my drink outside.

He listened for a moment. "About the homogeneity of Muslim and Christian island blood."

"You don't mean you are the same race after all this."

"That's right. They proved it with a DNA test. There is no physical difference between a Muslim and Christian Styxan. We're all the same after all. The funny thing is that the results also showed that our homogenous island blood is also distinctive from the mainland communities, Christian and Muslim."

"That's great! So what's the big secret?"

"The study. It was suppressed."

"Unbelievable."

"Nobody knows about it, and nobody wants to be the bearer of bad news."

"We *insist* on using faulty measuring sticks." I was still reeling from Hercules' contradictions over our backdoor, and now this. Styxan blood had evolved from some more complicated mix implicating Persians, Egyptians, Syrians, Italians, French and others — a source of embarrassment for the 'purebred'. To think that the melting pot attribute that Americans were so proud of was a source of embarrassment on Styxos!

We moved on to another group where the guests had taken up the issue of human trafficking. "It doesn't make sense to spend so much on infrastructure if there's no return for society," one woman was saying. She had an influential ear bent to her like a vine around a thistle. "Why not improve Styxos in exchange for all the investment? Think of it as an opportunity cost."

Good work! And there was Farouk, his shoulders square in a black suit. My heart leapt. He was still here. Farouk was the one person who would understand the emotional commerce underway. He was on his cell phone speaking to someone in Russian. He would understand that if caveats weren't added to the tender proposals, the island women would make life hell. This time, they would have to listen.

"Mac," he said at last.

"Farouk. It's been —" I looked at my shoes. "A long time."

"Yesss."

I caught my breath, and laughed. He touched me from a distance again! I found my bearings. "How are you bearing the weight of your occupational hazards?"

Farouk watched me out of the corner of his eye. "With a sense of duty and freedom."

"We met each other too late. What did my husband advise you to do?"

"To marry Niovi. If she becomes a good wife, I'll be happy. If not, I'll become a philosopher."

"Is that what I should do?"

"Apparently."

"My husband can have me but he can't see me. You can see me, but you can't have me." I saw my reflection in Farouk's sparkling eyes. "Maybe it's better this way."

"It's definitely much better this way." He remembered his gallantry in the warm summer breeze and held up his plate. He offered me his charred meat. I lunged for his eggplant.

The entire island will be free.

Chapter 44

Mirage Transfer

The reception buzzed with pushy women, *Imagine the good publicity for the transport company if it cleans up Styxos.* Farouk moved us into the circle around the President of Styxos and his wife. I told them that white slavery had caught the interest of European Union human rights groups. "Big business is *avec nous* on this one."

"You are French!" It was the Styxan First Lady.

"Franco-American."

"You are the person I wanted to talk to. It's so hard finding people around here who speak French. Now that Styxos is in the European Union, we really need to know what is going on in meetings held in French."

"And it's not enough to understand. You have to participate."

The First Lady was indulgent, but the president had almost turned away.

"Respectfully, Mr. President," I said, grabbing his arm. "Have you seen the women's infrastructure proposal?"

The president's expression hardened. "My wife handles most of the women's issues."

"Respectfully, Mr. President, it's not just a women's issue. Forced labour on Styxos includes men and boys, too. The police just found a container full of Roman men and boys who had been abducted and forced to work on a construction site outside of the city. Surely you heard about it."

The president scoffed. "That proposal is the triumph of wishful thinking over reason. You call that an infrastructure project?" the president said. "Do you have any idea what percentage of Styxos's tourist industry depends on so-called forced labour?"

"None," said Farouk, appearing at my side. "The money is being funnelled off of Styxos. She is the net loser."

In Farouk's presence, the president's attitude toward me changed abruptly. I had his full attention and took the opportunity to describe the Ladies' Consortium demands. "We demanded that for each tender accepted, five percent of the overall project cost had to be spent on augmenting the police force to combat drugs, arms and human trafficking. Another five percent would go for shutting down cabarets, and two percent for additional staff for increased customs operations on Styxos with legitimate police officers, which would entail detailed interviews before, during and after anyone entered with a short-term work visa."

The president addressed me directly. "It is refreshing to meet a woman who is so sure of herself." His wife tried to cut me off, but the president ignored her. "Madam." The president touched my elbow when he said this. "Why don't you let me take you up in that tower for twenty minutes?" He indicated a stone staircase. He ogled me as he took a sip of his martini. "There is a distracting view of the harbour that you can watch."

Farouk's eyebrows rose.

The president's wife nodded at me in acquiescence.

"Yuck," I said.

"There goes your husband's transfer," said the president, excusing himself and his wife.

"What was that?" My husband came up and filled the presidential void.

"Small talk," Farouk said.

"So, we meet again, Farouk," my husband said. "I am glad to see you moving freely here on Bastille Day among the useless and the merely envious. How are you getting along?"

"Barely managing. Fortunately, I was able to remember an exhaustive list of Grushenka's clients," he glanced at a group of heavy hitter politicians crowded around the *hors d'oeuvres*, "who with a little, shall we say, encouragement, had the will to shorten the tender negotiations. Not to say that I am personally *out of the woods*, as you say. I'm not. This romantic nightmare is the kind of thing that I usually see happening to other people, not me. We are struggling. There is no doubt about that."

"The complexities of the Styxos woman cannot be underestimated," my husband said. "You've been bewitched, as I'm sure you are continuing to find out. I know a good doctor."

Farouk laughed. "We have come to an agreement."

"You are both lucky," I said. "She is delightfully charming."

"Fascinating is the word. I'm afraid I have fallen under her spell. Right now, Niovi is looking to buy a small building. She's upset that there is absolutely nothing for sale at any price in the 7th arrondissement of Paris."

"That won't stop her," said my husband. "She is a powerful woman. Her Styxan stubbornness can be useful under the right circumstances. Like shopping for real estate. You have figured out by now that in many ways, Styxos is more of a matriarchal society than what you're used to. The mainland's inquisition against women who were connected with Mother Earth left Styxos virtually untouched during three hundred years of your witch hunts. While you were burning a million women at the stake, we went on spoiling them. Beware of our modern witches."

Farouk ran his hand through his hair. "You're not suggesting that Niovi really could have —"

"No, of course she didn't kill Grushenka." My husband patted Farouk on the back. The Frenchman looked relieved.

"But," I said, "things are different here. You have already noticed that time passes much slower on the island."

"Yes, it has a cyclical quality."

"Exactly. It's redundant. While on the mainland, the medieval persecutors of feminine religiosity held devotion to Mary suspect, Styxans have always invoked the Mother of God on a daily basis, and still do. 'Mother Mary!'"

Charon went on, "And Styxan wives are not used to taking no for an answer. If you don't lay down the law, Niovi will take advantage of you."

"You must consider yourself lucky to have an American wife."

"American wives are another problem."

Here came Vanessa wiping the tears from her eyes. Vanessa's husband was going back to Africa, this time for good. It was no longer a secret. She had turned him out. It had already been decided without us, and there was nothing anyone could do. Just like Irma Nicholaides last year when her unfaithful husband ran over her foot as she was getting into his Mercedes. They weren't rich, but they managed to be spoiled anyway. Families crumbling all around us. Lawyers were crawling all over them. Was it my imagination, or was it the new middle-class that was the most manipulated?

Since she was crying, I tried to hold up the conversation myself, and told her that our children would be glad that her children would still be there to play with. "Alex's tummy is disappearing." I put my hand on my stomach and caressed it, to show her. "She's becoming a big girl." Vanessa nodded in sympathy, still crying. We hugged, and Farouk tried to cheer Vanessa up, making a little speech about having strength in the face of adversity. She nodded and slipped away.

Farouk turned to me. "What were you saying about your daughter?"

"Just that her big tummy is disappearing." I put my hand on my stomach again.

He looked at me inquisitively.

"She's not a baby anymore."

"And you? Are you going to have any more babies?"

"I would have liked to," I said, "But Charon didn't want anymore, and now . . ."

My husband had come back with another glass of wine. "And are you going to have children, Farouk?"

"I hope so. Certainly not now, though. Maybe in a few years. I come from a big, happy family. It was very hectic, it's true, but when we all sat down at the table, there was a very nice ambiance. My parents didn't plan it that way, and they understood the feeling of not wanting any children at all. That's how I felt for a long time. But from what I am told, when you see your first baby, you want to have another, and then the second leads to the third."

It sounded nice in principle, but I couldn't imagine Farouk settling down. I hoped he wasn't taking Niovi for another ride.

"Well, you are right about the first leading to the second," my husband said, "but the travelling life is hard on children," "They like stability and need roots. By the time you get set up in another country, there is almost no time left to do your work before you have to go."

"*Au contraire*," I said. "Travelling is a great education for children."

"Yes," Farouk said, "We can spread the *civilisation française*. Are you still involved with the women's group, Mac? There is a certain human trafficking problem you would like to see resolved. Isn't it?" Farouk was still looking at my tummy.

"Why *not* make Styxos a better place in exchange for all the investment?" I said. Farouk stood firm, but the conversation stopped there. Farouk seemed to have already given all he could. He politely agreed, "Everyone will do what they can, surely, especially knowing that if some caveats aren't added to the tender proposals, the women will make life hell. I know from personal experience."

It was time to go. Farouk reached for my bare arms and ended up having to catch me, swimming in his emotional wave. He kissed me on both cheeks. I was afraid to think how much of us Farouk would be taking with him. I was afraid to be alone.

Charon drove me home. Watching the mountain shadows in the dark, I wondered what happened to our impossible happiness. Didn't we have everything we needed? Or was it expectations? There was a wilderness of expectations that accompanied me into slumber, as if I were practicing for that final passage. I had had two children. Now we were marooned on Styxos, where the average number of children per family was two. In the EU, it was closer to three, maybe 2.8. Could all of our complex reasoning be a mere expression of the collective national emotion? Math: there were infinite wrong answers, and only one right answer. I'd slipped into counting children: 2 plus 2.8 equals 4.8 divided by 2 equals 2.4 . . .

The Last Laugh

Justin tried to wash his father's car with the hose. Charon came running out of the kitchen to yell at him. "Don't waste the water!" This shipwreck couldn't be the man I had married. It had to be the ghost of Charon's father. Where was my husband? I wanted a real man; I got a real animal. We had spent our youth in each other's arms, accompanied each other through the birth of our children, and since he had grown old at the age of forty seven, his ideals disappeared one by one. I watched him regress to childhood. Since he had his mother, the only role left for me was governess. He was ranting with all his might. His nervous outbursts had become frequent and damaging to the rest of us. Maybe acupuncture would help.

Now that I knew what was going on, I couldn't let him damage my son anymore. I headed Charon off. "No need to share your clairvoyance with us."

Charon's fit subsided, and he put the hose away. It hadn't occurred to me yet that his hysteria was a hopeful sign. It meant that his naughtiness had not yet ripened into evil.

"Guess who is pregnant," Charon said.

"Not me," I said.

"Correct."

I'd wanted a third child and got a teenager. "Alright, who?"

"Farouk."

Things were starting to make sense again. "Who's the mother?"

"Niovi, of course."

"Are they still moving to France?"

"Yes. He says they'll go back right after the wedding."

"You mean the wedding's on?"

"You have understood everything."

"Amazing! Your sister caught a fish. Maybe all that jealousy was just hormones."

"Hormones are the cause of a lot of trouble," he muttered.

I hung my head. Could I have been wrong about Farouk? "So, who told you about the baby?"

"Farouk. We had lunch. It just goes to show, you never know."

"And what about the infrastructure bid?"

"He thinks he has gotten it done."

"Really! Well, what did he say?"

"Not much."

"Well, what?"

"What do you think? He convinced them going ahead with the tender would be too risky without the 10% for the human trafficking issue. He says with the French train company making a provision in its bid to stop the skin trade, the other companies will have to follow suit in order to compete. It's part of the Grushenka package."

"Perfect. That ought to be enough to get the government to make it a requirement, I mean, as a gesture." I turned around, but Charon had walked off.

There had been a recent trafficking case in the European Union Court of Human Rights, and as a result, an important precedent had been set for dealing with structural tolerance for human trafficking on the continent.

Niovi leaned across the wall. "Mac, I have a small favour to ask you."

"I heard the good news! Is the wedding on?"

"It's on, and I need a bridesmaid."

"If you're asking me to be your bridesmaid, I'd love to." I was a little stunned.

"You got the role, Mac. I don't have many real friends, and since we are already distant . . . sisters—"

"You knew all along. Why didn't you tell me?"

"Because our mothers never talk about it, except the time my mother was crying over your father-in-law."

I reached over the wall to hug her. "I would love to do it, Niovi."

I found my husband waiting with a dignified air of distraction in his black Mercedes. I grinned at him from my camouflage, a beige dress. I got in beside him in his black suit and red tie, and we were off to the wedding.

Part of the *Niovi* package was a big wedding up in her mother's mountain village. We followed the line of cars up the winding road, my husband cursing and passing the cars in front of us on narrow curves. The views of the mountain lakes were breathtaking, but I was trying not to look out the window. My husband finally manoeuvred the Mercedes into a makeshift parking space and lanced off toward the church.

The ancient village was well preserved. Shops selling raw hazelnuts and lace lined the main thoroughfare in front of a Venetian church with pointed arches. The guests were decked out in all manner of gaud, and the flowers, though real, were garbled with so much gold tape and glitter that they looked plastic. The tall cobblestones in the street were a trap for those of us in high-heels. I noticed that the village women all wore flats. A few of the female guests climbed treacherously on tiptoe to the church in their high heels, but I had to take mine off. On the church steps, an old hunchback woman grabbed Niovi's mother's arm and inquired after all the children in Niovi's extended family.

I met Niovi at the side door as planned. My husband was already there beside Farouk, who was struggling to retie his tie. Farouk and Niovi were done up with lots of hair gel and starch and looked like photographs. I busied myself with arranging Niovi's veils and tried to get her to relax. "Where is my bouquet?" Niovi asked. The florist had forgotten to deliver it.

I thought fast. A small thing like this could send Niovi into one of her tempests. "Niovi, honestly, I didn't want to mention it, but as your bride's maid, I feel it's my duty to tell you that those bouquets over there look fake. I know it was a mistake for the florist to forget your bouquet, but it seems like a heaven-sent opportunity to me. Look at these bougainvilleas back here." Behind the church was a terrace laced with the brilliant pink flowers. "Let me cut you a bouquet of these. They're so natural and so vibrant, like you."

The terror vanished from her expression. "Mac, you're absolutely right. I'll help you. Let's hurry." Niovi slipped off her shoes and we used my nail scissors to gather together the blazing bouquet of pink flowers.

The church was full enough, but everyone fit in it, not like at other weddings in Styxos where most of the guests had to wait outside. Granted, the guests were all on the bride's side, but I would have thought the star would have attracted a much bigger crowd. So much for religion. Charon whispered, "The square looks like a football field with tables for two thousand. You'll see. The peasants skip the church ceremony, but they show up to eat." My husband laughed. "What about Niovi? She looks chubby."

"She's not chubby. She's glowing."

The ceremony began. It was a long wedding. Everyone noticed the groom's look of willing submission. Farouk made the fundamental promise of fidelity although he couldn't have understood the language. Smiles spread across our faces. Brave Niovi looked scared. She understood all of the holy jargon. To, "Do you reject the glamour of Satan?" She nodded in obeisance at the three priests, her ox-eyes wide under the black eyeliner and the emerald shadow we had picked out.

Charon seemed to take a diabolical pleasure in helping Niovi and Farouk get married. The ceremony was long. Beads of sweat rolled down my bare legs. In the heat of the church, I took back any question I'd raised on Styxan religiosity and prayed for conclusion. What a relief when the priest finally put the wreaths on Farouk's and Niovi's heads and led us in a circle around the altar. The photographers went wild over the wreaths attaching their heads with a white ribbon. As we completed our first circle around the altar Farouk's simple stare expressed his longing to believe, a reminder of the sanctity of our own marriage bonds, since what else is a marriage if not a building block of society? It's no coincidence that the French use the word for 'whore house' for the dissolution of business, morals and everything else in society . . . I kicked myself for thinking this in a church.

We led the handsome couple in our last circle with white wreaths on their heads connected by a ribbon, a timeless representation of their union. It could have been an ancient ritual scene from a Grecian urn. Niovi wore her white dress with classical elegance. It fit like a glove. Farouk had settled into his role like water in a glass. Everyone who saw him in his black tuxedo that day said he was a good catch.

The ceremony was over. The photographers crouched before us aiming their zoom lenses. "There's Niovi's mother," I said to my husband, "to the left in the stunning blue-silver dress, and the blonde must be Niovi's stepmother, there in the rust-colour dress from Taylord's. I'm glad she didn't wear the same dress as the new woman."

An elderly woman in front of me turned around and grinned. "Niovi's mother did wear that same rust-colour dress to the dinner we held for them *last night!* Here's her picture in the paper — pretty darn good for an octogenarian!" I noticed there were several women holding the same magazine picture. Hence, the new wife was wearing 'Niovi's mother's dress. It didn't fit quite right, as if it had been borrowed, like the father of the bride. "It's rusty!" the old woman laughed. *It's rusty,* ran through the chorus. The new wife's face flushed.

Church bells sounded. The newlyweds ducked, as the guests threw the rice into the breeze. My husband pressed into Farouk's hand a small envelope with our 20 shekels in it. Judging by the number of people present with similar envelopes the newlyweds had enough to buy a modest country house to go with their *pied à terre*. "Thanks, Mac!" Niovi beamed.

"Good catch, Niovi," I told her again. I guessed it *wouldn't* be me who Farouk would be carrying onto the Poseidon.

"I know. Sorry to take him away from you, Mac."

"Take him away? You didn't take him away. You married him."

A shape floated past my peripheral vision. I looked over my shoulder. Of course, there was no one, but I could have sworn I heard, *You goose. Now he's Mackenzie's forever.*

Suddenly, the crowd scattered. "Oh!" they all said. Niovi had fallen down.

"Somebody pushed me!" Niovi said. But there was no one behind her. "I felt a hand on my back."

There was a murmur in the crowd. *Evil eye.* The acolytes picked her up off the ground, and she arranged her white ruffles. The singer's manager stepped behind her to protect her back.

An envious spirit pushed her.

People advised the newlyweds from all angles, *You are too lucky. Be careful not to arouse their jealousy.*

Niovi raised her head above the crowd. She caught up her white skirts and proceeded like the crest of a wave from her birthplace.

Chapter 46

Passports

I was hoping for the kids' sake I could keep the family together until we got a transfer off of Styxos. In the morning, Charon was hostile about a mess the kids had left in the bathroom, and raised his voice. "You should have put their clothes away instead of leaving them on the floor!" Now he was never nice. Did something happen at work?

After he left, I searched his drawers. There was a purple box under his shirts that I didn't remember seeing, his hidden stash of condoms. The box had been opened, and there were five condoms in it.

What a fool he made of me. They say that men don't change, but mine was a shape shifter, always shifting for the worse. I had gone into emergency mode. I could feel my body metabolizing itself. I had lost three kilos since the business with the SMS messages. It was clear that the joint pain was permanent. Now my arms felt like they would drop off my body.

On the way home he phoned saying he was outside of the divorced mother of Justin's best friend's apartment, asking if he should pick up Justin. "The arrangement was that they would drop Justin off in an hour."

"Well I'm right here. I can get him."

"Please don't flirt with her in front of Justin."

"You must be joking."

"I don't want him to see any promiscuity."

"Drive this foolishness from your imagination!"

There was no convincing him. He would never give in. He was *unable* to control his beast. I wasn't going to bring the condoms up again. I would watch and wait, and when the time was right, I would outsmart him. We continued in our lie. As long as the truth was veiled, we were but a tragedy.

We dragged ourselves to the French embassy to pick up the children's passports. My shoulders stiffened when I saw Farouk enter the embassy. He told the security guard he had some business with the Ambassador, and caught me out of the corner of his eye. He realized that I was already watching him and came into the waiting room to say hello.

"Hello married man," I said. "You must be excited about the baby. You're going to be so happy."

"Yes, we will. Thank you. I feel much better. And you?"

"I'm here for the children's passports," I said. "It's done. They're French."

"Ah! It's finished. But what will you do when it comes time for your son's military service? If he comes back into the country, they will get him." On Styxos, the boys had to serve in the army for over two years before going to college.

I shook my head. "No."

"But even if he comes for a visit, to see his grandmother, they will get him."

"No." I was still shaking my head. It would all work out in the end.

"True, it's a long time away. I'm sure the laws are changing. But he has his *racines* here. Do you know what those are, Mac? Roots."

No. I had lived like a gypsy for a long time, always saying goodbye, always leaving.

"Ah, Niovi is here!" His eyes lit up. I heard her voice in the corridor. I went into the hallway, and he called, "Niovi!" from behind me.

She came into the room, brown eyes beaming. She was wearing a red coat, and her cheeks had grown rosy framed in shiny, black curls.

"You look radiant!" I said. "I am so glad about the baby. We are so happy for you." I suppose even *I* was a little jealous, but still very, very happy.

Niovi performed the sign of the cross once, and then twice, to ward off any evil spirit we might have invoked with our compliments. She was struggling to compose herself. She had to be modern and productive, to grow beyond herself now. She had already broadened her parameters, especially around her middle.

The singer enjoyed the extra attention. "I am hungry all the time. It's the funniest thing to be obliged to gain a kilo a month. I think I'm going to like it. So far I've been eating lots of yogurt, and I bring these crackers with me wherever I go. Would you like one?"

"Thank you." I took a cracker. "Maybe it will rub off on me." We munched them together, trying not to drop crumbs on the waiting room floor. "Where are you going on your honeymoon?"

"Jordan," Niovi said. "We're taking a boat, the Poseidon. It stops there for four days, and then goes on to France."

The Poseidon! My jaw must have dropped. He really was taking her to the boat in my dream. The conversation dwindled.

"We might not see you again before we go," said Farouk. "There are others I have to see, to say goodbye."

What others? Others like Ambassadors, surely, and business people who could affect his career back home. Or all the random people his eclectic taste had brought him over the past few years, an old man in the street where they lived, the mayor, democrats, socialists, atheists, machos. The theme wouldn't matter to someone who entered your reality, effortlessly making it his for the time he was with you. It was his closing move. He was going to say goodbye to all of them in succession, carrying out a necessary order of operations. I would just have to listen for the sound and fall with the dominos. "You say goodbye a lot."

He glared as if to say, *A lot of people love me.* He was immobilized under the weight of a responsibility his wife was learning to live with. The taming of Niovi would not be simple.

Monsieur Montaigne's door opened, and we kissed each other goodbye. M. Montaigne signalled me to follow him into his office. "It is done. They are French!" Thanks to M. Montaigne. The embassy was short of staff, and M. Montaigne struggled with registering the children at the consulate and filing their passport applications himself.

"I am sorry I am taking so long. There have been a few changes around here."

"We've been working on this for four years," I said. "*You* are the fastest official we've met." Outside the tinted embassy window, I watched my husband's dark figure cross the street. I went to get him from the waiting room and we showed him the passports. "Oh, good!" he said, overjoyed. Our heads were touching as we looked at the children' pictures in their new passports.

M. Montaigne laughed at us.

"Are you allowed to accept gifts?" I asked M. Montaigne.

"No."

"Then we won't tell." My husband placed a small blue box on the table in front of M. Montaigne. "It's just a token, not of great value." M. Montaigne took the box, touched. "But why are you giving me this?"

"Because we like you," Charon said. In it was a pair of silver cufflinks in the shape of the symbol of Menandros. "Do you know about Menandros? He ruled over the kingdom of Bactria, which is present-day Afghanistan, Uzbekistan, and Tajikistan. Menandros met a Buddhist holy man. Through Socratic questioning, they had a meeting of minds, and the process of the king's enlightenment began. The dialog between the two men continued for days with hundreds of questions, of which only a partial record remains. Suddenly, the whole world shook six times, lightning flashed, the ocean roared, and the gods rained flowers on the earth, as Greek logic encountered Buddhist wisdom, and the Dharma-truth, *dustless and stainless* flowed into Menandros." My husband had a Styxan phrase engraved on each of the cufflinks, *Whatever is of the nature to arise, is of the nature to stop.*

Chapter 47

Dharma-Chakra Wheel

At home, I had given up on getting Charon to come to the table. You can only fight back with so much loving-kindness, I thought as I laid all the food that his mother had cooked out on the terrace and spooned salad onto each plate. I cut up the children's lamb, and gave them spoons for their rice and poured the drinks. With a serving of each dish on each plate, I went to lie down on the bed and read. Pretty soon, my husband came to investigate, and then gruffly called everyone to come outside and eat on the terrace. We all sat down. Then I brought out a bottle of champagne and passed the passports around the table. I got my husband to pop the cork.

"Mommy, we're a family!" Alex said.

His mother walked by the table. "It might rain," she said looking at a puff of white in the blue sky.

"*Saba*, why don't you eat?" said Justin. There was plenty of room at the table, but there was still no getting her to sit down with us.

"I will eat later."

"When?" Justin persisted.

"Maybe tomorrow," my husband said without looking up from his plate. He soaked a piece of hard bread in olive oil and ate it with the salad of small cucumbers and deep red tomatoes with mint leaves sprinkled on top. The lonely cloud had floated in front of the sun. My husband looked up at it. "It might rain."

"It might rain somewhere, but not here," I said. Travel agencies were offering tourists their money back if it rained during their vacations to Styxos. It seemed like it hadn't rained in decades. "Do you want to bet?" I asked.

My husband looked up at the cloud in front of the sun. "It might rain in the mountains."

"It might rain in London."

His mother was carrying a ladder across the backyard to pick some figs. The fig tree spread its leaves like wide hands and several branches hung near the ground, but the purplest globes were on the top. She climbed up and down, washed the figs and sliced off the skins, she cut them in half, and placed a plate of the pink fruit on the table with four forks. We crunched on the fig seeds and tasted the ripeness of summer's end.

My husband opened the newspaper. "Another article about Israel. Look at this guy! He just discovered he's Jewish. Who else was it? That U.S. Secretary of State. She claimed she didn't know that she was Jewish. It's pretty much a prerequisite for working in the White House. Nobody believes she discovered that she was Jewish after she got into office. I'm sorry, but it doesn't happen that way!"

His mother set the ladder down. "My dear." She had an imploring look on her face as she went on in Styxan. "We didn't want to tell you, but since you bring it up . . ."

My husband quickly swallowed his fig whole.

His mother sat down at the table next to him. "My mother was Jewish."

His mouth dropped open. *Me?* He looked at his children. *Us?*

"Just like your father changed his name when he got his first job, and then converted when he married me, my mother had converted from Judaism the generation before. We didn't want to tell you because people are so hostile toward anyone who is not 'pure'."

"That's OK," I said, patting his hand. "We're all Styxans."

"Why didn't you tell me?" My husband exclaimed.

"The fruit is not in the roots of the tree," she said. She pointed up to the branches. The children followed her fingers up to the purple figs in the branches.

Charon came home late so he didn't have to see me that night, and slept late so he didn't have to see us in the morning. I gave up negotiating to get him to come to the table at lunchtime. Charon's father had eaten in a separate room from the rest of the family. The habit had been ingrained from birth. Charon came out of his mother's room and started cursing the kids' clothes on the bathroom floor. It was his father talking.

Never again would I let him, whoever he was, hurt me like this. Now I pre-empted his tantrums. I didn't ask what he thought or try to converse with him at all. That would be like opening a floodgate to the hatred he felt for me. Instead, I cut into his tirade, "Aren't you going to say good morning to Justin?" I said. I wasn't letting Charon get away with bullying Justin now that I knew there was no way out for Justin. Charon had never read a parenting book.

Now that I knew the extent of his promiscuity, when Charon came home, I would wake up and not be able to get back to sleep. Some nights, I felt nauseous and had to take medicine for my stomach. I had to do something. I couldn't have another of his temper explosions damage the kids any further.

Farouk's company won the bid for the railway construction with a provision for 'social stability' to stop the human trafficking. Everyone was excited about the new railway. He had to postpone his honeymoon to accept the contract. The Ladies' Consortium had won, and even looked forward to involving men in some of their upcoming functions.

The house was painted, and the children were in school. On some levels, our family was thriving, with the children growing fast and speaking three languages.

My husband took the next day off, so we'd had plenty of time to test each other's nerves. "I don't have anymore socks!" I informed Charon, who wasn't listening, but I went on, "You know, the average person loses 5 socks a year. There are 6 billion people in the world. That's 30 billion socks a year missing. Where are all those socks?" I opened Charon's drawer to find three times as many socks as he had ever had, apparently those of all the male members of the extended family, and none of mine.

The smell of burnt orange cake filled the kitchen. There was a letter waiting for me on the table. I opened it and read. " 'We are pleased to inform you' — Oh wow!

'Assistant Curator of Palaeolithic Archaeology at the museum of natural history in Paris'!" I sat down, about to evaporate. My turn to taste freedom. How much freedom would there be in just disappearing? Up until now, I'd resisted the seeping irony that we would only be free fulfilling our duty. I wondered whether Charon had learned that yet.

What would Niovi do?

I handed the letter to my husband and watched his eyes widen.

I had a wonderful feeling of wellbeing as I drifted off to sleep that night. I was woken in the middle of the night by the sound of Charon's talking on the terrace outside. I got out of bed and tiptoed across the floor where I could make out what he was saying.

"Of course she's still charming. She's blonde, with an excellent figure . . . . Yes, I'll bring her to the port at fourteen hundred hours on Wednesday. Yes, you have a deal. Two thousand will be fine. Just make sure she doesn't show up in town again…That's right. Take her under."

Chapter 48

Endgame

I lay awake the next three nights, my brain racing in my double bed with the children. It was Thursday. At least I knew where my children were: they were on either side of me holding my hands.

All that university education and travel had been lost on Charon. He was a spiritual peasant. He'd been educated beyond his intelligence. I had lost my shine since our marriage, and he could only see other women. When I was growing up, my mother always emphasized that one day I wouldn't have my looks to rely on. I'd been planning for this moment all my life. Time to do something ethereal.

My brain exercised the arguments I wasn't able to lay on him during the day. Despite the sadness for what could have been, I knew Charon was so sick he was gone. Under different circumstances, I might have felt that I should stay and take care of him. Lucky for me his evil had absolved me of the obligation. He was guilty. I was free to go. Time to cut my losses without bad conscience, if it wasn't too late.

When the light of dawn crept into the cracks in the shutters, I slid out from between my babies and stole from the room. I knew Niovi's number by heart. I listened to the ring tone and prayed that she was alone: I did not want to alert the male conspiracy. Niovi sounded sleepy. "I'm sorry to wake you up. Niovi, you're not going to believe what is going on here."

"What is it Mac?"

"Charon. He wants to get rid of me. I know this sounds crazy."

"What?"

"I think he's planning on selling me!"

Niovi gasped. "Mac, you need help."

I heard Farouk's voice in the background. "What is it, chérie?"

"Nothing. It's Mac."

"Is she in trouble?"

I bit my lip. How did he know?

"Yes, she's in trouble. Now let me see you *prove* that you can help a woman in need."

Niovi handed Farouk the phone. "Mackenzie, tell me exactly what has happened." After I explained, he said, "No, you don't sound that crazy. In fact, it makes sense, at least on Styxos. You were right not to let on that you suspect anything: Rule number one in the *Art of War* by Sun-Tzu. The enemy will not know how much force it needs to fight you if he doesn't know you are fighting back. Did you say he arranged a meeting at the port at fourteen hundred hours on Wednesday?"

"Yes."

"That is very useful information, Mackenzie. Thank you. You have helped tremendously, and they are going to get you out of there."

"They are?"

"Yes. In fact, I think the authorities are already working on it. It wouldn't have been helpful if you knew."

"I can't believe this is happening to my family. Knew what?"

"And you're sure you are in danger now?"

"Listen to me, Farouk. I'm in serious danger."

"They don't have time for wife-beaters. They're looking for Snake's boss. The Boss of the underworld. He's a real animal, Mackenzie. Men like him look at people in the street, and they see hamburger. You'll have to pretend you don't know what's happening until you can escape."

"What are you saying, Farouk?" I cried.

"OK," Farouk finally said. "We'll find out what boats are leaving at that time and be sure to get on the right one."

"Not again," Niovi's voice coaxed in the background.

"I'm sorry!" I cried. "You're supposed to be on your honeymoon! I could leave now."

"No Mac. You cannot leave. Not with the children."

I knew it was true. I had to be sure not to let Charon find out that I knew anything. That was my greatest weapon.

"You have to catch him in the act if you want to leave with your children," Farouk said. "It is the only way out."

I heard Niovi swearing in the background. "Thank you for rearranging your honeymoon," I said.

"Can you leave the house without arousing suspicions?" Farouk asked.

"I think so."

"Here is what you must do. You need to go to the travel agent and pick up the three tickets that will be waiting for you for the Wednesday boat," Farouk said.

"Tickets for our boat!" Niovi groaned in the background.

"You said help her. What do you suggest?" Farouk countered.

"Three tickets?" I asked.

"For you and the children. I will be there watching in case anything goes wrong."

I hung up the phone. The last thing I remember was the smell of rotten apples.

Chapter 49

The Boat

At the travel agent, I prayed that Farouk had found the right tickets. I kept them hidden under the rug. Wednesday came around, and Charon said that he wanted to go to the beach. I announced it to the kids immediately. "Yay!" They cheered, and it did seem that there was no way out.

"Let's just go the two of us," Charon said.

I had to nail him right there: "Since when have you wanted to go anywhere just the two of us? What's gotten into you?"

I watched him try to look natural. "Fine. Get the kids ready."

I searched the tickets for the name of the boat. The ink was blurred. I could just make out the word 'POSEIDON', just as I had dreamed of it. I tried to steady my breathing as I packed the beach gear and double stroller into the car. We got on the highway. Charon swore all the way. The Mercedes stopped at the port on the outskirts of the city. I immediately recognized where we were:

the slave market of Styxos. Life congregated in a single cove of terraces with cottages stepping up to the skyline. There were three yachts and one cruise ship moored in the harbour. I could see a large '-DON' on the side of the cruise ship. That was the one.

"We'll just stop here for a minute." Charon said. As we approached, the rest of the blue letters on the side of the ship came into view: 'POSEIDON'. I looked at my watch. It would be leaving in fifteen minutes. A strange wave of cool air enveloped me. I froze in horror. Just beyond the ship, the cliffs opened onto an enormous cavern. The dank air that crept from its mouth chilled me. My body let go of the midday heat and contracted into a clammy sweat. The mouth of the cave was impressive. Precipitous fifty-metre slopes formed a natural wall. Massive rocks stood suspended on their smallest side as if they had been put there. Inside their small cracks plants tried to live with remarkable patience and persistence. Six men in black guarded the opening. The mouth of hell. An anthropologist's dream. I hadn't imagined it like this. The find of a lifetime, and no time for pictures.

I heard a sound that chilled me to the bones: chains sliding along the ground. I caught a glimpse of them through the crowd: a group of naked women trudging single file into the mouth of the cave, their ankles shackled and chained together. Pretending not to see them, I averted my gaze to a tree branch above the car. The tree was screeching. A black bird flew out of the mouth of the cave and into the tree where it hung upside down. I saw then that the tree was full of creatures hanging upside down, their demon faces watching. Bats. They sprang into the air. I covered my head.

Charon laughed as the bats swooped over the car. "Let's go," he said. "The kids can wait in the car."

I felt my legs instinctively lock into place. I forced myself to let go of the seat. Everything depended on my performance. I had to appear ignorant of his real designs. How would I have acted if I hadn't known? I pretended not to hear him. "Hang on. I'm looking for Alex's sunglasses."

He swore again.

I opened the trunk and yanked the double stroller out. "Oh here they are." The children had wandered out of the car by now. They climbed into the stroller. I held up the glasses.

Anxiety washed across his face. He shook it off with a curse. For a moment I thought he was going to start yelling at the children to get back in the car. But, just as wives refuse to believe their husbands are cheating, husbands refuse to believe the wives are leaving them. Instead, he cursed me and led us through the harbour. He made no attempt to hide the fact that he had arranged a meeting. I went along with his big lie, thinking, things could have happened this way; he is always arranging meetings. He was a good 50 feet ahead of us and didn't bother to look back. The group of men in black surrounded a couple up ahead, shackled the woman and herded her off to join the others at the mouth of the cave. It was as if the cave were inhaling. I heard a scream. The chains rattled in the wind that arose from the cave. My head spun. It resounded in the depths of the cave. For a terrifying moment, I couldn't move my limbs. I knew that if I stepped any closer to the mouth of the cave, I would be sucked in. The wind died down: my signal to bolt.

Charon went to meet the men in black. I was surprised that my body had responded to the emergency. It could have melted under me, but here it was running us forward toward the boat. I was afraid to look back until I got to the boat. Then I saw that the men had started haggling. I pushed the stroller up to the Poseidon. On the dock, one of the men opened his jacket and showed Charon a roll of money. The front wheel of the stroller found the boat's ramp. "We're going on a boat!" Justin cheered. My muscles heaved against the stroller.

There was a commotion on the landing. The men yelled and pointed. Charon whirled around. His eyes locked onto mine. He started running toward us. The men in black followed him.

A steward in a starched uniform nodded at me. I handed him the tickets Farouk had bought. It was then that I saw, the steward was Farouk! A feeling of security washed over me. So much for bonds of flesh. At least I had a friend. I *had* been wrong about Farouk, and felt ashamed of myself.

Too late! Charon was running toward us, the money flapping in his fist. As his hairy arm closed on my waist, the bills flew into the air. Confetti fell into the sea. Charon dragged me backward. A smile peeled across Farouk's face. It pierced me like a stab in the back. I instinctively whirled around.

Four international police cars screeching to a halt blocked the two roads coming into the port. The police officers leapt out and aimed their guns at the men in black. As one of the wheels fell off the stroller and clattered down the gangway, a shot rang out. Farouk hiked the stroller into the corridor before the children could see a man in black crumble to the pavement. In a flash, Farouk leapt halfway down the ramp, yanking Charon's arm. Charon released me to swing at Farouk and knocked him down the ramp into me. I used the momentum to heave Charon to the side as hard as I could. He lost his balance, grasped at the air, then fell backward off of the ramp and into the sea. The crowd that stood gaping broke into applause. One of the tourists was videotaping the fight. The last thing I saw, two police officers were wrestling Charon to the shore.

Niovi was there in the entrance to the boat! She threw her arm around me and led the babies to a cabin. "You're safe now, Mac. Don't cry. It's alright. You lost your husband a long time ago. If you ever had him. Your marriage was a bad dream."

Chapter 50

Theory of Light

The land disappeared. The blue horizon line rose and fell in the round window of our cabin. The water bottles slid to the left and right. The children were jumping on the top bunk and promised to sleep there quietly together. The sea sprayed the window. I prayed that we were headed for safety and not another trap. "I want Papa to put me to bed!" Alex cried.

"Me too!" Justin said.

I didn't have an answer to that. There didn't seem to be any point in telling them that their father was a bad man. I finally got them tucked into opposite ends of the top bunk. They fell asleep with the rocking of the boat.

An hour later, there was a gentle knock on the door. It was Niovi, followed by Farouk. "Come in!" I whispered. I motioned for them to sit on one of the beds, and I sat on the other. "I guess we won't be needing this stroller."

"You can make it without the stroller," Niovi said. "They can both walk, now, Mac."

"I don't know how I can thank you both enough."

"It is we who should be thanking you," Farouk said.

Niovi looked baffled. The children breathed evenly through the uncomfortable silence.

"You exaggerate, Farouk," I said. "I'm ruining your honeymoon."

"Yes, but you are wrapping up my investigation." Farouk took out a black wallet and flipped it open. A blue and gold police badge glared up at us. We stared. There was a special police ID card opposite the badge. Niovi and I looked at each other and then at Farouk. He *was* different.

A nervous laugh escaped my throat. "Are we under arrest?"

"No. The case has been closed," Farouk said, "Thanks to you. There's no more need for secrecy."

"Secrecy?" Niovi asked.

Farouk didn't offer an apology, but looked very sorry when Niovi took the badge in her hand.

"It says 'special police agent'."

"That's right. I was working undercover. I have a few identities."

"I married a detective?"

"Yes."

"How dare you not tell me until now!" She hit him with the pillow.

"Shhh," he said. "You'll wake the children. The time was never right, *chérie,* and you wanted to get married immediately."

"Do you have any children?" Niovi asked.

"No."

"But you went to prison. Didn't you? They sprung you from prison," I said.

"It was part of my cover. You could say that they sprung my cover."

"Did I marry your cover?" Niovi asked.

Farouk's eyes sparkled.

So much for *my* threadbare morality. I regretted half of the things I had ever said to Farouk. My implication that he condoned Gru's death at the gala must have been torture for him.

"But you looked awful when you came out of prison," Niovi said.

"Because I had lost you, *chérie*. Everything is fine, now. Don't be so angry. We have caught the Boss of the underworld. "

"You have?" I asked. "Who?"

"Charon."

"Charon! Snake's boss? the Big Boss? You don't mean—"

"The deadliest enemy is beloved."

"No! Doesn't he care about our children?"

"He has had other children with other women."

Charon of the underworld!

The boat lurched, and I tumbled onto the floor.

I didn't sleep again that night. I waited for dawn to break the sky. I took the children to meet Niovi and Farouk for croissants in the restaurant at a table with a white tablecloth on it. I ordered a decaf coffee with milk. The waiter called out in front of everyone, "Here is the bizarre order of the day! Decaf coffee with milk!" The other passengers giggled.

The boat docked on the Egyptian shore. We all disembarked and stood on the quay. Niovi handed me a purse with some money in it and hugged me. "Goodbye, Mac. I know you'll be good."

"I know you will, too, Niovi. You'll have to, now. Thank you, Farouk. I felt safe with you here."

Farouk said. "You did it yourself."

"You did, Mac," Niovi said. "You let your light shine and made the rest of us shine." It felt like a part of me was leaving with them. Farouk lingered a second longer. His eyes let go of mine, just as they had in my dream. He scooped Niovi up, wide hips and all, and carried her up the gangplank above the enormous letters on the side of the boat: POSEIDON. *Her turn.* I was no longer in the loop.

Man and marriage had fallen away. I felt lighter. Had I separated from my former self? I felt as if I'd broken out of my trajectory. I was different this time. Something had changed this time around. At the top of the ramp, Niovi turned and looked for me among the people on the quay. I held up my hand. Niovi waved goodbye, her smile serene in her magazine face, as Farouk carried her away. I knew she was as happy for me as she was for herself. Farouk had never looked back before, so I was about to turn and go when he saw Niovi waving at me and turned around. He smiled and waved, his face as happy as the sun.

I took the children to the seaside for the rest of the day. It was evening when we taxied to the airport. The twilight sky was plaid with airplane trails. We held hands and walked into the lobby. A woman in a black headscarf stood behind the counter. "Are you checking any baggage today?"

I could hear the blood rushing to my ears. "No . . ." My words trailed off. I struggled to find my voice. "We're . . . travelling light."

She smiled and handed me the boarding passes.

THE BEGINNING

Afterword

Today, slaves are forced to destroy coastal ecosystems and to mine profitable metals for industry spreading mercury into the environments of Ghana and Congo. Slave labourers raze entire forests in Western Africa and the Amazon. There is a correlation between this damage to our environment and the erosion of our human rights. Buying the fruits of slavery degrades freedom.

Most of today's slaves toil under debt bondage incurred by 'lenders', often for generations. Human trafficking is the fastest growing criminal industry on the planet and is predicted to outgrow drug trafficking. Human traffickers prey on children and women prostituted into the sex industry.

Free the Slaves has found slavery practiced in every country in the world except Iceland and Greenland, and has calculated that it would cost $10.8 billion to eradicate slavery, the same amount spent on potato chips and pretzels for one year in America. Free the Slaves estimates that it costs an average of $400 to sustainably free one slave. It would be relatively cheap to eradicate slavery. Our generation can shut down this hell on earth. Find out more.[1]

---

1. Free the Slaves   www.freetheslaves.net
   The UN Voluntary Trust Fund for Victims of Trafficking in Persons
       http://www.unodc.org/unodc/human-trafficking-fund.html
   Free the Children   www.freethechildren.com
   Stop Child Slavery   www.stopchildslavery.com
   Anti-Slavery International   www.antislavery.org
   Anti-Slavery Society   www.anti-slaverysociety.addr.com
   Human Rights Watch   www.hrw.org
   Help Stop Child Slavery   www.helpstopchildslavery.org

About the Author

Travelling Light is J. L. Morin's second novel. Morin wrote the award-winning Japan novel *Sazzae* as a creative thesis at Harvard and was nominated for the Pushcart Prize in 2011. Morin's writing has appeared in the *Voice from the Planet* and *Above Ground* anthologies, *The Harvard Advocate, Harvard Yisei, The Detroit News, Agence France Presse, Livonia Observer Eccentric Newspapers,* and *The Harvard Crimson.*

J. L. Morin grew up in inner city Detroit and traded currency derivatives in New York for six years while studying nights at New York University's Stern School of Business (MBA '97) culminating in a job at the Federal Reserve Bank posted to the 103rd floor of the World Trade Center. After 9/11, Morin became a TV newscaster and diplomatic spouse and is currently adjunct faculty at Boston University.